PENGUIN POETS

THE PENGUIN BOOK OF
BALLADS

Geoffrey Grigson was born in Pelynt, Cornwall, in 1905. He was the editor and founder of *New Verse*. He also worked as literary editor of the *Morning Post*, on the staff of the *Yorkshire Post*, in the BBC Talks Department, and in publishing. A prolific writer, he has had a great many books published. Among these are *Discoveries of Bones and Stones and Other Poems* (1971), which won the Duff Cooper Memorial Prize in 1972; a volume of criticism, *Poems and Poets* (1968); *Unrespectable Verse*, published by Allen Lane (1971), *The Contrary View* (1974), *Britain Observed* (1975) and *The Goddess of Love: The Birth, Triumph, Death and Return of Aphrodite* (1976). He has also edited and contributed to *Penguin Modern Poets 23* (1973) and *Charles Cotton Selected by Geoffrey Grigson*, which was published simultaneously with this volume. His own first choice among his books is *Notes from an Odd Country* (1970).

THE PENGUIN BOOK OF
BALLADS

CHOSEN AND INTRODUCED BY
GEOFFREY GRIGSON

PENGUIN BOOKS

Penguin Books Ltd, Harmondsworth, Middlesex, England
Penguin Books, 625 Madison Avenue, New York, New York 10022, U.S.A.
Penguin Books Australia Ltd, Ringwood, Victoria, Australia
Penguin Books Canada Ltd, 2801 John Street, Markham, Ontario, Canada L3R 1B4
Penguin Books (N.Z.) Ltd, 182–190 Wairau Road, Auckland 10, New Zealand

—

First published 1975
Reprinted 1977

—

—

Made and printed in Great Britain by
Hazell Watson & Viney Ltd, Aylesbury, Bucks
Set in Monotype Fournier

CONTENTS

68759

ACKNOWLEDGEMENTS

For permission to reprint poems in copyright thanks are due to the following:

For Rudyard Kipling, 'The Widow's Lament' and 'Danny Deever', from *Barrack-room Ballads*, to Mrs George Bambridge, Eyre Methuen Ltd, Macmillan Co. of Canada and Doubleday & Company Inc.; for Louis MacNeice, 'The Streets of Laredo', from the *Collected Poems*, to Faber & Faber Ltd and OUP New York; for W. H. Auden, 'Victor was a Little Baby' (copyright 1940 and renewed 1968 by W. H. Auden), from *Collected Shorter Poems 1927–1957*, to Faber & Faber Ltd and Random House Inc.; for Adrian Mitchell, 'Song about Mary' and 'Fifteen Million Plastic Bags', from *Poems*, to the author and Jonathan Cape Ltd.

INTRODUCTION

PERHAPS more mystery is made of ballads, or at least of the 'traditional' ballads, than their case requires. Ballads are – or were – versified stories in alliance with music. The 'traditional' ballads, the older ones – the ballads of the first part of this selection – belonged to a stage of society, not a particularly ancient one, and to areas of society in which few people at any level depended greatly on written and printed words. The people of the time resembled all mankind in liking stories. Coming from whatever source, domestic or overseas, the ballad-stories they enjoyed were as various as modern fiction, as various for instance as the common fictions of radio and television. They included stories of the supernatural, stories of successful and thwarted love, stories of triumphs, defeat, revenge, murder, betrayal, cattle-reiving, stories of the upset of oppressors and of encounters (as between Haroun-al-Rashid and his subjects) between naïve common folk and kings in disguise who could prove kind and merciful and generous.

The audience liked to hear of life in court, castle, and manor house. Wicked queens turned their handsome stepchildren into loathly creatures, were found out and burnt on faggots of dry gorse and thorn. Demons and elf-knights were encountered and worsted. Highborn girls were with child and paid the price, together with their lovers; or they murdered their babies and were hanged. Or murdered lovers returned with clay-cold lips and at dawn drew back into the grey realm of the dead. More edifying (and of monastic authorship?) were English ballad-stories limpidly retelling legends of the life of Christ and the Virgin. (The existence of ballads of this kind warns us against too modern an identification of 'illiterate' with the poor and the deprived. The apocryphal – or extra-apocryphal – legends retold in ballads like 'St Stephen and Herod' [No. 1], 'The Cherry-Tree Carol' [No. 2] or 'The Bitter Withy' [No. 5] were often presented in another medium – the illumination of manuscripts – hardly within reach of the poor.)

Such stories required to be memorable, whether the tellers of them, as our northern world moved late out of the Middle Ages into the Renaissance, made a living by their art, as minstrels, or carried on the tradition, in its gradual decay, as amateurs with a gift for the dual performance of word and music, amateurs who inherited an unstable repertoire of old favourites.

The means of memorability were verse for the words and music for the verse – verse and music with all their tricks.

To begin with the verse, embodying the story which people wanted to hear, it was natural (if the word can be used of the unnaturalness of art) that its ballad form should be far from complex. Our ballads – though ballads elsewhere were often told in forms of a different simplicity – are most of them simply measured verse in a succession of simply rhymed stanzas of four lines apiece. The measure and the rhyme and the succession of small units helped the memorability; so did the various other tricks, various other repetitions such as the stock formulae of introduction, episode, action, and signing off. But then in art means of such a kind are also part and parcel of the ends, are themselves part of the totality of the enjoyment. Broadly we may say that the tunes to which ballads were fitted and told were also essential aids to memorability and at the same time a major part of that enjoyability which held a fireside audience for generation after generation.

So much said, does it matter greatly how each of the old ballads – all this is part of the surrounding mystery tackled by scholars – came actually into existence, how the ballad was transmitted, how it was varied, in oral succession, in Scotland, in England, in Ireland, and then further overseas, wherever the English, Scotch and Irish emigrated (or were transported)?

Not really. Somewhere, of course, at the back of every ballad there was an originator, a primal inventor, a 'poet' who put the words together in a primary version. I remember Verrier Elwin, who lived with the more or less 'primitive' Gonds of Bastur State in the Central Provinces of India, saying of their folksongs (folksongs are people's songs, and ballads are folksongs of a particular kind) that a young man would invent a new song – especially under the stimulus of love – and sing it around his village. If it caught on, soon everybody was singing it, and it passed among the Gonds from village to village, quickly becoming common property. If it didn't catch on, it died. So it must have been with the earlier ballads.

Then came variation, 'recomposition', and in the end degeneracy – all subjects for investigation, along with the ballad socially, historically, and psychologically, along with the ballad in migration, and the folklore in the ballad.

Fascinating – but something else than the ballads; and I have to shake my head a little when I find a ballad scholar writing like this:

> So far, we have considered the three kinds of ballad transmission and the three kinds of ballad-story; when correlated, they provide us with the various kinds of ballad text. The oral ballad-story produces, by oral transmission, oral texts; by transitional transmission, oral-transitional texts; and by modern transmission, memorised reproductions of oral and oral-transitional texts. The chap ballad-story appears initially in a printed text, and then produces, by transitional transmission, chap-transitional texts, and by modern transmission, memorised reproductions of printed and chap-transitional texts. The modern ballad-story appears initially in a written or printed text, or even a record, and then produces, by modern transmission, memorised reproductions of this modern text.*

Ballad archaeology, in whatever shape, is not the first thrilling encounter with 'Thomas Rymer' (No. 22) wading through red blood to the knee, is not the channerin worm of 'The Wife of Usher's Well' (No. 24) or Clark Sanders crying for a bed (No. 30), or the sun shining on the feet of Brown Robin and the king's only daughter (No. 58) as they lie in bed too long for safety, or the king's daughter in 'Willie o Winsbury' (No. 45) having to stand naked on the stone to show if she is pregnant. Ballad archaeology is not the so adequately and curtly expressed pathos of the seal husband and his young son (Nos. 74 and 75), or the earl's lady going off with the gypsy and being stared at by the black gypsy crew in the barn (No. 18), or the glitter of the plate armour in 'Chevy Chace' (No. 71), or the breathless raising and riding of the Scotch in 'Jamie Telfer of the Fair Dodhead' (No. 67). These we have as poems of a special kind. And every poem is its own secret, or proffers its own secret in the immediate terms of its effect.

What matters is that the best of the older ballads (of course, of the later ones as well) continue to 'work', even for the reader.

All the same it is human to wish to know when, more or less, our great traditional ballads were invented, when their careers so to

* David Buchan, *A Scottish Ballad Book* (Routledge, 1973).

say, or their voyage through time and populace, began. Something, though rather negatively, may be learnt from the stanzaic forms in which they have their being. The forms appear to have come from medieval France, in the Normanizing of the English. That at once crosses out notions of extreme antiquity for the ballads. What is clear is that by the time ballad-making began, popular songs had familiarized everyone, illiterate or literate, with stanzas in four lines or couplets. So the obvious way of telling and singing a story was to add four-line stanza to stanza, or couplet to couplet. What tells us more or most about the date of the oral ballads is the kind of feeling which compels and animates them; and the aesthetic feeling of the oral ballads, the great traditionals, whether tragical or lyrical, is that of the High Tudor time, equally discernible in the great poetic drama and lyricism of our delayed Renaissance.

In the illiterate as in the literate milieu, the narrative, dramatic impact of the same elements: love, incest, transgression of the divisions of class and rank, violence, bloodshed, revenge, requital, in court and in castle.

Whatever he adds, however he subtilizes them and uses them in human depth, Shakespeare works lyrically and tragically and dramatically in the same elements as the inventor of ballads. A time-related *frisson* arises from *Hamlet* and 'The Unquiet Grave' (No. 31). And in 'Janet' (No. 40), that version of 'Lady Maisry' which begins so savagely

> In came her sister,
>   Stepping on the floor;
> Says, It's telling me, my sister Janet,
>   That you've become a whore.

> A whore, sister, a whore, sister?
>   That's what I'll never be;
> I'm no so great a whore, sister,
>   As liars does on me lee.

> In came her brother,
>   Stepping on the floor;
> Says, It's telling me, my sister Janet,
>   That you've become a whore,

we are in a world of time and feeling shared by the terrible ingenuity of *'Tis Pity She's a Whore*, or *The Duchess of Malfi*, or *The Revenger's Tragedy*.

Other evidence than this relationship (rather than identity) of spirit, evidence of manuscripts and known and datable happenings described in some ballads, indicates as well that the chief age of ballad-making for the people of the various 'ballad areas' of England and Scotland was this more or less Shakespearean time, after the Middle Ages and before the (relative) exorcism or disowning of violence, from 1550 or thereabouts to the first decades of the seventeenth century; which does not contradict the fact that a few of the surviving 'traditionals' are of an older and a few more of a later time. Then to primary invention must be added the secondary invention, the re-creative invention, of the still-vigorous and skilful ballad performers. David Buchan, in his book *The Ballad and the Folk**, concludes that in the supreme 'ballad area' of North-East Scotland this period of composition and re-composition comes within the wide limits of 1350 and 1750. Conditions there especially favoured its continuance.

The degeneration of ballad-singing and the traditional ballads was caused and complicated by a score of things – by social changes, by the spread of cheap printing and of cheaply printed prose stories and prose 'reporting', the extension of a basic literacy, the sophisticated discovery of ballads from their later singers, and their collection and polite or learned publication from the eighteenth century onwards, particularly in Bishop Percy's *Reliques of Ancient English Poetry*, which appeared in 1765. Gapped or fragmented ballads were joined and tidied up by poets of the literate tradition, among them Burns (alive in both traditions) and Sir Walter Scott. Poets captivated by ballad substance and stylization imitated old ballads or found their own ballad manner under this recovered stimulus. The short story in verse became, and remains, an always possible mode, especially for poets gifted with, at any rate, verbal melody.

Then followed the passage of emigrants to new countries and new eras of insecurity, violence and rough justice, away from, or little touched by, literacy. Ballads, new as well as transferred, were an entertainment the emigrants could provide for themselves;

* Routledge, 1972.

13

though the emigrant cultures without literacy were a cruder and coarser affair, with ballads to match, than the old culture without literacy in which the ballads had matured.

Times changed at home. There was still hanging; there was imprisonment, and the workhouse. In balladry old themes of social injustice and the underdog and fantasies of escape persisted, especially in the extra-heavy circumstances of agrarian and industrial oppression and urban rookeries. But England divided more and more into two worlds, and at home as well the popular balladry of the poorer of these worlds coarsened along with the coarsening, in some ways, of its conditions of life. The old drama, and certainly the old lyricism, of the ballads dwindled. In the printer's ballads sold by the thousands round and round the British Isles in the nineteenth century the sentimental and the maudlin increased. More ballads conveyed the comic and the grotesque, the taste for which was not always satisfied at the ingenious level of George Colman's comic ghost story of poor Miss Bailey (No. 88), first sung at the Haymarket Theatre in one of his plays, in 1803, or the young W. S. Gilbert's 'Yarn of the "Nancy Bell"', of the 1860s (No. 105), which *Punch* had declined as 'too cannibalistic' –

> When I ups with his heels, and smothers his squeals
> In the scum of the boiling broth

– for the taste of its middle-class readers. Published in the magazine *Fun*, it was soon afterwards on sale as a sheet ballad, fitted to its tune.

The popular balladry of particular working communities in and after the nineteenth century, as well as commercial popular balladry, is on the whole depressed and depressing. Exploring it is like picking through a vast rubbish dump, in which a glittering good thing is occasionally to be found – something in ballad-making which corresponds to the canvases, or cardboards, of that very rare bird, the good Sunday painter. The second part of this selection is shared, on the whole, between the poet indulging in balladry and the 'Sunday balladist', the Sunday poet.

There remains an inevitable consideration which, perhaps in a cowardly-cautious way, I have put off till last.

This is one more selection of ballad words without ballad tunes. Certainly it is true that the ballad without its tune is less than it-

14

self, less than complete. Certainly it is true that literary concern for ballads has always – until recently – elbowed the music aside. But then musicians (especially now that Child's great *English and Scottish Popular Ballads* has been supplemented by Bronson's great *Traditional Tunes of the Child Ballads*) are inclined to elbow the words, the poems, the stories, aside.

Knowing about the tunes* will often save the unrepentant *reader* from imagining metrical deficiencies where they do not really exist, in lines fitted to the music. But in mediation between the way in which poets or literary appreciators look at ballads and the way musicians look at them, let it be emphasized that the story was, after all, the *raison d'être* of the old balladry.

It was the story that the traditional singers wished to tell, and hung on to, however much they 're-created' the telling; and those who are not musicians – most of us, that is to say – may still want to read them; and reading them aloud is a great pleasure.

Why object? Nobody knows the music to which bards sang the *Homeric Hymns*, but poems they remain. Poems – if of a peculiar, simple, open, direct, unambiguous, story-telling kind – the ballads remain; the best of them have long, and justly, been included in the canon of our poetry.

Coming to the later ballads, in the more slender, second part of this ballad-book, readers might recollect some clarifying remarks on ballads, and especially modern ballads, which T. S. Eliot made when he introduced his *Choice of Kipling's Verse* in 1941. He realized that an unbroken thread runs through balladry from first to latest. He wrote that 'the ballad persists and develops in its own way, and corresponds to a permanent level of enjoyment of literature' – the ballad, he insisted, has its appeal without distinction of class.

To have heard him sing – but did I say sing? – 'Frankie and Johnny' would have alarmed some of the purists of the high snows of poetry.

GEOFFREY GRIGSON

* The ordinary unmusical reader will get as much as he wishes to know about the tunes from Matthew Hodgart's *The Ballads* (Hutchinson, 1962), which is a brilliant little guide to ballad virtues and to the maze and imbroglio of ballad studies.

I
_____

EARLIER BALLADS,
ENGLISH AND SCOTCH

_____

SAINT STEPHEN AND HEROD

Seynt Stevene was a clerk
   In kyng Herowdes halle,
And servyd him of bred and cloth
   As every kyng befalle.

Stevyn out of kechone cam
   Wyth boris hed on honde,
He saw a sterre was fayr and bryght
   Over Bedlem stonde.

He kyst adoun the boris hed
   And went in to the halle:
I forsak the, kyng Herowdes,
   And thi werkes alle.

I forsak the, kyng Herowdes,
   And thi werkes alle,
Ther is a chyld in Bedlem born
   Is beter than we alle.

Quat eylyt the, Stevene?
   Quat is the befalle?
Lakkyt the eyther mete or drynk
   In kyng Herowdes halle?

Lakit me neyther mete ne drynk
   In kyng Herowdes halle,
Ther is a chyld in Bedlem born
   Is beter than we alle.

servyd him of bred and cloth served
  him with bread and clothes, i.e.
  at meals and at robing
As every kyng befalle As happens
  with every king

kechone kitchen
boris hed boar's head
kyst cast
Quat eylyt the What aileth thee

Quat eylyt the, Stevyn? art thu wod,
    Or thu gynnyst to brede?
Lakkyt the eyther gold or fe,
    Or ony ryche wede?

Lakyt me neyther gold ne fe
    Ne non ryche wede,
Ther is a chyld in Bedlem born
    Sal helpyn us at our nede.

That is al so soth, Stevyn,
    Al so soth, iwys,
As this capoun crowe sal
    That lyth here in myn dysh.

That word was not so sone seyd,
    That word in that halle,
The capoun crew *Cristus natus est*
    Among the lordes alle.

Rysyt up, myn turmentowres,
    Be to and al be on,
And ledyt Stevyn out of this town
    And stonyt hym wyth ston.

Tokyn he Stevene
    And stonyd hym in the way,
And therfore is his evyn
    On Crystes owyn day.

wod mad
brede breed fever, feel ill
wede weed, garment
soth sooth, true
iwys indeed

capoun capon, chicken
Cristus natus est Christ is born
be to . . . be on by two . . . by one
way road
evyn even, eve

THE CHERRY-TREE CAROL

Joseph was an old man,
  And an old man was he,
When he wedded Mary
  In the land of Galilee.

Joseph and Mary walked
  Through an orchard good,
Where was cherries and berries
  So red as any blood.

Joseph and Mary walked
  Through an orchard green,
Where was berries and cherries
  As thick as might be seen.

O then bespoke Mary
  So meek and so mild,
Pluck me one cherry, Joseph,
  For I am with child.

O then bespoke Joseph
  With words most unkind,
Let him pluck thee a cherry
  That brought thee with child.

O then bespoke the babe
  Within his mother's womb,
Bow down then the tallest tree
  For my mother to have some.

Then bowed down the highest tree
  Unto his mother's hand.
Then she cried, See, Joseph,
  I have cherries at command.

O then bespake Joseph,
　I have done Mary wrong,
But cheer up, my dearest,
　And be not cast down.

Then Mary plucked a cherry
　As red as the blood,
Then Mary went home
　With her heavy load.

Then Mary took her babe
　And sat him on her knee,
Saying, My dear Son, tell me
　What this world will be.

O I shall be as dead, Mother,
　As the stones in the wall,
O the stones in the streets, Mother,
　Shall mourn for me all.

Upon Easter-day, Mother,
　My uprising shall be,
O the sun and the moon, Mother,
　Shall both rise with me.

3
THE MAID AND THE PALMER

The maid shee went to the well to washe,
  Lillumwham, lillumwham!
The mayd shee went to the well to washe,
  Whatt then? what then?
The maid shee went to the well to washe,
Dew ffell of her lilly white fleshe.
  Grandam boy, grandam boy, heye!
Leg a derry, leg a merry, mett, mer, whoope, whir!
  Driuance, larumben, grandam boy, heye!

While shee washte and while shee ronge,
While shee hangd o the hazle wand.

There came an old palmer by the way,
Sais, God speed thee well, thou faire maid!

Hast either cupp or can,
To give an old palmer drinke therin?

Sayes, I have neither cupp nor cann,
To give an old palmer drinke therin.

But an thy lemman came from Roome,
Cupps and canns thou wold ffind soone.

Shee sware by God and good St John,
Lemman had shee never none.

Saies, Peace, ffaire mayd, you are fforsworne.
Nine children you have borne.

palmer pilgrim   *lemman* lover
an if

23

Three were buryed under thy bed's head,
Other three under thy brewing leade.

Other three on yon play greene;
Count, maid, and there be nine.

But I hope you are the good old man
That all the world beleeves upon.

Old palmer, I pray thee,
Pennaunce that thou wilt give to me.

Penance I can give thee none,
But seaven yeere to be a stepping-stone.

Other seaven a clapper in a bell,
Other seaven to lead an ape in hell.

When thou hast thy penance done,
Then thoust come a mayden home.

---

brewing leade a built-in cauldron
   for brewing ale

to lead an ape in hell the fate of
   women who die unmarried

4
THE SEVEN VIRGINS

All under the leaves, the leaves of life,
  I met with the virgins seven,
And one of them was Mary mild,
  Our Lord's mother from heaven.

O what are you seeking, you seven fair maids,
  All under the leaves of life?
Come tell, come tell me what seek you
  All under the leaves of life.

We're seeking for no leaves, Thomas,
  But for a friend of thine,
We're seeking for sweet Jesus Christ,
  To be our guide and thine.

Go you down, go you down to yonder town,
  And sit in the gallery,
And there you'll find sweet Jesus Christ
  Nailed to a big yew-tree.

So down they went to yonder town
  As fast as foot could fall,
And many a grievous bitter tear
  From the virgins' eyes did fall.

O peace, mother, O peace, mother,
  Your weeping doth me grieve.
O I must suffer this, he said,
  For Adam and for Eve.

O how can I my weeping leave
  Or my sorrows undergo
Whilst I do see my own son die,
  When sons I have no mo'?

Dear mother, dear mother, you must take John,
   All for to be your son,
And he will comfort you sometimes,
   Mother, as I have done.

O come, thou John Evangelist,
   Thou'rt welcome unto me,
But more welcome my own dear son
   That I nursed upon my knee.

Then he laid his head on his right shoulder,
   Seeing death it struck him nigh:
The Holy Ghost be with your soul,
   I die, mother dear, I die.

Oh the rose, the rose, the gentle rose,
   And the fennel that grows so green,
God give us grace in every place
   To pray for our king and queen.

Furthermore for our enemies all
   Our prayers they should be strong.
Amen, Good Lord. Your charity
   Is the ending of my song.

THE BITTER WITHY

As it befell on a bright holiday
Small hail from the sky did fall.
Our Saviour asked his mother dear
If he might go play at ball.

At ball, at ball, my own dear son,
It's time that you were gone,
But don't let me hear of any mischief
At night when you come home.

So up the hill and down the hill
Our sweet young Saviour run,
Until he met three rich young lords –
Good morning to each one.

Good morn, good morn, good morn, said they,
Good morning, then said he,
And which of you three rich young lords
Will play at ball with me?

We are all lords' and ladies' sons
Born in our bower and hall,
And you are nothing but a poor maid's child
Born in an ox's stall.

It's if I'm nothing but a poor maid's child,
Born in an ox's stall,
I'll make you believe in your latter end
I'm an angel above you all.

So he made him a bridge of the beams of the sun,
And over the water run he,
The rich young lords chased after him,
And drowned they were all three.

So up the hill and down the hill
Three rich young mothers run,
Crying, Mary mild, fetch home your child,
For ours he's drowned each one.

So Mary mild fetched home her child,
And laid him across her knee,
And with a handful of willow twigs
She gave him slashes three.

Ah bitter withy, ah bitter withy,
You have caused me to smart,
And the willow shall be the very first tree
To perish at the heart.

IN DESSEXSHIRE AS IT BEFEL

In Dessexshire as it befel
A farmer there as I knew well
On a Christmas day as it happened so
Down in the meadows he went to plough.

As he was a ploughing on so fast
Our Saviour Christ came by at last;
He said, O man, why dost thou plough
So hard as it do blow and snow?

The man he answered the Lord with speed,
For to work we have great need,
If we wasn't to work all on that day
We should want some other way.

For his hands did tremble and pass to and fro,
He ran so fast that he could not plough;
And the ground did open and let him in
Before he could repent his sin.

His wife and children were out at play;
And all the world consumed at last.
And his beasts and cattle all died away
For breaking of the Lord's birthday.

THE ROYAL FISHERMAN

As I walked out one May morning,
  When May was all in bloom,
O there I spied a bold fisherman,
  Come fishing all alone.

I said to this bold fisherman,
  How come you fishing here?
I'm fishing for your own sweet sake
  All down the river clear.

He drove his boat towards the side,
  Which was his full intent,
Then he laid hold of her lily-white hand
  And down the stream they went.

Then he pulled off his morning gown
  And threw it over the sea,
And there she spied three robes of gold
  All hanging down his knee.

Then on her bended knees she fell:
  Pray, sir, pardon me
For calling you a fisherman
  And a rover down the sea.

Rise up, rise up, my pretty fair maid,
  Don't mention that to me,
For not one word that you have spoke
  Has the least offended me.

Then we'll go to my father's hall,
  And married we shall be,
And you shall have your fisherman
  To row you on the sea.

Then they went to his father's house,
    And married now they be;
And now she's got her fisherman
    To row her down the sea.

BROWN ROBYN'S CONFESSION

It fell upon a Wodensday
   Brown Robyn's men went to sea,
But they saw neither moon nor sun,
   Nor starlight wi their ee.

We'll cast kevels us amang,
   See wha the unhappy man may be.
The kevel fell on Brown Robyn,
   The master-man was he.

It is nae wonder, said Brown Robyn,
   Altho I dinna thrive,
For wi my mither I had twa bairns,
   And wi my sister five.

But tie me to a plank o wude,
   And throw me in the sea,
And if I sink, ye may bid me sink,
   But if I swim, just lat me be.

They've tied him to a plank o wude,
   And thrown him in the sea.
He didna sink, tho they bade him sink,
   He swimd, and they bade lat him be.

He hadna been into the sea
   An hour but barely three
Till by it came Our Blessed Lady,
   Her dear young son her wi.

kevels lots

Will ye gang to your men again,
  Or will ye gang wi me?
Will ye gang to the high heavens,
  Wi my dear son and me?

I winna gang to my men again,
  For they would be feared at me,
But I would gang to the high heavens,
  Wi thy dear son and thee.

It's for nae honour ye did to me, Brown Robyn,
  It's for nae guid ye did to me,
But a' is for your fair confession
  You've made upon the sea.

THE HOLY WELL

As it fell out one May morning,
  And upon one bright holiday,
Sweet Jesus asked of his mother dear,
  If he might go to play.

To play, to play, sweet Jesus shall go,
  And to play pray get you gone,
And let me hear of no complaint
  At night when you come home.

Sweet Jesus went down to yonder town,
  As far as the Holy Well,
And there did see as fine children
  As any tongue can tell.

He said, God bless you every one,
  And your bodies Christ save and see:
Little children, shall I play with you,
  And you shall play with me.

But they made answer to him, No:
  They were lords' and ladies' sons;
And he, the meanest of them all,
  Was but a maiden's child, born in an ox's stall.

Sweet Jesus turned him around,
  And he neither laugh'd nor smil'd,
But the tears came trickling from his eyes
  Like water from the skies.

Sweet Jesus turned him about,
  To his mother's dear home went he,
And said, I have been in yonder town,
  As far as you may see.

I have been down in yonder town
   As far as the Holy Well,
There did I meet as fine children
   As any tongue can tell.

I bid God bless them every one,
   And their bodies Christ save and see:
Little children, shall I play with you,
   And you shall play with me.

But they made answer to me, No:
   They were lords' and ladies' sons,
And I, the meanest of them all,
   Was but a maiden's child, born in an ox's stall.

Though you are but a maiden's child,
   Born in an ox's stall,
Thou art the Christ, the King of Heaven,
   And the Saviour of them all.

Sweet Jesus, go down to yonder town
   As far as the Holy Well,
And take away those sinful souls,
   And dip them deep in Hell.

Nay, nay, sweet Jesus said,
   Nay, nay, that may not be;
For there are too many sinful souls
   Crying out for the help of me.

RIDDLES WISELY EXPOUNDED

There was a knicht riding frae the east,
   Sing the Cather banks, the bonnie brume
Wha had been wooing at monie a place.
   And ye may beguile a young thing sune.

He came unto a widow's door.
And speird whare her three dochters were.

The auldest ane's to the washing gane,
The second's to a baking gane.

The youngest ane's to a wedding gane,
And it will be nicht or she be hame.

He sat him doun upon a stane,
Till thir three lasses came tripping hame.

The auldest ane's to the bed making,
And the second ane's to the sheet spreading.

The youngest ane was bauld and bricht,
And she was to lye wi this unco knicht.

Gin ye will answer me questions ten,
This morn ye sall be made my ain.

O what is heigher nor the tree?
And what is deeper nor the sea?

Or what is heavier nor the lead?
And what is better nor the breid?

speird asked   *unco* strange

O what is whiter nor the milk?
Or what is safter nor the silk?

Or what is sharper nor a thorn?
Or what is louder nor a horn?

Or what is greener nor the grass?
Or what is waur nor a woman was?

O heaven is higher nor the tree,
And hell is deeper nor the sea.

O sin is heavier nor the lead,
The blessing's better than the bread.

The snaw is whiter nor the milk,
And the down is safter nor the silk.

Hunger is sharper nor a thorn,
And shame is louder nor a horn.

The pies are greener nor the grass,
And Clootie's waur nor a woman was.

As sune as she the fiend did name,
He flew awa in a blazing flame.

want worse   *Clootie* the Devil whose hoof is
pies magpies   cloven into two cloots

THE WEE WEE MAN

As I was walking all alone
  Between the water and the green,
There I spied a wee wee man,
  The least wee man that ever was seen.

His legs were scarce an effet's length,
  But thick his arms as any tree.
Between his brows there was a span,
  Between his shoulders there were three.

He took up a boulder stone,
  And flung it as far as I could see.
Though I had been a miller's man,
  I could not lift it to my knee.

O wee wee man, but thou art strang!
  O tell me where thy haunt may be.
My dwelling's down by yon bonny bower,
  O will you mount and ride with me?

On we leapt, and off we rode,
  Till we came to far away,
We lighted down to bait our horse,
  And out there came a bonny may.

Four and twenty at her back,
  And they were all dressed out in green,
And though King Harry had been there,
  The worst o them might be his queen.

effet eft, newt   *may* maid

38

On we leapt, and off we rode,
  Till we came to yon bonny hall.
The roof was o the beaten gold,
  Of gleaming crystal was the wall.

When we came to the door of gold,
  The pipes within did whistle and play,
But ere the tune of it was told,
  My wee wee man was clean away.

LADY ISOBEL AND THE ELF-KNIGHT

Fair lady Isabel sits in her bower sewing,
   Aye as the gowans grow gay
There she heard an elf-knight blawing his horn.
   The first morning in May.

If I had yon horn that I hear blawing,
And yon elf-knight to sleep in my bosom.

This maiden had scarcely these words spoken,
Till in at her window the elf-knight has luppen.

It's a very strange matter, fair maiden, said he,
I canna blaw my horn but ye call on me.

But will ye go to yon greenwood side?
If ye canna gang, I will cause you to ride.

He leapt on a horse, and she on another,
And they rode on to the greenwood together.

Light down, light down, lady Isabel, said he,
We are come to the place where ye are to die.

Hae mercy, hae mercy, kind sir, on me,
Till ance my dear father and mother I see.

Seven king's-daughters here hae I slain,
And ye shall be the eight o them.

O sit down a while, lay your head on my knee,
That we may hae some rest before that I die.

bower room   *luppen* leapt
gowans daisies

She stroakd him sae fast, the nearer he did creep,
Wi a sma charm she lulld him fast asleep.

Wi his ain sword-belt sae fast as she ban him,
Wi his ain dag-durk sae sair as she dang him.

If seven king's-daughters here ye hae slain,
Lye ye here, a husband to them a'.

ban bound   *dang* struck
dag-durk dagger

HARPKIN

Harpkin gaed up to the hill,
And blew his horn loud and shrill,
   And by came Fin.

What for stand you there? quo Fin.
Spying the weather, quo Harpkin.

What for had you your staff on your shouther? quo Fin.
To haud the cauld frae me, quo Harpkin.

Little cauld will that haud frae you, quo Fin.
As little will it win through me, quo Harpkin.

I came by your door, quo Fin.
It lay in your road, quo Harpkin.

Your dog barkit at me, quo Fin.
It's his use and custom, quo Harpkin.

I flang a stane at him, quo Fin.
I'd rather it had been a bane, quo Harpkin.

Your wife's lichter, quo Fin.
She'll clim the brae brichter, quo Harpkin.

Of a braw lad bairn, quo Fin.
There'll be the mair men for the king's wars, quo Harpkin.

There's a strae at your beard, quo Fin.
I'd rather it had been a thrave, quo Harpkin.

strae straw   *thrave* twenty-four sheaves
brae hill

The ox is eating at it, quo Fin.
If the ox were i' the water, quo Harpkin.

And the water were frozen, quo Fin.
And the smith and his fore-hammer at it, quo Harpkin.

And the smith were dead, quo Fin.
And another in his stead, quo Harpkin.

Giff, gaff, quo Fin.
Your mou's fou o draff, quo Harpkin.

fore-hammer sledge hammer   *draff* rubbish

14

THE FALSE KNIGHT UPON THE ROAD

O whare are ye gaun?
  Quo the fause knicht upon the road.
I'm gaun to the scule,
  Quo the wee boy, and still he stude.

What is that upon your back?
  Quo the fause knicht upon the road.
Atweel it is my bukes,
  Quo the wee boy, and still he stude.

What's that ye've got in your arm?
  Quo the fause knicht upon the road.
Atweel it is my peit,
  Quo the wee boy, and still he stude.

Wha's aucht they sheep?
  Quo the fause knicht upon the road.
They are mine and my mither's,
  Quo the wee boy, and still he stude.

How monie o them are mine?
  Quo the fause knicht upon the road.
A' they that hae blue tails,
  Quo the wee boy, and still he stude.

I wiss ye were on yon tree,
  Quo the fause knicht upon the road.
And a gude ladder under me,
  Quo the wee boy, and still he stude.

Atweel To be sure   *Wha's aucht* Whose are
peit piece of peat (for the school
  fire)

And the ladder for to break,
    Quo the fause knicht upon the road.
And you for to fa down,
    Quo the wee boy, and still he stude.

I wiss ye were in yon sie,
    Quo the fause knicht upon the road.
And a gude bottom under me,
    Quo the wee boy, and still he stude.

And the bottom for to break,
    Quo the fause knicht upon the road.
And ye to be drowned,
    Quo the wee boy, and still he stude.

15

THE ELFIN KNIGHT

My plaid awa, my plaid awa,
And ore the hill and far awa,
And far awa to Norrowa,
My plaid shall not be blown awa.

The elphin knight sits on yon hill,
   Ba, ba, lilli ba.
He blaws his horn both lowd and shrill.
   The wind hath blown my plaid awa.

He blowes it east, he blowes it west,
He blowes it where he lyketh best.

I wish that horn were in my kist,
Yea, and the knight in my armes two.

She had no sooner these words said,
When that the knight came to her bed.

Thou art over young a maid, quoth he,
Married with me thou il wouldst be.

I have a sister younger than I,
And she was married yesterday.

Married with me if thou wouldst be,
A courtesie thou must do to me.

For thou must shape a sark to me,
Without any cut or heme, quoth he.

---

plaid cloak   *sark* shirt
kist chest, box

Thou must shape it knife-and-sheerlesse,
And also sue it needle-threadlesse.

If that piece of courtesie I do to thee,
Another thou must do to me.

I have an aiker of good ley-land,
Which lyeth low by yon sea-strand.

For thou must eare it with thy horn,
So thou must sow it with thy corn.

And bigg a cart of stone and lyme,
Robin Redbreast he must trail it hame.

Thou must barn it in a mouse-holl,
And thrash it into thy shoes' soll.

And thou must winnow it in thy looff,
And also seck it in thy glove.

For thou must bring it over the sea,
And thou must bring it dry home to me.

When thou hast gotten thy turns well done,
Then come to me and get thy sark then.

I'l not quit my plaid for my life,
It haps my seven bairns and my wife.
 The wind shall not blow my plaid awa.

My maidenhead I'l then keep still,
Let the elphin knight do what he will.
 The wind's not blown my plaid awa.

bigg build   *seck* sack
looff palm

16

THE BROOMFIELD HILL

There was a knight and a lady bright,
　　Had a true tryste at the broom;
The ane gaed early in the morning,
　　The other in the afternoon.

And ay she sat in her mother's bower door,
　　And ay she made her mane:
O whether should I gang to the Broomfield Hill,
　　Or should I stay at hame?

For if I gang to the Broomfield Hill,
　　My maidenhead is gone;
And if I chance to stay at hame,
　　My love will ca me mansworn.

Up then spake a witch-woman,
　　Ay from the room aboon:
O ye may gang to the Broomfield Hill,
　　And yet come maiden hame.

For when ye gang to the Broomfield Hill,
　　Ye'll find your love asleep,
With a silver belt about his head,
　　And a broom-cow at his feet.

Take ye the blossom of the broom,
　　The blossom it smells sweet,
And strew it at your true-love's head,
　　And likewise at his feet.

ca me mansworn say I have broken　　*aboon* above
　my word　　　　　　　　　　*broom-cow* spray of broom

Take ye the rings off your fingers,
   Put them on his right hand,
To let him know, when he doth awake,
   His love was at his command.

She pu'd the broom flower on Hive Hill,
   And strewd on 's white hals-bane,
And that was to be wittering true
   That maiden she had gane.

O where were ye, my milk-white steed,
   That I hae coft sae dear,
That wadna watch and waken me
   When there was maiden here?

I stamped wi my foot, master,
   And gard my bridle ring,
But na kin thing wald waken ye,
   Till she was past and gane.

And wae betide ye, my gay goss-hawk,
   That I did love sae dear,
That wadna watch and waken me
   When there was maiden here.

I clapped wi my wings, master,
   And aye my bells I rang,
And aye cry'd, Waken, waken, master,
   Before the ladye gang.

But haste and haste, my gude white steed,
   To come the maiden till,
Or a' the birds of gude green wood
   Of your flesh shall have their fill.

hals-bane neck-bone, Adam's   *coft* bought
  apple   *gard* made
wittering sign   *kin* kind of

Ye need na burst your gude white steed
    Wi racing oer the howm;
Nae bird flies faster through the wood,
    Than she fled through the broom.

howm river-flat, river-meadow

17

ALLISON GROSS

O Allison Gross, that lives in yon towr,
  The ugliest witch i the north country,
Has trysted me ae day up till her bowr,
  An monny fair speech she made to me.

She stroaked my head, an she kembed my hair,
  An she set me down saftly on her knee;
Says, Gin ye will be my lemman so true,
  Saw monny braw things as I would you gi.

She showd me a mantle o red scarlet,
  Wi gouden flowrs an fringes fine;
Says, Gin ye will be my lemman so true,
  This goodly gift it sal be thine.

Awa, awa, ye ugly witch,
  Haud far awa, an lat me be;
I never will be your lemman sae true,
  An I wish I were out o your company.

She neist brought a sark o the saftest silk,
  Well wrought wi pearles about the ban;
Says, Gin you will be my ain true love,
  This goodly gift you sal comman.

She showed me a cup of the good red gold,
  Well set wi jewels sae fair to see;
Says, Gin you will be my lemman sae true,
  This goodly gift I will you gi.

trysted enticed	*neist* next
ae one	*sark* shirt
bowr room	*ban* band
lemman lover	

Awa, awa, ye ugly witch,
   Had far awa, and lat me be;
For I woudna ance kiss your ugly mouth
   For a' the gifts that ye coud gi.

She's turnd her right and roun about,
   An thrice she blaw on a grass-green horn,
An she sware by the meen and the stars abeen,
   That she'd gar me rue the day I was born.

Then out has she taen a silver wand,
   An she's turnd her three times roun and roun;
She's muttered sich words till my strength it faild,
   An I fell down senceless upon the groun.

She's turnd me into an ugly worm,
   And gard me toddle about the tree;
An ay, on ilka Saturdays night,
   My sister Maisry came to me,

Wi silver bason an silver kemb,
   To kemb my heady upon her knee;
But or I had kissd her ugly mouth,
   I'd rather a toddled about the tree.

But as it fell out on last Hallow-even,
   When the seely court was ridin by,
The queen lighted down on a gowany bank,
   Nae far frae the tree where I wont to lye.

She took me up in her milk-white han,
   An she's stroakd me three times oer her knee;
She chang'd me again to my ain proper shape,
   An I nae mair maun toddle about the tree.

gar make	*seely* happy, i.e. fairy
ilka every	*gowany* daisied

18

THE GYPSY LADDIE

The gypsies they came to my lord Cassilis' yett,
  And O but they sang bonnie!
They sang so sweet and so complete
  Till down came our fair ladie.

She came tripping down the stairs,
  And all her maids before her;
As soon as they saw her weel-far'd face,
  They cast their glamourie owre her.

She gave them the good wheat bread,
  And they gave her the ginger;
But she gave them a fair better thing,
  The gold rings of her fingers.

Will ye go with me, my hinny and my heart?
  Will you go with me, my dearie?
And I will swear by the hilt of my spear,
  That your lord shall no more come near thee.

Gar take from me my silk manteel,
  And bring to me a plaidie,
For I will travel the world owre
  Along with the gypsie laddie.

I could sail the seas with my Jackie Faa,
  I could sail the seas with my dearie;
I could sail the seas with my Jackie Faa,
  And with pleasure could drown with my dearie.

yett gate   *hinny* honey
glamourie spell   *plaidie* cloak

They wandred high, they wandred low,
    They wandred late and early,
Untill they came to an old farmer's barn,
    And by this time she was weary.

Last night I lay in a weel-made bed,
    And my noble lord beside me,
And now I most ly in an old farmer's barn,
    And the black crae glowring owre me.

Hold your tongue, my hinny and my heart,
    Hold your tongue, my dearie,
For I will swear, by the moon and the stars,
    That thy lord shall no more come near thee.

They wandred high, they wandred low,
    They wandred late and early,
Untill they came to that on water,
    And by this time she was wearie.

Many a time I have rode that on water,
    And my lord Cassilis beside me,
And now I must set in my white feet and wade,
    And carry the gypsie laddie.

By and by came home this noble lord,
    And asking for his ladie,
The one did cry, the other did reply
    She is gone with the gypsie laddie.

Go saddle to me the black, he says,
    The brown rides never so speedie,
And I will neither eat nor drink
    Till I bring home my ladie.

crae crew   *on water* wan water
glowring staring

He wandred high, he wandred low,
  He wandred late and early,
Untill he came to that on water,
  And there he spied his ladie.

O wilt thou go home, my hinny and my heart,
  O wilt thou go home, my dearie?
And I'll close thee in a close room,
  Where no man shall come near thee.

I will not go home, my hinny and my heart,
  I will not go home, my dearie;
If I have brewn good beer, I will drink of the same,
  And my lord shall no more come near me.

But I will swear, by the moon and the stars,
  And the sun that shines so clearly,
That I am as free of the gypsie gang
  As the hour my mother bore me.

They were fifteen valiant men,
  Black, but very bonny,
They lost all their lives for one,
  The Earl of Cassillis' ladie.

19

THE JOVIAL HUNTER OF BROMSGROVE

Old Sir Robert Bolton had three sons,
  Wind well thy horn, good hunter;
And one of them was Sir Ryalas,
  For he was a jovial hunter.

He ranged all round down by the wood side,
  Wind well thy horn, good hunter,
Till in a tree-top a gay lady he spied,
  For he was a jovial hunter.

Oh, what dost thee mean, fair lady? said he,
  Wind well thy horn, good hunter;
The wild boar's killed my lord, and has thirty men gored,
  And thou beest a jovial hunter.

Oh, what shall I do this wild boar for to see?
  Wind well thy horn, good hunter;
Oh, thee blow a blast and he'll come unto thee,
  As thou beest a jovial hunter.

Then he blowed a blast, full north, east, west, and south,
  Wind well thy horn, good hunter;
And the wild boar then heard him full in his den,
  As he was a jovial hunter.

Then he made the best of his speed unto him,
  Wind well thy horn, good hunter;
  .   .   .   .
  To Sir Ryalas, the jovial hunter.

Then the wild boar, being so stout and so strong,
  Wind well thy horn, good hunter;
Thrashed down the trees as he ramped him along,
  To Sir Ryalas, the jovial hunter.

Oh, what dost thee want of me? wild boar said he,
  Wind well thy horn, good hunter;
Oh, I think in my heart I can do enough for thee,
  For I am the jovial hunter.

Then they fought four hours in a long summer day,
  Wind well thy horn, good hunter;
Till the wild boar fain would have got him away
  From Sir Ryalas, the jovial hunter.

Then Sir Ryalas drawed his broad sword with might,
  Wind well thy horn, good hunter;
And he fairly cut the boar's head off quite,
  For he was a jovial hunter.

Then out of the wood the wild woman flew,
  Wind well thy horn, good hunter;
Oh, my pretty spotted pig thou hast slew,
  For thou beest a jovial hunter.

There are three things, I demand them of thee,
  Wind well thy horn, good hunter;
It's thy horn, and thy hound, and thy gay lady,
  As thou beest a jovial hunter.

If these three things thou dost ask of me,
  Wind well thy horn, good hunter;
It's just as my sword and thy neck can agree,
  For I am a jovial hunter.

Then into his long locks the wild woman flew,
  Wind well thy horn, good hunter;
Till she thought in her heart to tear him through,
  Though he was a jovial hunter.

Then Sir Ryalas drawed his broad sword again,
  Wind well thy horn, good hunter,
And he fairly split her head into twain,
  For he was a jovial hunter.

In Bromsgrove church, the knight he doth lie,
    Wind well thy horn, good hunter;
And the wild boar's head is pictured thereby,
    Sir Ryalas, the jovial hunter.

20

THE LAILY WORM AND THE
MACHREL OF THE SEA

I was but seven year auld
  When my mither she did die;
My father married the ae warst woman
  The warld did ever see.

For she has made me the laily worm,
  That lies at the fit o the tree,
An my sister Masery she's made
  The machrel of the sea.

On every Saturday at noon
  The machrel comes to me,
An she takes my laily head
  An lays it on her knee,
She kaims it wi a siller kaim,
  An washes 't in the sea.

Seven knights hae I slain,
  Sin I lay at the fit of the tree,
An ye war na my ain father,
  The eight ane ye should be.

Sing on your song, ye laily worm,
  That ye did sing to me:
I never sung that song but what
  I would it sing to thee.

ae one   *worm* serpent, dragon
laily loathsome

I was but seven year auld,
    When my mither she did die;
My father married the ae warst woman
    The warld did ever see.

For she changed me to the laily worm,
    That lies at the fit o the tree,
And my sister Masery
    To the machrel of the sea.

And every Saturday at noon
    The machrel comes to me,
An she takes my laily head
    An lays it on her knee,
An kames it wi a siller kame,
    An washes it i the sea.

Seven knights hae I slain,
    Sin I lay at the fit o the tree,
An ye war na my ain father,
    The eighth ane ye should be.

He sent for his lady,
    As fast as send could he:
Whar is my son that ye sent frae me,
    And my daughter, Lady Masery?

Your son is at our king's court,
    Serving for meat an fee,
An your daughter's at our queen's court,
    A mary sweet an free.

Ye lie, ye ill woman,
    Sae loud as I hear ye lie;
My son's the laily worm,
    That lies at the fit o the tree,
And my daughter, Lady Masery,
    Is the machrel of the sea.

mary maid-of-honour   *free* beautiful

She has tane a siller wan,
    An gien him strokes three,
And he has started up the bravest knight
    That ever your eyes did see.

She has taen a small horn,
    An loud an shrill blew she,
An a' the fish came her untill
    But the proud machrel of the sea:
Ye shapeit me ance an unseemly shape,
    An ye's never mare shape me.

He has sent to the wood
    For whins and for hawthorn,
An he has taen that gay lady,
    An there he did her burn.

21

HIND ETIN

May Margret stood in her bouer door,
    Kaiming doun her yellow hair;
She spied some nuts growin in the wud,
    And wishd that she was there.

She has plaited her yellow locks
    A little abune her bree,
And she has kilted her petticoats
    A little below her knee,
And she's aff to Mulberry wud,
    As fast as she could gae.

She had na pu'd a nut, a nut,
    A nut but barely ane,
Till up started the Hynde Etin,
    Says, Lady, let thae alane!

Mulberry wuds are a' my ain;
    My father gied them me,
To sport and play when I thought lang;
    And they sall na be tane by thee.

And ae she pu'd the tither berrie,
    Na thinking o' the skaith,
And said, To wrang ye, Hynde Etin,
    I wad be unco laith.

But he has tane her by the yellow locks,
    And tied her till a tree,
And said, For slichting my commands,
    An ill death sall ye dree.

hind young   *bree* brow
May Maid   *thae* them
abune above   *skaith* harm

He pu'd a tree out o the wud,
  The biggest that was there,
And he howkit a cave monie fathoms deep,
  And put May Margret there.

Now rest ye there, ye saucie may;
  My wuds are free for thee;
And gif I tak ye to mysell,
  The better ye'll like me.

Na rest, na rest May Margret took,
  Sleep she got never nane;
Her back lay on the cauld, cauld floor,
  Her head upon a stane.

O tak me out, May Margret cried,
  O tak me hame to thee,
And I sall be your bounden page
  Until the day I dee.

He took her out o the dungeon deep,
  And awa wi him she's gane;
But sad was the day an earl's dochter
  Gaed hame wi Hynde Etin.

It fell out ance upon a day
  Hynde Etin's to the hunting gane,
And he has tane wi him his eldest son,
  For to carry his game.

O I wad ask ye something, father,
  An ye wadna angry be;
Ask on, ask on, my eldest son,
  Ask onie thing at me.

howkit dug

My mother's cheeks are aft times weet,
    Alas! they are seldom dry;
Na wonder, na wonder, my eldest son,
    Tho she should brast and die.

For your mother was an earl's dochter,
    Of noble birth and fame,
And now she's wife o Hynde Etin,
    Wha neer got christendame.

But we'll shoot the laverock in the lift,
    The buntlin on the tree,
And ye'll tak them hame to your mother,
    And see if she'll comforted be.

I wad ask ye something, mother,
    An ye wadna angry be;
Ask on, ask on, my eldest son,
    Ask onie thing at me.

Your cheeks they are aft times weet,
    Alas! they're seldom dry;
Na wonder, na wonder, my eldest son,
    Tho I should brast and die.

For I was ance an earl's dochter,
    Of noble birth and fame,
And now I am the wife of Hynde Etin,
    Wha neer got christendame.

brast burst   *buntlin* bunting
laverock lark

22

THOMAS RYMER

True Thomas lay oer yond grassy bank,
  And he beheld a ladie gay,
A ladie that was brisk and bold,
  Come riding oer the fernie brae.

Her skirt was of the grass-green silk,
  Her mantel of the velvet fine,
At ilka tett of her horse's mane
  Hung fifty silver bells and nine.

True Thomas he took off his hat,
  And bowed him low down till his knee:
All hail, thou mighty Queen of Heaven!
  For your peer on earth I never did see.

O no, O no, True Thomas, she says,
  That name does not belong to me;
I am but the queen of fair Elfland,
  And I'm come here for to visit thee.

But ye maun go wi me now, Thomas,
  True Thomas, ye maun go wi me,
For ye maun serve me seven years,
  Thro weel or wae as may chance to be.

She turned about her milk-white steed,
  And took True Thomas up behind,
And aye wheneer her bridle rang,
  The steed flew swifter than the wind.

Rymer (the) Poet   *ilka tett* every lock
brae brow of a hill

O they rade on, and further on,
  Until they came to a garden green:
Light down, light down, ye ladie free,
  Some of that fruit let me pull to thee.

O no, O no, True Thomas, she says,
  That fruit maun not be touched by thee,
For a' the plagues that are in hell
  Light on the fruit of this countrie.

But I have a loaf here in my lap,
  Likewise a bottle of claret wine,
And now ere we go farther on,
  We'll rest a while, and ye may dine.

When he had eaten and drunk his fill,
  Lay down your head upon my knee,
The lady sayd, ere we climb yon hill,
  And I will show you fairlies three.

O see not ye yon narrow road,
  So thick beset wi thorns and briers?
That is the path of righteousness,
  Tho after it but few enquires.

And see not ye that braid braid road,
  That lies across yon lillie leven?
That is the path of wickedness,
  Tho some call it the road to heaven.

And see not ye that bonny road,
  Which winds about the fernie brae?
That is the road to fair Elfland,
  Where you and I this night maun gae.

fairlies wonders   *brae* hill
lillie leven lovely glade

66

But Thomas, ye maun hold your tongue,
  Whatever you may hear or see,
For gin ae word you should chance to speak,
  You will neer get back to your ain countrie.

For forty days and forty nights
  He wade thro red blude to the knee,
And he saw neither sun nor moon,
  But heard the roaring of the sea.

He has gotten a coat of the even cloth,
  And a pair of shoes of velvet green,
And till seven years were past and gone
  True Thomas on earth was never seen.

ae one   *even cloth* smooth cloth (such as
                            noblemen wear)

23

TAM LIN

O I forbid you, maidens a',
  That wear gowd on your hair,
To come or gae by Carterhaugh,
  For young Tam Lin is there.

There's nane that gaes by Carterhaugh,
  But they leave him a wad,
Either their rings, or green mantles,
  Or else their maidenhead.

Janet has kilted her green kirtle
  A little aboon her knee,
And she has broded her yellow hair
  A little aboon her bree,
And she's awa to Carterhaugh,
  As fast as she can hie.

When she came to Carterhaugh
  Tam Lin was at the well,
And there she fand his steed standing,
  But away was himsel.

She had na pu'd a double rose,
  A rose but only twa,
Till up then started young Tam Lin,
  Says, Lady, thou pu's nae mae.

Why pu's thou the rose, Janet,
  And why breaks thou the wand?
Or why comes thou to Carterhaugh
  Withoutten my command?

wad forfeit   *bree* brow

Carterhaugh, it is my ain,
    My daddie gave it me;
I'll come and gang by Carterhaugh,
    And ask nae leave at thee.

Janet has kilted her green kirtle
    A little aboon her knee,
And she has snooded her yellow hair
    A little aboon her bree,
And she is to her father's ha,
    As fast as she can hie.

Four and twenty ladies fair
    Were playing at the ba,
And out then cam the fair Janet,
    Ance the flower among them a'.

Four and twenty ladies fair
    Were playing at the chess,
And out then cam the fair Janet,
    As green as onie glass.

Out then spak an auld grey knight,
    Lay o'er the castle wa,
And says, Alas, fair Janet, for thee
    But we'll be blamed a'.

Haud your tongue, ye auld facd knight,
    Some ill death may ye die!
Father my bairn on whom I will,
    I'll father nane on thee.

Out then spak her father dear,
    And he spak meek and mild:
And ever alas, sweet Janet, he says,
    I think thou gaes wi child.

If that I gae wi child, father,
  Mysel maun bear the blame;
There's neer a laird about your ha
  Shall get the bairn's name.

If my love were an earthly knight,
  As he's an elfin grey,
I wad na gie my ain true-love
  For nae lord that ye hae.

The steed that my true-love rides on
  Is lighter than the wind;
Wi siller he is shod before,
  Wi burning gowd behind.

Janet has kilted her green kirtle
  A little aboon her knee,
And she has snooded her yellow hair
  A little aboon her bree,
And she's awa to Carterhaugh,
  As fast as she can hie.

When she cam to Carterhaugh,
  Tam Lin was at the well,
And there she fand his steed standing,
  But away was himsel.

She had na pu'd a double rose,
  A rose but only twa,
Till up then started young Tam Lin,
  Says, Lady, thou pu's nae mae.

Why pu's thou the rose, Janet,
  Amang the groves saw green,
And a' to kill the bonnie babe,
  That we gat us between?

elfin grey grey elf

O tell me, tell me, Tam Lin, she says,
    For's sake that died on tree,
If eer ye was in holy chapel,
    Or christendom did see?

Roxburgh he was my grandfather,
    Took me with him to bide,
And ance it fell upon a day
    That wae did me betide.

And ance it fell upon a day,
    A cauld day and a snell,
When we were frae the hunting come,
    That frae my horse I fell;
The Queen o Fairies she caught me,
    In yon green hill to dwell.

And pleasant is the fairy land,
    But, an eerie tale to tell,
Ay at the end of seven years
    We pay a tiend to hell;
I am sae fair and fu o flesh,
    I'm feard it be mysel.

But the night is Halloween, lady,
    The morn is Hallowday;
Then win me, win me, an ye will,
    For weel I wat ye may.

Just at the mirk and midnight hour
    The fairy folk will ride,
And they that wad their tru-love win,
    At Miles Cross they maun bide.

snell sharp   *tiend* tithe

But how shall I thee ken, Tam Lin,
  Or how my true-love know,
Amang sae mony unco knights
  The like I never saw?

O first let pass the black, lady,
  And syne let pass the brown,
But quickly run to the milk-white steed,
  Pu ye his rider down.

For I'll ride on the milk-white steed,
  And ay nearest the town;
Because I was an earthly knight
  They gie me that renown.

My right hand will be glovd, lady,
  My left hand will be bare,
Cockt up shall my bonnet be,
  And kaimd down shall my hair,
And thae's the takens I gie thee,
  Nae doubt I will be there.

They'll turn me in your arms, lady,
  Into an esk and adder;
But hold me fast, and fear me not,
  I am your bairn's father.

They'll turn me to a bear sae grim,
  And then a lion bold;
But hold me fast, and fear me not,
  As ye shall love your child.

Again they'll turn me in your arms
  To a red hot gaud of airn;
But hold me fast, and fear me not,
  I'll do to you nae harm.

unco unknown, strange   *esk* eft, newt
syne then   *gaud* bar

And last they'll turn me in your arms
    Into the burning gleed;
Then throw me into well water,
    O throw me in wi speed.

And then I'll be your ain true-love,
    I'll turn a naked knight;
Then cover me wi your green mantle,
    And cover me out o sight.

Gloomy, gloomy was the night,
    And eerie was the way,
As fair Jenny in her green mantle
    To Miles Cross she did gae.

About the middle o the night
    She heard the bridles ring;
This lady was as glad at that
    As any earthly thing.

First she let the black pass by,
    And syne she let the brown;
But quickly she ran to the milk-white steed,
    And pu'd the rider down.

Sae weel she minded what he did say,
    And young Tam Lin did win;
Syne coverd him wi her green mantle,
    As blythe's a bird in spring.

Out then spak the Queen o Fairies,
    Out of a bush o broom:
Them that has gotten young Tam Lin
    Has gotten a stately groom.

gleed red-hot coal   *syne* then

Out then spak the Queen o Fairies,
  And an angry woman was she:
Shame betide her ill-far'd face,
  And an ill death may she die,
For she's taen awa the bonniest knight
  In a' my companie.

But had I kend, Tam Lin, she says,
  What now this night I see,
I wad hae taen out thy twa grey een,
  And put in twa een o tree.

tree wood

24

THE WIFE OF USHER'S WELL

There lived a wife at Usher's Well,
    And a wealthy wife was she;
She had three stout and stalwart sons,
    And sent them oer the sea.

They hadna been a week from her,
    A week but barely ane,
Whan word came to the carline wife
    That her three sons were gane.

They hadna been a week from her,
    A week but barely three,
Whan word came to the carlin wife
    That her sons she'd never see.

I wish the wind may never cease,
    Nor fashes in the flood,
Till my three sons come hame to me,
    In earthly flesh and blood.

It fell about the Martinmass,
    When nights are lang and mirk,
The carlin wife's three sons came hame,
    And their hats were o the birk.

It neither grew in syke nor ditch,
    Nor yet in ony sheugh;
But at the gates o Paradise,
    That birk grew fair eneugh.

carline old woman   *syke* water-course
birk birch   *sheugh* wood

Blow up the fire, my maidens!
    Bring water from the well!
For a' my house shall feast this night,
    Since my three sons are well.

And she has made to them a bed,
    She's made it large and wide,
And she's taen her mantle her about,
    Sat down at the bed-side.

Up then crew the red, red cock,
    And up and crew the gray;
The eldest to the youngest said,
    'Tis time we were away.

The cock he hadna crawd but once,
    And clappd his wings at a',
When the youngest to the eldest said,
    Brother, we must awa.

The cock doth craw, the day doth daw,
    The channerin worm doth chide;
Gin we be mist out o our place,
    A sair pain we maun bide.

Fare ye weel, my mother dear!
    Fareweel to barn and byre!
And fare ye weel, the bonny lass
    That kindles my mother's fire!

channerin fretting

25

THE TWA MAGICIANS

The lady stands in her bower door,
  As straight as willow wand;
The blacksmith stood a little forebye,
  Wi hammer in his hand.

Weel may ye dress ye, lady fair,
  Into your robes o red;
Before the morn at this same time,
  I'll gain your maidenhead.

Awa, awa, ye coal-black smith,
  Would ye do me the wrang
To think to gain my maidenhead,
  That I hae kept sae lang!

Then she has hadden up her hand,
  And she sware by the mold,
I wudna be a blacksmith's wife
  For the full o a chest o gold.

I'd rather I were dead and gone,
  And my body laid in grave,
Ere a rusty stock o coal-black smith
  My maidenhead shoud have.

But he has hadden up his hand,
  And he sware be the mass,
I'll cause ye be my light leman
  For the hauf o that and less.

forebye apart   *stock* lump
mold earth   *leman* lover
rusty surly

O bide, lady, bide,
And aye he bade her bide;
The rusty smith your leman shall be,
For a' your muckle pride.

Then she became a turtle dow,
To fly up in the air,
And he became another dow,
And they flew pair and pair.
O bide, lady, bide, etc.

She turnd hersell into an eel,
To swim into yon burn,
And he became a speckled trout,
To gie the eel a turn.
O bide, lady, bide, etc.

Then she became a duck, a duck,
To puddle in a peel,
And he became a rose-kaimd drake,
To gie the duck a dreel.
O bide, lady, bide, etc.

She turnd hersell into a hare,
To rin upon yon hill,
And he became a gude grey-hound,
And boldly he did fill.
O bide, lady, bide, etc.

Then she became a gay grey mare,
And stood in yonder slack,
And he became a gilt saddle.
And sat upon her back.
Was she wae, he held her sae,
And still he bade her bide;
The rusty smith her leman was,
For a' her muckle pride.

peel pool
dreel flurry, stir

fill follow
slack low ground

78

Then she became a het girdle,
　　And he became a cake,
And a' the ways she turnd hersell,
　　The blacksmith was her make.
　　　　Was she wae, etc.

She turnd hersell into a ship,
　　To sail out ower the flood;
He ca'ed a nail intill her tail,
　　And syne the ship she stood.
　　　　Was she wae, etc.

Then she became a silken plaid,
　　And stretchd upon a bed,
And he became a green covering,
　　And gaind her maidenhead.
　　　　Was she wae, etc.

het girdle hot griddle　　　　*syne* then
make mate　　　　　　　　　　*plaid* cloak

26

KEMP OWYNE

Her mother died when she was young,
　　Which gave her cause to make great moan;
Her father married the warst woman
　　That ever lived in Christendom.

She served her with foot and hand,
　　In every thing that she could dee,
Till once, in an unlucky time,
　　She threw her in ower Craigy's sea.

Says, Lie you there, dove Isabel,
　　And all my sorrows lie with thee;
Till Kemp Owyne come ower the sea,
　　And borrow you with kisses three,
Let all the warld do what they will,
　　Oh borrowed shall you never be!

Her breath grew strang, her hair grew lang,
　　And twisted thrice about the tree,
And all the people, far and near,
　　Thought that a savage beast was she.

These news did come to Kemp Owyne,
　　Where he lived, far beyond the sea;
He hasted him to Craigy's sea,
　　And on the savage beast lookd he.

Her breath was strang, her hair was lang,
　　And twisted was about the tree,
And with a swing she came about:
　　Come to Craigy's sea, and kiss with me.

borrowed set free

Here is a royal belt, she cried,
  That I have found in the green sea;
And while your body it is on,
  Drawn shall your blood never be;
But if you touch me, tail or fin,
  I vow my belt your death shall be.

He stepped in, gave her a kiss,
  The royal belt he brought him wi;
Her breath was strang, her hair was lang,
  And twisted twice about the tree,
And with a swing she came about:
  Come to Craigy's sea, and kiss with me.

Here is a royal ring, she said,
  That I have found in the green sea;
And while your finger it is on,
  Drawn shall your blood never be;
But if you touch me, tail or fin,
  I swear my ring your death shall be.

He stepped in, gave her a kiss,
  The royal ring he brought him wi;
Her breath was strang, her hair was lang,
  And twisted ance about the tree,
And with a swing she came about:
  Come to Craigy's sea, and kiss with me.

Here is a royal brand, she said,
  That I have found in the green sea;
And while your body it is on,
  Drawn shall your blood never be;
But if you touch me, tail or fin,
  I swear my brand your death shall be.

He stepped in, gave her a kiss,
  The royal brand he brought him wi;
Her breath was sweet, her hair grew short,
  And twisted nane about the tree,
And smilingly she came about,
  As fair a woman as fair could be.

27

THE CRUEL MOTHER

She sat down below a thorn,
   Fine flowers in the valley;
And there she has her sweet babe born,
   And the green leaves they grow rarely.

Smile na sae sweet, my bonie babe:
And ye smile sae sweet, ye'll smile me dead.

She's taen out her little penknife
And twinn'd the sweet babe o its life.

She's howket a grave by the light o the moon
And there she's buried her sweet babe in.

As she was going to the church
She saw a sweet babe in the porch.

O sweet babe and thou were mine
I wad cleed thee in the silk so fine.

O mother dear, when I was thine,
You didna prove to me sae kind.

O cursed mother, heaven's high,
And that's where thou will neer win nigh.

O cursed mother, hell is deep,
   Fine flowers in the valley;
And there thou'll enter step by step,
   And the green leaves they grow rarely.

---

twinn'd deprived   *howket* dug

28

THE THREE RAVENS

There were three ravens sat on a tree,
  Downe a downe, hay downe, hay downe,
There were three ravens sat on a tree,
  With a downe,
There were three ravens sat on a tree,
They were as black as they might be,
  With a downe derrie, derrie, derrie, downe, downe.

The one of them said to his make,
Where shall we our breakfast take?

Down in yonder greene field,
There lies a knight slain under his shield.

His hounds they lie down at his feete,
So well they can their master keepe.

His haukes they flie so eagerly,
There's no fowle dare him come nie.

Downe there comes a fallow doe,
As great with yong as she might goe.

She lift up his bloudy hed,
And kist his wounds that were so red.

She got him up upon her backe,
And carried him to earthen lake.

make mate   *lake* grave

She buried him before the prime,
She was dead herselfe ere even-song time.

God send every gentleman
Such haukes, such hounds, and such a leman.

the prime 6 a.m., or sunrise, the   *leman* lover
   hour of the first prayer and
   worship

29

THE LAMENT OF THE BORDER WIDOW

My love he built me a bonny bower,
And clad it a wi lilye flower.
A brawer bower ye ne'er did see
Than my true love he built for me.

There came a man by middle day,
He spied his sport and went away,
And brought the king that very night,
Who brake my bower, and slew my knight.

He slew my knight to me sae dear.
He slew my knight and poind his gear.
My servants all for life did flee
And left me in extremitie.

I sewd his sheet, making my mane,
I watched the corpse myself alane,
I watched his body night and day.
No living creature came that way.

I took his body on my back,
And whiles I gaed, and whiles I sat.
I diggd a grave and laid him in,
And happd him with the sod sae green.

But think na ye my heart was sair
When I laid the moul on his yellow hair?
O think na ye my heart was wae
When I turnd about, away to gae?

---

poind his gear seized and sold his   *moul* mould, earth
   possessions

Nae living man I'll love again,
Since that my lovely knight is slain.
Wi ae lock of his yellow hair
I'll chain my heart for evermair.

30

CLARK SANDERS

i

Clark Sanders and May Margret
  Walkt ower yon graveld green,
And sad and heavy was the love,
  I wat, it fell this twa between.

A bed, a bed, Clark Sanders said,
  A bed, a bed for you and I;
Fye no, fye no, the lady said,
  Until the day we married be.

For in it will come my seven brothers,
  And a' their torches burning bright;
They'll say, We hae but ae sister,
  And here her lying wi a knight.

Ye'l take the sourde fray my scabbord,
  And lowly, lowly lift the gin,
And you may say, your oth to save,
  You never let Clark Sanders in.

Yele take a napken in your hand,
  And ye'l ty up baith your een,
An ye may say, your oth to save,
  That ye saw na Sandy sen late yestreen.

Yele take me in your armes twa,
  Yele carrey me ben into your bed,
And ye may say, your oth to save,
  In your bower-floor I never tread.

graveld green gravelly grass	*sen* since
ae one	*ben* inside
gin latch	*bower* chamber

She has taen the sourde fray his scabbord,
   And lowly, lowly lifted the gin;
She was to swear, her oth to save,
   She never let Clark Sanders in.

She has tain a napkin in her hand,
   And she ty'd up baith her een;
She was to swear, her oth to save,
   She saw na him sene late yestreen.

She has taen him in her armes twa,
   And carried him ben into her bed;
She was to swear, her oth to save,
   He never in her bower-floor tread.

In and came her seven brothers,
   And all their torches burning bright;
Says thay, We hae but ae sister,
   And see there her lying wi a knight.

Out and speaks the first of them,
   A wat they hay been lovers dear;
Out and speaks the next of them,
   They hay been in love this many a year.

Out an speaks the third of them,
   It wear great sin this twa to twain;
Out an speaks the fourth of them,
   It wear a sin to kill a sleeping man.

Out an speaks the fifth of them,
   A wat they'll near be twaind by me:
Out an speaks the sixt of them,
   We'l tak our leave an gae our way.

A wat I wot   *twain* part

Out an speaks the seventh of them,
　　Altho there wear no a man but me,
[I'se bear the brand into my hand
　　Shall quickly gar Clark Sanders die.]

Out he has taen a bright long brand,
　　And he has striped it throw the strae,
And throw and throw Clarke Sanders' body
　　A wat he has gard cold iron gae.

Sanders he started, an Margret she lapt
　　Intill his arms whare she lay,
And well and wellsom was the night,
　　A wat it was between these twa.

And they lay still, and sleeped sound,
　　Untill the day began to daw;
And kindly till him she did say
　　It's time, trew-love, ye wear awa.

They lay still, and sleeped sound,
　　Untill the sun began to shine;
She lookt between her and the wa,
　　And dull and heavy was his eeen.

She thought it had been a loathsome sweat,
　　A wat it had fallen this twa between;
But it was the blood of his fair body,
　　A wat his life days wair na lang.

O Sanders, I'le do for your sake
　　What other ladys would na thoule;
When seven years is come and gone,
　　There's near a shoe go on my sole.

gar make　　　　　　　　thoule endure
the strae the bed-straw　lapt folded (herself)

O Sanders, I'le do for your sake
    What other ladies would think mare;
When seven years is come an gone,
    Ther's nere a comb go in my hair.

O Sanders, I'le do for your sake
    What other ladies would think lack;
When seven years is come an gone,
    I'le wear nought but dowy black.

The bells gaed clinking throw the towne,
    To carry the dead corps to the clay,
An sighing says her May Margret,
    A wat I bide a doulfou day.

In an come her father dear,
    Stout steping on the floor;
Hold your toung, my doughter dear,
    Let all your mourning a bee;
I'le carry the dead corps to the clay,
    An I'le come back an comfort thee.

Comfort well your seven sons,
    For comforted will I never bee;
For it was neither lord nor loune
    That was in bower last night wi mee.

ii

Whan bells war rung, an mass was sung,
    A wat a' man to bed were gone,
Clark Sanders came to Margret's window,
    With mony a sad sigh and groan.

dowy mournful   *bower* room, bedroom

Are ye sleeping, Margret, he says,
  Or are ye waking, presentlie?
Give me my faith and trouthe again,
  A wat, trew love, I gied to thee.

Your faith and trouth ye's never get,
  Now our trew love shall never twain,
Till ye come with me in my bower,
  And kiss me both cheek and chin.

My mouth it is full cold, Margret.
  It has the smell now of the ground;
And if I kiss thy comely mouth,
  Thy life-days will not be long.

Cocks are crowing a merry midl-arf,
  I wat the wild fule boded day;
Gie me my faith and trouthe again,
  And let me fare me on my way.

Thy faith and trouthe thou shall na get,
  Nor our trew love shall never twain,
Till ye tell me what comes of women
  Awat that dy's in strong traveling.

Their beds are made in the heavens high,
  Down at the foot of our good Lord's knee,
Well set about wi gilly-flowers,
  A wat sweet company for to see.

O cocks are crowing a merry middl-arf,
  A wat the wilde foule boded day;
The salms of Heaven will be sung,
  And ere now I'le be misst away.

bower room	*wild fule boded day* wild fowls
a merry midl-arf on merry	announced day
middle-earth (earth as the	*twain* part
middle of the universe)	*traveling* travail (childbirth)
	gily-flowers clove-scented pinks

Up she has tain a bright long wand,
    And she has straked her trouth thereon;
She has given him out at the shot-window,
    Wi many a sad sigh and heavy groan.

I thank you, Margret, I thank you, Margret,
    And I thank you hartilie;
Gine ever the dead come for the quick,
    Be sure, Margret, I'll come again for thee.

It's hose an shoon an gound alane
    She clame the wall and followed him,
Untill she came to a green forest,
    On this she lost the sight of him.

Is their any room at your head, Sanders?
    Is their any room at your feet?
Or any room at your twa sides?
    Whare fain, fain woud I sleep.

Their is na room at my head, Margret,
    Their is na room at my feet;
There is room at my twa sides,
    For ladys for to sleep.

Cold meal is my covering owre,
    But an my winding sheet;
My bed it is full low, I say,
    Down among the hongerey worms I sleep.

Cold meal is my covering owre,
    But an my winding sheet;
The dew it falls na sooner down
    Then ay it is full weet.

wand staff   shot-window hinged window
straked her trouth pledged (struck)   which can be opened and shut
  her troth   Cold meal Cold earth
                                    But an And also

92

THE UNQUIET GRAVE

The wind doth blow today, my love,
   And a few small drops of rain.
I never had but one true-love,
   In cold grave she was lain.

I'll do as much for my true-love
   As any young man may,
I'll sit and mourn all at her grave
   For a twelvemonth and a day.

The twelvemonth and a day being up,
   The dead began to speak:
Oh who sits weeping on my grave,
   And will not let me sleep?

'Tis I, my love, sits on your grave,
   And will not let you sleep,
For I crave one kiss of your clay-cold lips,
   And that is all I seek.

You crave one kiss of my clay-cold lips,
   But my breath smells earthy strong.
If you have one kiss of my clay-cold lips,
   Your time will not be long.

'Tis down in yonder garden green,
   Love, where we used to walk,
The finest flower that ere was seen
   Is withered to a stalk.

The stalk is withered dry, my love,
   So will our hearts decay.
So make yourself content, my love,
   Till God calls you away.

THE CRUEL BROTHER

There was three ladies playd at the ba,
  With a hey ho and a lillie gay.
There came a knight and played oer them a'.
  As the primrose spreads so sweetly.

The eldest was baith tall and fair,
But the youngest was beyond compare.

The midmost had a graceful mien,
But the youngest lookd like beautie's queen.

The knight bowd low to a' the three,
But to the youngest he bent his knee.

The ladie turned her head aside,
The knight he woo'd her to be his bride.

The ladie blushd a rosy red,
And sayd, Sir knight, I'm too young to wed.

O ladie fair, give me your hand,
And I'll make you ladie of a' my land.

Sir knight, ere ye my favor win,
You maun get consent frae a' my kin.

He's got consent frae her parents dear,
And likewise frae her sisters fair.

He's got consent frae her kin each one,
But forgot to spiek to her brother John.

played o er them a' played better than them all

Now, when the wedding day was come,
The knight would take his bonny bride home.

And many a lord and many a knight
Came to behold that ladie bright.

And there was nae man that did her see,
But wishd himself bridegroom to be.

Her father dear led her down the stair,
And her sisters twain they kissd her there.

Her mother dear led her thro the closs,
And her brother John set her on her horse.

She leand her oer the saddle-bow,
To give him a kiss ere she did go.

He has taen a knife, baith lang and sharp,
And stabbd that bonny bride to the heart.

She hadno ridden half thro the town,
Until her heart's blude staind her gown.

Ride softly on, says the best young man,
For I think our bonny bride looks pale and wan.

O lead me gently up yon hill,
And I'll there sit down, and make my will.

O what will you leave to your father dear?
The silver-shod steed that brought me here.

What will you leave to your mother dear?
My velvet pall and my silken gear.

pall mantle   *closs* closed courtyard

What will you leave to your sister Anne?
My silken scarf and my gowden fan.

What will you leave to your sister Grace?
My bloody cloaths to wash and dress.

What will you leave to your brother John?
The gallows-tree to hang him on.

What will you leave to your brother John's wife?
The wilderness to end her life.

This ladie fair in her grave was laid,
And many a mass was oer her said.

But it would have made your heart right sair,
To see the bridegroom rive his haire.

33

EARL BRAND

Did you ever hear of good Earl Brand,
Aye lally an lilly lally
And the king's daughter of fair Scotland?
   And the braw knights o Airly.

She was scarce fifteen years of age
When she came to Earl Brand's bed,
   Wi the braw knights o Airly.

O Earl Brand, I fain wad see
Our grey hounds run over the lea,
Mang the braw bents o Airly.

O, says Earl Brand, I've nae steads but one,
And you shall ride and I shall run,
   Oer the braw heights o Airly.

O, says the lady, I hae three,
And ye shall hae yeer choice for me,
Of the braw steeds o Airly.

So they lap on, and on they rade,
Till they came to auld Carle Hood,
   Oer the braw hills o Airly.

Carl Hood's aye for ill, and he's no for good,
He's aye for ill, and he's no for good,
   Mang the braw hills o Airly.

Where hae ye been hunting a' day,
And where have ye stolen this fair may,
   I the braw nights sae Airly?

may maid

She is my sick sister dear,
New comd home from another sister,
  I the braw nights sae early.

O, says the lady, if ye love me,
Gie him a penny fee and let him gae.
  I the braw nights sae early.

He's gane home to her father's bower,
Where is the lady o this ha?
She's out wi the young maids, playing at the ba.
I the braw nights so early.

No, says another, she's riding oer the moor,
And a' to be Earl Brand's whore.
  I the braw nights so early.

The king mounted fifteen weel armed men
A' to get Earl Brand taen,
  I the braw hills so early.

The lady looked over her white horse mane,
O Earl Brand, we will be taen.
  In the braw hills so early.

He says, If they come one by one,
Ye'll no see me so soon taen.
  In the braw hills so early.

So they came every one but one,
And he has killd them a' but ane,
  In the braw hills so early.

And that one came behind his back,
And gave Earl Brand a deadly stroke,
  In the braw hills of Airly.

For as sair wounded as he was,
He lifted the lady on her horse,
  In the braw nights so early.

O Earl Brand, I see thy heart's bluid!
It's but the shadow of my scarlet robe.
  I the braw nights so early.

He came to his mother's home;
She looked out and cryd her son was gone,
And a' for the sake of an English loon.

What will I do wi your lady fair?
Marry her to my eldest brother.
  The brawest knight i Airly.

loon whore

34

WILLIE AND LADY MARGERIE

Willie was a widow's son,
   And he wore a milk-white weed, O
And weel could Willie read and write,
   Far better ride on steed, O.

Lady Margerie was the first lady
   That drank to him the wine,
And aye as the healths gade round and round,
   Laddy, your love is mine.

Lady Margerie was the first ladye
   That drank to him the beer,
And aye as the healths gade round and round,
   Laddy, you're welcome here.

You must come into my bower
   When the evening bells do ring,
And you must come into my bower
   When the evening mass doth sing.

He's taen four and twenty braid arrows,
   And laced them in a whang,
And he's awa to Lady Margerie's bower,
   As fast as he can gang.

He set ae foot on the wall,
   And the other on a stane,
And he's killed a' the king's life-guards,
   And he's killed them every man.

bower room   *laced them in a whang*
                                    tied them in a thong

Oh open, open, Lady Margerie,
    Open and let me in;
The weet weets a' my yellow hair,
    And the dew draps on my chin.

With her feet as white as sleet
    She strode her bower within,
And with her fingers long and small
    She's looten Sweet Willie in.

She's louten down unto her foot
    To loose Sweet Willie's shoon;
The buckles were sa stiff they wudna lowse,
    The blood had frozen in.

O Willie, Willie, I fear that thou
    Has bred me dule and sorrow;
The deed that thou has dune this nicht
    Will kythe upon the morrow.

In then came her father dear,
    And a broad sword by his gare,
And he's gien Willie, the widow's son,
    A deep wound and a sair.

Lye yont, lye yont, Willie, she says,
    Your sweat weets a' my side;
Lye yont, lie yont, Willie, she says,
    For your sweat I downa bide.

She turned her back unto the wa,
    Her face unto the room,
And there she saw her auld father,
    Walking up and down.

louten bent   *kythe* be apparent

Woe be to you, father, she said,
  And an ill deed may you die!
For ye've killd Willie, the widow's son
  And he would have married me.

She turned her back unto the room,
  Her face unto the wa,
And with a deep and heavy sich
  Her heart it brak in twa.

sich sigh

35

BLOW THE WINDS, I-HO

There was a shepherd's son,
  He kept sheep on yonder hill;
He laid his pipe and his crook aside,
  And there he slept his fill.
    And blow the winds, I-ho!
      Sing, blow the winds, I-ho!
    Clear away the morning dew,
      And blow the winds, I-ho!

He looked east, and he looked west,
  He took another look,
And there he spied a lady gay,
  Was dipping in a brook.

She said, Sir, don't touch my mantle,
  Come, let my clothes alone;
I will give you as much money
  As you can carry home.

I will not touch your mantle,
  I'll let your clothes alone;
I'll take you out of the water clear,
  My dear, to be my own.

He did not touch her mantle,
  He let her clothes alone;
But he took her from the clear water,
  And all to be his own.

He set her on a milk-white steed,
  Himself upon another;
And there they rode, along the road,
  Like sister and like brother.

And as they rode along the road,
  He spied some cocks of hay;
Yonder, he says, is a lovely place
  For men and maids to play!

And when they came to her father's gate,
  She pulled at a ring;
And ready was the proud porter
  For to let the lady in.

And when the gates were open,
  This lady jumped in;
She says, You are a fool without,
  And I'm a maid within.

Good morrow to you, modest boy,
  I thank you for your care;
If you had been what you should have been,
  I would not have left you there.

There is a horse in my father's stable,
  He stands beyond the thorn;
He shakes his head above the trough,
  But dares not prie the corn.

There is a bird in my father's flock,
  A double comb he wears;
He flaps his wings, and crows full loud,
  But a capon's crest he bears.

There is a flower in my father's garden,
  They call it marygold;
The fool that will not when he may,
  He shall not when he wold.

---

stands beyond the thorn i.e. is
  harnessed to a bush-harrow,
  primitive arrangement of thorn
  bushes for 'bushing in' the seed
  corn. The horse would have been
an ordinary gelding, equivalent
to the capon in the next stanza.
prie taste, sample
capon castrated cockerel

Said the shepherd's son, as he doft his shoon,
    My feet they shall run bare.
And if ever I meet another maid,
    I rede that maid beware.

36

LITTLE MUSGRAVE AND LADY BARNARD

As it fell one holy-day,
  Hay downe
As many be in the yeare,
When young men and maids together did goe,
  Their mattins and masse to heare,

Little Musgrave came to the church-dore;
  The preist was at private masse;
But he had more minde of the faire women
  Then he had of Our Lady's grace.

The one of them was clad in green,
  Another was clad in pall,
And then came in my lord Bernard's wife,
  The fairest amonst them all.

She cast an eye on Little Musgrave,
  As bright as the summer sun;
And then bethought this Little Musgrave,
  This lady's heart have I woonn.

Quoth she, I have loved thee, Little Musgrave,
  Full long and many a day;
So have I loved you, fair lady,
  Yet never word durst I say.

I have a bower at Buckelsfordbery,
  Full daintyly it is deight:
If thou wilt wend thither, thou Little Musgrave,
  Thou's lig in mine armes all night.

pall fine cloth   *bower* house

Quoth he, I thank yee, faire lady,
　　This kindnes thou showest to me;
But whether it be to my weal or woe,
　　This night I will lig with thee.

With that he heard, a little tyne page,
　　By his ladye's coach as he ran:
All though I am my ladye's foot-page,
　　Yet I am Lord Barnard's man.

My lord Barnard shall knowe of this,
　　Whether I sink or swim;
And ever where the bridges were broake
　　He laid him downe to swimme.

A sleepe or wake, thou Lord Barnard,
　　As thou art a man of life,
For Little Musgrave is at Bucklesfordbery,
　　A bed with thy own wedded wife.

If this be true, thou little tinny page,
　　This thing thou tellest to me,
Then all the land in Bucklesfordbery
　　I freely will give to thee.

But if it be a ly, thou little tinny page,
　　This thing thou tellest to me,
On the hyest tree in Bucklesfordbery
　　Then hanged shalt thou be.

He called up his merry men all:
　　Come saddle me my steed;
This night must I go to Buckellsfordbery,
　　For I never had greater need.

And some of them whistld, and some of them sung,
　　And some these words did say,
And ever when my lord Barnard's horn blew,
　　Away, Musgrave, away!

Methinks I hear the thresel-cock,
   Methinks I hear the jaye;
Methinks I hear my lord Barnard,
   And I would I were away.

Lye still, lye still, thou Little Musgrave,
   And huggell me from the cold;
'Tis nothing but a shephard's boy,
   A driving his sheep to the fold.

Is not thy hawke upon a perch?
   Thy steed eats oats and hay;
And thou a fair lady in thine armes,
   And wouldst thou bee away?

With that my lord Barnard came to the dore,
   And lit a stone upon;
He plucked out three silver keys,
   And he opend the dores each one.

He lifted up the coverlett,
   He lifted up the sheet:
How now, thou Littell Musgrave,
   Doest thou find my lady sweet?

I find her sweet, quoth Little Musgrave,
   The more 'tis to my paine;
I would gladly give three hundred pounds
   That I were on yonder plaine.

Arise, arise, thou Littell Musgrave,
   And put thy clothes on;
I shall nere be said in my country
   I have killed a naked man.

I have two swords in one scabberd,
   Full deere they cost my purse;
And thou shalt have the best of them,
   And I will have the worse.

The first stroke that Little Musgrave stroke,
　　He hurt Lord Barnard sore;
The next stroke that Lord Barnard stroke,
　　Little Musgrave nere struck more.

With that bespake the faire lady,
　　In bed whereas she lay:
Although thou'rt dead, thou Little Musgrave,
　　Yet I for thee will pray.

And wish well to thy soule will I,
　　So long as I have life;
So will I not for thee, Barnard,
　　Although I am thy wedded wife.

He cut her paps from off her brest;
　　Great pitty it was to see
That some drops of this ladie's heart's blood
　　Ran trickling downe her knee.

Woe worth you, woe worth, my mery men all,
　　You were nere borne for my good;
Why did you not offer to stay my hand,
　　When you see me wax so wood?

For I have slaine the bravest sir knight
　　That ever rode on steed;
So have I done the fairest lady
　　That ever did woman's deed.

A grave, a grave, Lord Barnard cryd,
　　To put these lovers in;
But lay my lady on the upper hand,
　　For she came of the better kin.

wax so wood grew so mad with anger

37

LADY DIAMOND

There was a king, and a very great king,
  And a king of meikle fame;
He had not a child in the world but ane,
  Lady Daisy was her name.

He had a very bonnie kitchen-boy,
  And William was his name;
He never lay out o Lady Daisy's bower,
  Till he brought her body to shame.

When een-birds sung, and een-bells rung,
  And a' men were boune to rest,
The king went on to Lady Daisy's bower,
  Just like a wandering ghaist.

He has drawn the curtains round and round,
  And there he has sat him down;
To whom is this, Lady Daisy, he says,
  That now you gae so round?

Is it to a laird? or is it to a lord?
  Or a baron of high degree?
Or is it William, my bonnie kitchen-boy?
  Tell now the truth to me.

It's no to a laird, and it's no to a lord,
  Nor a baron of high degree;
But it's to William, your bonnie kitchen-boy:
  What cause hae I to lee?

O where is all my merry, merry men,
  That I pay meat and fee,
That they will not take out this kitchen-boy,
  And kill him presentlie?

They hae taen out this bonnie kitchen-boy,
  And killd him on the plain;
His hair was like the threads o gold,
  His een like crystal stane;
His hair was like the threads o gold,
  His teeth like ivory bane.

They hae taen out this bonnie boy's heart,
  Put it in a cup o gold;
Take that to Lady Daisy, he said,
  For she's impudent and bold;
And she washd it with the tears that ran from her eye
  Into the cup of gold.

Now fare ye weel, my father the king!
  You hae taen my earthly joy;
Since he's died for me, I'll die for him,
  My bonnie kitchen-boy.

O where is all my merry, merry men,
  That I pay meat and wage,
That they could not withold my cruel hand,
  When I was mad with rage?

I think nae wonder, Lady Daisy, he said,
  That he brought your body to shame;
For there never was man of woman born
  Sae fair as him that is slain.

38

LIZIE WAN

Lizie Wan sits at her father's bower-door,
  Weeping and making a mane,
And by there came her father dear:
  What ails thee, Lizie Wan?

I ail, and I ail, dear father, she said,
  And I'll tell you a reason for why;
There is a child between my twa sides,
  Between my dear billy and I.

Now Lizie Wan sits at her father's bower-door,
  Sighing and making a mane,
And by there came her brother dear:
  What ails thee, Lizie Wan?

I ail, I ail, dear brither, she said,
  And I'll tell you a reason for why;
There is a child between my twa sides,
  Between you, dear billy, and I.

And hast thou tald father and mother o that?
  And hast thou tald sae o me?
And he has drawn his gude braid sword,
  That hang down by his knee.

And he has cutted aff Lizie Wan's head,
  And her fair body in three,
And he's awa to his mothers bower,
  And sair aghast was he.

billy brother   *bower* room
bower-door house door

What ails thee, what ails thee, Geordy Wan?
  What ails thee sae fast to rin?
For I see by thy ill colour
  Some fallow's deed thou hast done.

Some fallow's deed I have done, mother,
  And I pray you pardon me;
For I've cutted aff my greyhound's head;
  He wadna rin for me.

Thy greyhound's bluid was never sae red,
  O my son Geordy Wan!
For I see by thy ill colour
  Some fallow's deed thou hast done.

Some fallow's deed I hae done, mother,
  And I pray you pardon me;
For I hae cutted aff Lizie Wan's head
  And her fair body in three.

O what wilt thou do when thy father comes hame,
  O my son Geordy Wan?
I'll set my foot in a bottomless boat,
  And swim to the sea-ground.

And when will thou come hame again,
  O my son Geordy Wan?
The sun and the moon shall dance on the green
  That night when I come hame.

fallow (low) fellow   *sea-ground* bottom of the sea

39

LORD THOMAS AND FAIR ANNET

Lord Thomas and Fair Annet
   Sate a' day on a hill;
Whan night was cum, and sun was sett,
   They had not talkt their fill.

Lord Thomas said a word in jest,
   Fair Annet took it ill:
A, I will nevir wed a wife
   Against my ain friends' will.

Gif ye wull nevir wed a wife,
   A wife wull neir wed yee.
Sae he is hame to tell his mither,
   And knelt upon his knee.

O rede, O rede, mither, he says,
   A gude rede gie to mee;
O sall I tak the nut-browne bride,
   And let Fair Annet bee?

The nut-browne bride has gowd and gear,
   Fair Annet she has gat nane;
And the little beauty Fair Annet haes
   O it wull soon be gane.

And he has till his brother gane:
   Now, brother, rede ye mee;
A, sall I marrie the nut-browne bride,
   And let Fair Annet bee?

rede advice

The nut-browne bride has oxen, brother,
   The nut-browne bride has kye;
I wad hae ye marrie the nut-browne bride,
   And cast Fair Annet bye.

Her oxen may dye i' the house, billie,
   And her kye into the byre,
And I sall hae nothing to mysell
   Bot a fat fadge by the fyre.

And he has till his sister gane:
   Now, sister, rede ye mee;
O sall I marrie the nut-browne bride,
   And set Fair Annet free?

I'se rede ye tak Fair Annet, Thomas,
   And let the browne bride alane;
Lest ye sould sigh and say, Alace,
   What is this we brought hame?

No, I will tak my mither's counsel,
   And marrie me owt o hand;
And I will tak the nut-browne bride,
   Fair Annet may leive the land.

Up then rose Fair Annet's father,
   Twa hours or it were day.
And he is gane into the bower
   Wherein Fair Annet lay.

Rise up, rise up, Fair Annet, he says,
   Put on your silken sheene;
Let us gae to St Marie's kirke,
   And see that rich weddeen.

billie brother   *sheene* shoes
fadge baggage

My maides, gae to my dressing-room,
   And dress to me my hair;
Whaireir yee laid a plait before,
   See yee lay ten times mair.

My maides, gae to my dressing-room,
   And dress to me my smock;
The one half is o the holland fine,
   The other o needle-work.

The horse Fair Annet rade upon,
   He amblit like the wind;
Wi siller he was shod before,
   Wi burning gowd behind.

Four and twenty siller bells
   Wer a' tyed till his mane,
And yae tift o the norland winde,
   They tinkled ane by ane.

Four and twenty gay gude knichts
   Rade by Fair Annet's side,
And four and twenty fair ladies,
   As gin she had bin a bride.

And whan she cam to Marie's kirk,
   She sat on Marie's stean:
The cleading that Fair Annet had on
   It skinkled in their een.

And whan she cam into the kirk,
   She shimmerd like the sun;
The belt that was about her waist
   Was a' wi pearles bedone.

yae tift every puff   *skinkled* glittered
As gin As if

She sat her by the nut-browne bride,
    And her een they were sae clear,
Lord Thomas he clean forgat the bride,
    When Fair Annet drew near.

He had a rose into his hand,
    He gae it kisses three,
And reaching by the nut-browne bride,
    Laid it on Fair Annet's knee.

Up than spak the nut-browne bride,
    She spak wi meikle spite:
And whair gat ye that rose-water,
    That does mak yee sae white?

O I did get the rose-water
    Whair ye wull neir get nane,
For I did get that very rose-water
    Into my mither's wame.

The bride she drew a long bodkin
    Frae out her gay head-gear,
And strake Fair Annet unto the heart,
    That word spak nevir mair.

Lord Thomas he saw Fair Annet wex pale,
    And marvelit what mote bee;
But whan he saw her dear heart's blude,
    A' wood-wroth wexed hee.

He drew his dagger, that was sae sharp,
    That was sae sharp and meet,
And drave it into the nut-browne bride,
    That fell deid at his feit.

Now stay for me, dear Annet, he sed,
    Now stay, my dear, he cry'd;
Then strake the dagger untill his heart,
    And fell deid by her side.

A' wood-wroth All mad with wrath

117

Lord Thomas was buried without kirk-wa,
  Fair Annet within the quiere,
And o the tane thair grew a birk,
  The other a bonny briere.

And ay they grew, and ay they threw,
  As they wad faine be neare;
And by this ye may ken right weil
  They were twa luvers deare.

birk birch

40

JANET
(LADY MAISRY)

In came her sister,
　Stepping on the floor;
Says, It's telling me, my sister Janet,
　That you're become a whore.

A whore, sister, a whore, sister?
　That's what I'll never be;
I'm no so great a whore, sister,
　As liars does on me lee.

In came her brother,
　Stepping on the floor;
Says, It's telling me, my sister Janet,
　That you're become a whore.

A whore, brother, a whore, brother?
　A whore I'll never be;
I'm no so bad a woman, brother,
　As liars does on me lee.

In came her mother,
　Stepping on the floor:
They are telling me, my daughter,
　That you're so soon become a whore.

A whore, mother, a whore, mother?
　A whore I'll never be;
I'm only with child to an English lord,
　Who promised to marry me.

In came her father,
　Stepping on the floor;
Says, They tell me, my daughter Janet,
　That you are become a whore.

A whore, father, a whore, father?
    A whore I'll never be;
I'm but with child to an English lord,
    Who promisd to marry me.

Then in it came an old woman,
    The lady's nurse was she,
And ere she could get out a word
    The tear blinded her ee.

Your father's to the fire, Janet,
    Your brother's to the whin;
All for to kindle a bold bonfire,
    To burn your body in.

Where will I get a boy, she said,
    Will gain gold for his fee,
That would run unto fair England
    For my good lord to me?

O I have here a boy, she said,
    Will gain gold to his fee,
For he will run to fair England
    For thy good lord to thee.

Now when he found a bridge broken,
    He bent his bow and swam,
And when he got where grass did grow,
    He slacked it and ran.

And when he came to that lord's gate,
    Stopt not to knock or call,
But sent his bent bow to his breast
    And lightly leapt the wall;
And ere the porter could open the gate,
    The boy was in the hall,

whin (dried) gorse

In presence of that noble lord,
  And fell down on his knee:
What is it, my boy, he cried,
  Have you brought unto me?

Is my building broke into?
  Or is my towers won?
Or is my true-love delivered
  Of daughter or of son?

Your building is not broke, he cried,
  Nor is your towers won,
Nor is your true-love delivered
  Of daughter nor of son;
But if you do not come in haste,
  Be sure she will be gone.

Her father is gone to the fire,
  Her brother to the whin,
To kindle up a bold bonfire,
  To burn her body in.

Go saddle to me the black, he cried,
  And do it very soon;
Get unto me the swiftest horse
  That ever rade from the town.

The first horse that he rade upon,
  For he was raven black,
He bore him far, and very far,
  But failed in a slack.

The next horse that he rode upon,
  He was a bonny brown;
He bore him far, and very far,
  But did at last fall down.

slack low wet ground

The next horse that he rode upon,
    He as the milk was white;
Fair fall the mare that foaled that foal
    Took him to Janet's sight!

And boots and spurs, all as he was,
    Into the fire he lap,
Got one kiss of her comely mouth,
    While her body gave a crack.

O who has been so bold, he says,
    This bonfire to set on?
Or who has been so bold, he says,
    Her body for to burn?

O here are we, her brother said,
    This bonfire who set on;
And we have been so bold, he said,
    Her body for to burn.

O I'll cause burn for you, Janet,
    Your father and your mother;
And I'll cause die for you, Janet,
    Your sister and your brother.

And I'll cause mony back be bare,
    And mony shed be thin,
And mony wife be made a widow,
    And mony ane want their son.

lap leapt   *shed be thin* ? field be barren

41

GLASGERION

Glasgerion was a kings owne sonne,
  And a harper he was good,
He harped in the kings chamber
  Where cappe and candle yoode;
And soe did hee in the queens chamber
  Till ladies waxed wood.

And then bespake the kings daughter,
  And these words thus sayd shee,
Saide, Strike on, strike on, Glasgerrion,
  Of thy striking doe not blinne;
Theres never a stroke comes over this harpe
  But it glads my hart within.

Faire might you fall, lady, quoth hee;
  Who taught you now to speake?
I have loved you, lady, seven yeere,
  My hart I durst neere breake.

But come to my bower, my Glasgerryon,
  When all men are att rest;
I am a ladie true of my promise,
  Thou shalt bee a welcome guest.

But hom then came Glasgerryon,
  A glad man, Lord, was hee:
And come thou hither, Iacke, my boy,
  Come hither unto mee;

cappe cup   *waxed wood* waxed wild with
yoode weat   pleasure
           blinne cease

For the kings daughter of Normandye,
   Her love is granted mee,
And before the cocke have crowen
   Att her chamber must I bee.

But come you hither, master, quoth hee,
   Lay your head downe on this stone,
For I will waken you, master deere,
   Afore it be time to gone.

But upp then rose that lither ladd
   And did on hose and shoone;
A coller he cast upon his necke,
   Hee seemed a gentleman.

And when he came to that ladies chamber
   He thrild upon a pinn.
The lady was true of her promise,
   Rose up and lett him in.

He did not take the lady gay
   To boulster nor to bedd,
But downe upon her chamber-flore
   Full soone he hath her layd.

He did not kisse that lady gay
   When he came nor when he youd;
And sore mistrusted that lady gay
   He was of some churles blood.

But home then came that lither ladd
   And did of his hose and shoone,
And cast that coller from about his necke;
   He was but a churles sonne:
Awaken, quoth hee, my master deere,
   I hold it time to be gone.

lither wicked   *thrild upon a pinn* rattled the pin
                        (of the door)
                        youd went

For I have sadled your horsse, master,
  Well bridled I have your steed;
Have not I served a good breakfast,
  When times comes I have need.

But up then rose good Glasgerryon
  And did on both hose and shoone,
And cast a coller about his necke;
  He was a kinges sonne.

And when he came to that ladies chamber
  He thrild upon a pinn;
The lady was more then true of promise,
  Rose up and let him in.

Saies, Whether have you left with me
  Your braclett or your glove?
Or are you returned backe againe
  To know more of my love?

Glasgerryon swore a full great othe
  By oake and ashe and thorne:
Lady, I was never in your chamber
  Sith the time that I was borne.

O then it was your litle foote-page
  Falsly hath beguiled me:
And then she pulld forth a litle pen-knife
  That hanged by her knee,
Says, There shall never noe churles blood
  Spring within my body.

But home then went Glasgerryon,
  A woe man, Lord, was hee,
Sayes, Come hither, thou Iacke, my boy,
  Come thou hither to me.

For if I had killed a man to-night,
    Iacke, I wold tell it thee;
But if I have not killed a man to-night,
    Iacke, thou hast killed three!

And he puld out his bright browne sword
    And dryed it on his sleeve,
And he smote off that lither ladds head
    And asked noe man noe leave.

He sett the swords poynt till his brest,
    The pumill till a stone:
Thorrow that falsenese of that lither ladd
    These three lives werne all gone.

browne i.e. burnished

42

GIL BRENTON

Gil Brenton has sent oer the fame,
He's woo'd a wife an brought her hame.

Full sevenscore o ships came her wi,
The lady by the greenwood tree.

There was twal an twal wi beer an wine,
An twal an twal wi muskadine;

An twall an twall wi bouted flowr
An twall an twall wi paramour;

An twall an twall wi baken bread,
An twall an twall wi the goud sae red.

Sweet Willy was a widow's son,
An at her stirrup-foot he did run.

An she was dress'd i the finest pa,
But ay she loot the tears down fa.

An she was deck'd wi the fairest flowrs,
But ay she loot the tears down pour.

O is there water i your shee?
Or does the win blaw i your glee?

Or are you mourning i your meed
That eer you left your mither gueede?

fame foam
twal twelve
muskadine muscatel (wine)
bouted flowr sifted flour

paramour (meaning unknown)
pa pall, cloth
shee shoe
meed mood

Or are ye mourning i your tide
That ever ye was Gil Brenton's bride?

There is nae water i my shee,
Nor does the win blaw i my glee:

Nor am I mourning i my tide
That eer I was Gil Brenton's bride:

But I am mourning i my meed
That ever I left my mither gueede.

But, bonny boy, tell to me
What is the customs o your country.

The customs o 't, my dame, he says,
Will ill a gentle lady please.

Seven king's daughters has our king wedded,
An seven king's daughters has our king bedded.

But he's cutted the paps frae their breastbane
An sent them mourning hame again.

But whan you come to the palace yate,
His mither a golden chair will set.

An be you maid or be you nane,
O sit you there till the day be dane.

An gin you're sure that you are a maid
Ye may gang safely to his bed.

But gin o that you be na sure,
Then hire some woman o youre bowr.

tide time   *yate* gate

O whan she came to the palace yate,
His mither a golden chair did set.

An was she maid or was she nane,
She sat in it till the day was dane.

An she's calld on her bowr woman
That waiting was her bowr within:

Five hundred pound, maid, I'll gi to thee,
An sleep this night wi the king for me.

Whan bells was rung an mass was sung
An a' man unto bed was gone,

Gill Brenton an the bonny maid,
Intill ae chamber they were laid.

O speak to me, blankets, an speak to me, sheets,
An speak to me, cods, that under me sleeps:

Is this a maid that I ha wedded?
Is this a maid that I ha bedded?

It's nae a maid that you ha wedded,
But it's a maid that you ha bedded.

Your lady's in her bigly bowr,
An for you she drees mony sharp showr.

O he has taen him thro the ha,
And on his mither he did ca.

I am the most unhappy man
That ever was in christend lan.

ae one
cods pillows
bigly fine, pleasant

drees mony sharp showr endures
many sharp pains

I woo'd a maiden meek an mild,
An I've marryed a woman great wi child.

O stay, my son, intill this ha
An sport you wi your merry men a';

An I'll gang to yon painted bowr
An see how 't fares wi yon base whore.

The auld queen she was stark an strang,
She gard the door flee aff the ban;

The auld queen she was stark an steer,
She gard the door lye i the fleer.

O is your bairn to laird or loon,
Or is it to your father's groom?

My bairn's na to laird or loon,
Nor is it to my father's groom;

But hear me, mither, on my knee,
An my hard wierd I'll tell to thee.

O we were sisters, sisters seven,
We was the fairest under heaven;

We had nae mair for our seven years wark
But to shape an sue the king's son a sark.

O it fell on a Saturday's afternoon,
Whan a' our langsome wark was done,

We keist the cavils us amang,
To see which shoud to the green wood gang.

stark an strang tough and strong   *wierd* fate
ban hinge   *sark* shirt
steer strong   *keist the cavils* cast lots
fleer floor

130

Ohone, alas, for I was youngest,
An ay my wierd it was the hardest.

The cavil it did on me fa,
Which was the cause of a' my wae.

For to the green wood I must gae
To pu the nut but an the slae,

To pu the red rose an the thyme
To strew my mother's bowr and mine.

I had na pu'd a flowr but ane
Till by there came a jelly hind graeme

Wi high-colld hose and laigh-colld shoone,
An he 'peard to be some kingis son.

An be I maid or be I nane,
He kept me there till the day was dane;

An be I maid or be I nae,
He kept me there till the close of day.

He gae me a lock of yallow hair
An bade me keep it for ever mair.

He gae me a carket o gude black beads
An bade me keep them against my needs.

He gae to me a gay gold ring
An bade me keep it aboon a thing.

He gae to me a little penknife
An bade me keep it as my life.

but an and also   *carket* necklace
jelly hind graeme handsome (jolly) *aboon* above
  young man (groom)   *a thing* everything
-colld cut

What did you wi these tokens rare
That ye got frae that young man there?

O bring that coffer hear to me
And a' the tokens ye sal see.

An ay she ranked, an ay she flang,
Till a' the tokens came till her han.

O stay here, daughter, your bowr within,
Till I gae parley wi my son.

O she has taen her thro the ha
An on her son began to ca:

What did you wi that gay gold ring
I bade you keep aboon a' thing?

What did you wi that little penknife
I bade you keep while you had life?

What did you wi that yallow hair
I bade you keep for ever mair?

What did you wi that good black beeds
I bade you keep against your needs?

I gae them to a lady gay
I met i the green wood on a day.

An I would gi a' my father's lan
I had that lady my yates within.

I would gi a' my ha's an towrs
I had that bright burd i my bowrs.

ranked raged   *flang* flung

O son, keep still your father's lan;
You hae that lady your yates within.

An keep you still your ha's an towrs;
You hae that bright burd i your bowrs.

Now or a month was come an gone
This lady bare a bonny young son;

An it was well written on his breastbane,
Gil Brenton is my father's name.

43

THE GAY GOSHAWK

O well's me o my gay goss-hawk,
    That he can speak and flee;
He'll carry a letter to my love,
    Bring back another to me.

O how can I your true-love ken,
    Or how can I her know?
Whan frae her mouth I never heard couth,
    Nor wi my eyes her saw.

O well sal ye my true-love ken,
    As soon as you her see;
For, of a' the flowrs in fair Englan,
    The fairest flowr is she.

At even at my love's bowr-door
    There grows a bowing birk,
An sit ye down and sing thereon,
    As she gangs to the kirk.

An four-and-twenty ladies fair
    Will wash and go to kirk,
But well shall ye my true-love ken,
    For she wears goud on her skirt.

An four and twenty gay ladies
    Will to the mass repair,
But well sal ye my true-love ken,
    For she wears goud on her hair.

O even at that lady's bowr-door
    There grows a bowin birk,
An she set down and sang thereon,
    As she ged to the kirk.

couth word   *birk* birch

O eet and drink, my marys a',
    The wine flows you among,
Till I gang to my shot-window,
    An hear yon bonny bird's song.

Sing on, sing on, my bonny bird,
    The song ye sang the streen,
For I ken by your sweet singin
    You're frae my true-love sen.

O first he sang a merry song,
    An then he sang a grave,
An then he peckd his feathers gray,
    To her the letter gave.

Ha, there's a letter frae your love,
    He says he sent you three;
He canna wait your love langer,
    But for your sake he'll die.

He bids you write a letter to him;
    He says he's sent you five;
He canno wait your love langer,
    Tho you're the fairest woman alive.

Ye bid him bake his bridal-bread,
    And brew his bridal-ale,
An I'll meet him in fair Scotlan
    Lang, lang or it be stale.

She's doen her to her father dear,
    Fa'n low down on her knee:
A boon, a boon, my father dear,
    I pray you, grant it me.

marys maids-of-honour   *the streen* yestreen, last night
shot-window hinged window   *doen her* taken herself
    which opens and shuts

Ask on, ask on, my daughter,
    An granted it sal be;
Except ae squire in fair Scotlan,
    An him you sall never see.

The only boon, my father dear,
    That I do crave of the,
Is, gin I die in southin lands,
    In Scotland to bury me.

An the firstin kirk that ye come till,
    Ye gar the bells be rung,
An the nextin kirk that ye come till,
    Ye gar the mess be sung.

An the thirdin kirk that ye come till,
    You deal gold for my sake,
An the fourthin kirk that ye come till,
    You tarry there till night.

She is doen her to her bigly bowr,
    As fast as she coud fare,
An she has tane a sleepy draught,
    That she had mixed wi care.

She's laid her down upon her bed,
    An soon she's fa'n asleep,
And soon oer every tender limb
    Cauld death began to creep.

Whan night was flown, an day was come,
    Nae ane that did her see
But thought she was as surely dead
    As ony lady could be.

ae one   *gar* cause
gin if   *bigly* fine, pleasant

Her father an her brothers dear
    Gard make to her a bier;
The tae half was o guide red gold,
    The tither o silver clear.

Her mither and her sisters fair
    Gard work for her a sark;
The tae half was o cambrick fine,
    The tither o needle wark.

The firstin kirk that they came till,
    They gard the bells be rung,
An the nextin kirk that they came till,
    They gard the mess be sung.

The thirdin kirk that they came till,
    They dealt gold for her sake,
An the fourthin kirk that they came till,
    Lo, there they met her make!

Lay down, lay down the bigly bier,
    Lat me the dead look on;
Wi cherry cheeks and ruby lips
    She lay an smil'd on him.

O ae sheave o your bread, true-love,
    An ae glass o your wine,
For I hae fasted for your sake
    These fully days is nine.

Gang hame, gang hame, my seven bold brothers,
    Gang hame and sound your horn;
An ye may boast in southin lans
    Your sister's playd you scorn.

Gard make caused to be made   *make* mate
Gard work Had worked   *ae sheave* one slice
sark shirt

44

YOUNG HUNTING

O lady, rock never your young son young
  One hour longer for me,
For I have a sweetheart in Garlick's wells
  I love thrice better than thee.

The very sols of my love's feet
  Is whiter than thy face;
But never the less na, Young Hunting,
  Ye'l stay wi me all night.

She has birld in him Young Hunting
  The good ale and the beer
Till he was as fou drucken
  As any wild-wood steer.

She has birld in him Young Hunting
  The good ale and the wine
Till he was as fou drunken
  As any wild-wood swine.

Up she has tain him Young Hunting
  And she has had him to her bed;
And she has minded her on a little penknife
  That hangs low down by her gare
An she has gin him Young Hunting
  A deep wound and a sare.

Out an spake the bonny bird
  That flew abon her head:
Lady keep well thy green clothing
  Fra that good lords blood.

birld poured   *gare* skirt
fou full   *abon* above

O better I'll keep my green clothing
    Fra that good lords blood
Nor thou can keep thy flattering toung
    That flatters in thy head.

Light down, light down, my bonny bird,
    Light down upon my hand,
O siller, O siller shall be thy hire
    An goud shall be thy fee,
An every month into the year
    Thy cage shall changed bee.

I winna light down, I shanna light down,
    I winna light on thy hand,
For soon, soon wad ye do to me
    As ye done to Young Hunting.

She has booted ane spird him, Young Hunting,
    As he had been gan to ride,
A hunting horn about his neck,
    An the sharp sourd by his side.
An she has had him to yon wan water,
    For a' man calls it Clyde.

The deepest pot intill it all
    She has puten Young Hunting in;
A green truff upon his breast,
    To hold that good lord down.

It fell ance upon a day
    The king was going to ride,
And he sent for him Young Hunting,
    To ride on his right side.

She has turnd her right and round about,
    She sware now by the corn,
I saw na thy son, Young Hunting
    Sen yesterday at morn.

pot hole   *truff* turf

She has turnd her right and round about,
　　She swear now by the moon,
I saw na thy son, Young Hunting,
　　Sen yesterday at noon.

It fears me sair in Clydes water
　　That he is dround therein.
O thay ha sent for the king's duckers,
　　To duck for Young Hunting.

Thay ducked in at the tae water bank,
　　Thay ducked out at the tither:
We'll duck no more for Young Hunting,
　　All tho he wear our brother.

Out an speake the bonny bird,
　　That flew abon their heads,
O he's na drownd in Clyde's Water,
　　He is slain and put therein;
The lady that lives in yon castil
　　Slew him and put him in.

Leave off your ducking on the day,
　　And duck upon the night;
Whear ever that sakeless knight lys slain,
　　The candels will shine bright.

They left off their ducking o the day,
　　And ducked upon the night,
And where that sakeless knight lay slain
　　The candles shone full bright.

The deepest pot intill it a'
　　They got Young Hunting in;
A green turff upon his brest,
　　To hold that good lord down.

duckers divers　　　　　*sakeless* innocent
the tae the one

O thay ha sent aff men to the wood
  To hew down baith thorn an fern,
That thay might get a great bonefire
  To burn that lady in.
Put na the wyte on me, she says,
  It was her May Catheren.

When thay had tane her May Catheren,
  In the bonefire set her in;
It wad na take upon her cheeks
  Nor take upon her chin
Nor yet upon her yallow hair
  To healle the deadly sin.

Out thay ha tain her May Catheren
  An thay hay put that lady in,
O it took upon her cheek, her cheek,
  An it took upon her chin,
An it took on her fair body,
  She burnt like holly gren.

wyte blame   *may* maid

45

WILLIE O WINSBURY

The king he hath been a prisoner,
  A prisoner lang in Spain, O
And Willie o the Winsbury
  Has lain lang wi his daughter at hame, O.

What aileth thee, my daughter Janet,
  Ye look so pale and wan?
Have ye had any sore sickness,
  Or have ye been lying wi a man?
Or is it for me, your father dear,
  And biding sae lang in Spain?

I have not had any sore sickness,
  Nor yet been lying wi a man;
But it is for you, my father dear,
  In biding sae lang in Spain.

Cast ye off your berry-brown gown,
  Stand straight upon the stone,
That I may ken ye by yere shape,
  Whether ye be a maiden or none.

She's coosten off her berry-brown gown,
  Stooden straight upo yon stone;
Her apron was short, and her haunches were round,
  Her face it was pale and wan.

Is it to a man o might, Janet?
  Or is it to a man of fame?
Or is it to any of the rank robbers
  That's lately come out o Spain?

It is not to a man of might, she said.
  Nor is it to a man of fame;
But it is to William of Winsburry;
  I could lye nae langer my lane.

The king's called on his merry men all,
  By thirty and by three:
Go fetch me William of Winsburry,
  For hanged he shall be.

But when he cam the king before,
  He was clad o the red silk;
His hair was like to threeds o gold,
  And his skin was as white as milk.

It is nae wonder, said the king,
  That my daughter's love ye did win;
Had I been a woman, as I am a man,
  My bedfellow ye should hae been.

Will ye marry my daughter Janet,
  By the truth of thy right hand?
I'll gie ye gold, I'll gie ye money,
  And I'll gie ye an earldom o land.

Yes, I'll marry yere daughter Janet,
  By the truth of my right hand;
But I'll hae nane o yer gold, I'll hae nane o yer money,
  Nor I winna hae an earldom o land.

For I hae eighteen corn-mills,
  Runs all in water clear,
And there's as much corn in each o them
  As they can grind in a year.

my lane alone

46

EDOM O GORDON

It fell about the Martinmas,
  When the wind blew schrile and cauld,
Said Edom o Gordon to his men,
  We maun draw to a hald.

And what an a hald sall we draw to,
  My merry men and me?
We will gae to the house of the Rhodes,
  To see that fair lady.

She had nae sooner busket her sell,
  Nor putten on her gown,
Till Edom o Gordon and his men
  Were round about the town.

They had nae sooner sitten down,
  Nor sooner said the grace,
Till Edom o Gordon and his men
  Were closed about the place.

The lady ran up to her tower-head,
  As fast as she could drie,
To see if by her fair speeches
  She could with him agree.

As soon he saw the lady fair,
  And hir yates all locked fast,
He fell into a rage of wrath,
  And his heart was aghast.

maun draw must move	*town* home-place
hald lodging	*could drie* was able
buske. dressed	*yates* gates

Cum down to me, ye lady fair,
    Cum down to me; let's see;
This night ye's ly by my ain side,
    The morn my bride sall be.

I winnae cum down, ye fals Gordon,
    I winnae cum down to thee;
I winnae forsake my ane dear lord,
    That is sae far frae me.

Gi up your house, ye fair lady,
    Gi up your house to me,
Or I will burn yoursel therein,
    Bot and your babies three.

I winnae gie up, you fals Gordon,
    To nae sik traitor as thee,
Tho you should burn myself therein,
    Bot and my babies three.

Set fire to the house, quoth fals Gordon,
    Sin better may nae bee;
And I will burn hersel therein,
    Bot and her babies three.

And ein wae worth ye, Jock my man!
    I paid ye weil your fee;
Why pow ye out my ground-wa-stane,
    Lets in the reek to me?

And ein wae worth ye, Jock my man!
    For I paid you weil your hire;
Why pow ye out my ground-wa-stane,
    To me lets in the fire?

Bot an And also   *wae worth ye* woe betide you
sik such   *reek* smoke
ein now, to be sure   *pow* pull

Ye paid me weil my hire, lady,
  Ye paid me weil my fee,
But now I'm Edom of Gordon's man,
  Maun either do or die.

O then bespake her youngest son,
  Sat on the nurses knee,
Dear mother, gie owre your house, he says,
  For the reek it worries me.

I winnae gie up my house, my dear,
  To nae sik traitor as he;
Cum weil, cum wae, my jewels fair,
  Ye maun tak share wi me.

O then bespake her dochter dear,
  She was baith jimp and sma;
O row me in a pair o shiets,
  And tow me owre the wa.

They rowd her in a pair of shiets,
  And towd her owre the wa,
But on the point of Edom's speir
  She gat a deadly fa.

O bonny, bonny was hir mouth,
  And chirry were her cheiks,
And clear, clear was hir yellow hair,
  Whereon the reid bluid dreips.

Then wi his speir he turnd hir owr;
  O gin hir face was wan!
He said, You are the first that eer
  I wist alive again.

jimp slender   *tow* lower

He turned hir owr and owr again;
    O gin hir skin was whyte!
He said, I might ha spard thy life
    To been some mans delyte.

Busk and boon, my merry men all,
    For ill dooms I do guess;
I cannae luik in that bonny face,
    As it lyes on the grass.

Them luiks to freits, my master deir,
    Then freits will follow them;
Let it neir be said brave Edom o Gordon
    Was daunted with a dame.

O then he spied hir ain deir lord,
    As he came owr the lee;
He saw his castle in a fire,
    As far as he could see.

Put on, put on, my mighty men,
    As fast as ye can drie!
For he that's hindmost of my men
    Sall neir get guid o me.

And some they raid, and some they ran,
    Fu fast out-owr the plain,
But lang, lang eer he coud get up
    They were a' deid and slain.

But mony were the mudie men
    Lay gasping on the grien;
For o fifty men that Edom brought out
    There were but five ged heme.

Busk and boon Get ready to go   *drie* manage
Them luiks to freits Those who   *mudie* bold
look to portents

And mony were the mudie men
  Lay gasping on the grien,
And mony were the fair ladys
  Lay lemanless at heme.

And round and round the waes he went,
  Their ashes for to view;
At last into the flames he flew,
  And bad the world adieu.

lemanless without lovers   *waes* walls

CHILD WATERS

I warn ye all, ye gay ladies,
    That wear scarlet an brown,
That ye dinna leave your father's house,
    To follow young men frae town.

O here am I, a lady gay,
    That wears scarlet an brown,
Yet I will leave my father's house,
    An follow Lord John frae the town.

Lord John stood in his stable-door,
    Said he was bound to ride;
Burd Ellen stood in her bowr-door,
    Said she'd rin by his side.

He's pitten on his cork-heeled shoone,
    An fast awa rade he;
She's clade hersel in page array,
    An after him ran she.

Till they came till a wan water,
    An folks do ca it Clyde;
Then he's lookit oer his left shoulder,
    Says, Lady, can ye wide?

O I learnt it i my father house,
    An I learnt it for my weal,
Wenneer I came to a wan water,
    To swim like ony eel.

But the firstin stap the lady stappit,
    The water came til her knee;
Ohon, alas! said the lady,
    This water's oer deep for me.

The nextin stap the lady stappit,
  The water came till her middle;
An sighin says that gay lady,
  I've wat my gouden girdle.

The nextin stap the lady stappit,
  The water came till her pap;
An the bairn that was in her twa sides
  For caul began to quake.

Lye still, lye still, my ain dear babe,
  Ye work your mither wae;
Your father rides on high horse-back,
  Cares little for us twae.

O about the midst o Clyden water
  There was a yeard-fast stane;
He lightly turnd his horse about,
  An took her on him behin.

O tell me this now, good Lord John,
  An a word ye dinna lee,
How far it is to your lodgin,
  Whare we this night maun be?

O see you nae yon castle, Ellen,
  That shines sae fair to see?
There is a lady in it, Ellen,
  Will sunder you and me.

There is a lady in that castle
  Will sunder you and I:
Betide me well, betide me wae,
  I sal go there an try.

O my dogs sal eat the good white bread,
  An ye sal eat the bran;
Then will ye sigh, an say, alas!
  That ever I was a man!

yeard-fast earth-fast, firmly fixed

O I sal eat the good white bread,
  An your dogs sal eat the bran;
An I hope to live an bless the day,
  That ever ye was a man.

O my horse sal eat the good white meal,
  An ye sal eat the corn;
Then will ye curse the heavy hour
  That ever your love was born.

O I sal eat the good white meal,
  An your horse sal eat the corn;
An I ay sall bless the happy hour
  That ever my love was born.

O four an twenty gay ladies
  Welcomd Lord John to the ha,
But a fairer lady then them a'
  Led his horse to the stable sta.

An four an twenty gay ladies
  Welcomd Lord John to the green,
But a fairer lady than them a'
  At the manger stood alane.

Whan bells were rung, an mass was sung,
  An a' men boun to meat,
Burd Ellen at a bye-table
  Amo the foot-men was set.

O eat an drink, my bonny boy,
  The white bread an the beer:
The never a bit can I eat or drink,
  My heart's sae full of fear.

O eat an drink, my bonny boy,
  The white bread an the wine:
O I canna eat nor drink, master,
  My heart's saw full of pine.

But out it spake Lord John's mother,
    An a wise woman was she:
Whare met ye wi that bonny boy,
    That looks sae sad on thee?

Sometimes his cheek is rosy red,
    An sometimes deadly wan;
He's liker a woman big wi bairn,
    Than a young lord's serving man.

O it makes me laugh, my mother dear,
    Sic words to hear fra thee;
He is a squire's ae dearest son,
    That for love has followd me.

Rise up, rise up, my bonny boy,
    Gi my horse corn an hay:
O that I will, my master dear,
    As quickly as I may.

She's taen the hay under her arm,
    The corn intill her han,
An she's gane to the great stable,
    As fast as eer she can.

O room ye roun, my bonny broun steeds,
    O room ye near the wa;
For the pain that strikes me thro my sides
    Full soon will gar me fa.

She's leand her back against the wa;
    Strong travail seizd her on;
An even amo the great horse feet
    Burd Ellen brought forth her son.

room ye roun move round and   *gar* make
    make room

Lord John's mither intill her bowr
    Was sitting all alone,
Whan, i the silence o the night,
    She heard fair Ellen's moan.

Won up, won up, my son, she says,
    Go se how a' does fare;
For I think I hear a woman's groans,
    An a bairn greeting sair.

O hastily he gat him up,
    Stayd neither for hose nor shoone,
An he's doen him to the stable-door,
    Wi the clear light o the moon.

He strack the door hard wi his foot,
    An sae has he wi his knee,
An iron locks an iron bars
    Into the floor flung he:
Be not afraid, Burd Ellen, he says,
    There's nane come in but me.

Up he has taen his bonny young son,
    An gard wash him wi the milk;
An up has he taen his fair lady,
    Gard row her in the silk.

Cheer up your heart, Burd Ellen, he says,
    Look nae mair sad nor wae;
For your marriage an your kirkin too
    Sal baith be in ae day.

Won up Get up
greeting crying
gard wash had (him) washed

Gard row Had (her) wrapped
kirkin churching (of women after childbirth)

THE DUKE OF GRAFTON

As two men were a-walking, down by the sea-side
O the brave Duke of Grafton they straightway espied,
Said the one to the other, and thus did they say,
It is the brave Duke of Grafton that is now cast away.

They brought him to Portsmouth, his fame to make known,
And from thence to fair London, so near to the Crown,
They pull'd out his bowels, and they stretch'd forth his feet,
They embalm'd his body with spices so sweet.

All things were made ready, his funeral for to be,
Where the royal Queen Mary came there for to see,
Six lords went before him, six bore him from the ground,
Six Dukes walk'd before him in black velvet gowns.

So black was their mourning, so white were their bands!
So yellow were the flamboys they carried in their hands!
The drums they did rattle, the trumpets sweetly sound,
While the muskets and cannons did thunder all around.

In Westminster Abbey 'tis now call'd by name,
There the great Duke of Grafton does lie in great fame;
In Westminster Abbey he lies in cold clay
Where the royal Queen Mary went weeping away.

THE DOUGLAS TRAGEDY

Rise up, rise up, now, Lord Douglas, she says,
  And put on your armour so bright;
Let it never be said that a daughter of thine
  Was married to a lord under night.

Rise up, rise up, my seven bold sons,
  And put on your armour so bright,
And take better care of your youngest sister,
  For your eldest's awa the last night.

He's mounted her on a milk-white steed,
  And himself on a dapple grey,
With a bugelet horn hung down by his side,
  And lightly they rode away.

Lord William lookit oer his left shoulder,
  To see what he could see,
And there he spy'd her seven brethren bold,
  Come riding over the lee.

Light down, light down, Lady Margret, he said,
  And hold my steed in your hand,
Until that against your seven brethren bold,
  And your father, I mak a stand.

She held his steed in her milk-white hand,
  And never shed one tear,
Until that she saw her seven brethren fa,
  And her father hard fighting, who loved her so dear.

under night in the night

O hold your hand, Lord William! she said,
  For your strokes they are wondrous sair;
True lovers I can get many a ane,
  But a father I can never get mair.

O she's taen out her handkerchief,
  It was o the holland sae fine,
And aye she dighted her father's bloody wounds,
  That were redder than the wine.

O chuse, O chuse, Lady Margret, he said,
  O whether will ye gang or bide?
I'll gang, I'll gang, Lord William, she said,
  For ye have left me no other guide.

He's lifted her on a milk-white steed,
  And himself on a dapple grey,
With a bugelet horn hung down by his side,
  And slowly they baith rade away.

O they rade on, and on they rade,
  And a' by the light of the moon,
Until they came to yon wan water,
  And there they lighted down.

They lighted down to tak a drink
  Of the spring that ran sae clear,
And down the stream ran his gude heart's blood,
  And sair she gan to fear.

Hold up, hold up, Lord William, she says,
  For I fear that you are slain;
'Tis naething but the shadow of my scarlet cloak,
  That shines in the water sae plain.

O they rade on, and on they rade,
  And a' by the light of the moon,
Until they cam to his mother's ha door,
  And there they lighted down.

Get up, get up, lady mother, he says,
    Get up, and let me in!
Get up, get up, lady mother, he says,
    For this night my fair lady I've win.

O mak my bed, lady mother, he says,
    O mak it braid and deep,
And lay Lady Margret close at my back,
    And the sounder I will sleep.

Lord William was dead lang ere midnight,
    Lady Margret lang ere day,
And all true lovers that go thegither,
    May they have mair luck than they!

50

FAIR ANNIE

It's narrow, narrow, make your bed,
  And learn to lie your lane;
For I'm ga'n oer the sea, Fair Annie,
  A braw bride to bring hame.
Wi her I will get gowd and gear;
  Wi you I neer got nane.

But wha will bake my bridal bread,
  Or brew my bridal ale?
And wha will welcome my brisk bride,
  That I bring oer the dale?

It's I will bake your bridal bread,
  And brew your bridal ale,
And I will welcome your brisk bride,
  That you bring oer the dale.

But she that welcomes my brisk bride
  Maun gang like maiden fair;
She maun lace on her robe sae jimp,
  And braid her yellow hair.

But how can I gang maiden-like,
  When maiden I am nane?
Have I not born seven sons to thee,
  And am with child again?

She's taen her young son in her arms,
  Another in her hand,
And she' s up to the highest tower,
  To see him come to land.

lie your lane lie alone   *jimp* slender

Come up, come up, my eldest son,
    And look oer yon sea-strand,
And see your father's new-come bride,
    Before she come to land.

Come down, come down, my mother dear,
    Come frae the castle wa!
I fear, if langer ye stand there,
    Ye'll let yoursell down fa.

And she gaed down, and farther down,
    Her love's ship for to see,
And the topmast and the mainmast
    Shone like the silver free.

And she 's gane down, and farther down,
    The bride's ship to behold,
And the topmast and the mainmast
    They shone just like the gold.

She's taen her seven sons in her hand,
    I wot she didna fail;
She met Lord Thomas and his bride,
    As they came oer the dale.

You're welcome to your house, Lord Thomas,
    You're welcome to your land;
You're welcome with your fair ladye,
    That you lead by the hand.

You're welcome to your ha's, ladye,
    You're welcome to your bowers;
You're welcome to your hame, ladye,
    For a' that's here is yours.

I thank thee, Annie; I thank thee, Annie,
    Sae dearly as I thank thee;
You're the likest to my sister Annie,
    That ever I did see.

There came a knight out oer the sea
  And steald my sister away;
The shame scoup in his company,
  And land whereer he gae!

She hang ae naplin at the door,
  Another in the ha,
And a' to wipe the trickling tears,
  Sae fast as they did fa.

And aye she served the lang tables,
  With white bread and with wine,
And aye she drank the wan water,
  To had her colour fine.

And aye she served the lang tables,
  With white bread and with brown;
And ay she turned her round about,
  Sae fast the tears fell down.

And he's taen down the silk napkin,
  Hung on a silver pin,
And aye he wipes the tear trickling
  A' down her cheek and chin.

And aye he turn'd him round about,
  And smiled amang his men;
Says, Like ye best the old ladye,
  Or her that's new come hame?

When bells were rung, and mass was sung,
  And a' men bound to bed,
Lord Thomas and his new-come bride
  To their chamber they were gaed.

The shame scoup The devil skip   *To had her colour* To hold, keep,
                                                her colour

Annie made her bed a little forbye,
    To hear what they might say;
And ever alas! Fair Annie cried,
    That I should see this day!

Gin my seven sons were seven young rats,
    Running on the castle wa,
And I were a grey cat mysell,
    I soon would worry them a'.

Gin my seven sons were seven young hares,
    Running oer yon lilly lee,
And I were a grew hound mysell,
    Soon worried they a' should be.

And wae and sad Fair Annie sat,
    And drearie was her sang,
And ever, as she sobbd and grat,
    Wae to the man that did the wrang!

My gown is on, said the new-come bride,
    My shoes are on my feet,
And I will to Fair Annie's chamber,
    And see what gars her greet.

What ails ye, what ails ye, Fair Annie,
    That ye make sic a moan?
Has your wine barrels cast the girds,
    Or is your white bread gone?

O wha was't was your father, Annie,
    Or wha was't was your mother?
And had ye ony sister, Annie,
    Or had ye ony brother?

forbye near by   *grat* cried
lilly lee charming lea   *girds* hoops

The Earl of Wemyss was my father,
    The Countess of Wemyss my mother;
And a' the folk about the house
    To me were sister and brother.

If the Earl of Wemyss was your father,
    I wot sae was he mine;
And it shall not be for lack o gowd
    That ye your love sall tyne.

For I have seven ships o mine ain,
    A' loaded to the brim,
And I will gie them a' to thee,
    Wi four to thine eldest son:
But thanks to a' the powers in heaven
    That I gae maiden hame!

tyne lose

51

EPPIE MORRIE

Four-and-twenty Highland men
  Came a' from Carrie side
To steal awa Eppie Morrie,
  Cause she would not be a bride.

Out it's came her mother,
  It was a moonlight night,
She could not see her daughter,
  Their swords they shin'd so bright.

Haud far awa frae me, mother,
  Haud far awa frae me;
There's not a man in a' Strathdon
  Shall wedded be with me.

They have taken Eppie Morrie,
  And horse back bound her on,
And then awa to the minister,
  As fast as horse could gang.

He's taken out a pistol,
  And set it to the minister's breast:
Marry me, marry me, minister,
  Or else I'll be your priest.

Haud far awa frae me, good sir,
  Haud far awa frae me;
For there's not a man in all Strathdon
  That shall married be with me.

Haud far awa frae me, Willie,
  Haud far awa frae me:
For I darna avow to marry you,
  Except she's as willing as ye.

They have taken Eppie Morrie,
    Since better could nae be,
And they're awa to Carrie side,
    As fast as horse could flee.

When mass was sung, and bells were rung,
    And all were bound for bed,
Then Willie an Eppie Morrie
    In one bed they were laid.

Haud far awa frae me, Willie,
    Haud far awa frae me:
Before I 'll lose my maidenhead,
    I'll try my strength with thee.

She took the cap from off her head
    And threw it to the way;
Said, Ere I lose my maidenhead,
    I'll fight with you till day.

Then early in the morning,
    Before her clothes were on,
In came the maiden of Scalletter,
    Gown and shirt alone.

Get up, get up, young woman,
    And drink the wine wi me;
You might have called me maiden,
    I'm, sure as leal as thee.

Wally fa you, Willie,
    That ye could nae prove a man
And taen the lassie's maidenhead!
    She would have hired your han.

___

to the way away, aside   *hired your han* paid for you to do it
Wally fa you Bad luck to you

Haud far awa frae me, lady,
  Haud far awa frae me;
There's not a man in a' Strathdon
  The day shall wed wi me.

Soon in there came Bellbordlane,
  With a pistol on every side:
Come awa hame, Eppie Morrie,
  And there you'll be my bride.

Go get to me a horse, Willie,
  And get it like a man,
And send me back to my mother
  A maiden as I cam.

The sun shines oer the westlin hills;
  By the light lamp of the moon,
Just saddle your horse, young John Forsyth,
  And whistle, and I 'll come soon.

52

LEESOME BRAND

My boy was scarcely ten years auld,
   Whan he went to an unco land,
Where wind never blew, nor cocks ever crew,
   Ohon for my son, Leesome Brand!

Awa to that king's court he went,
   It was to serve for meat an fee;
Gude red gowd it was his hire,
   And lang in that king's court stayd he.

He hadna been in that unco land
   But only twallmonths twa or three,
Till by the glancing o his ee,
   He gaind the love o a gay ladye.

This ladye was scarce eleven years auld,
   When on her love she was right bauld;
She was scarce up to my right knee,
   When oft in bed wi men I'm tauld.

But when nine months were come and gane,
This ladye's face turned pale and wane.

To Leesome Brand she then did say,
In this place I can nae mair stay.

Ye do you to my father's stable,
Where steeds do stand baith wight and able.

Strike ane o them upo the back,
The swiftest will gie his head a wap.

unco unknown, strange   *gie his head a wap* toss his head
wight strong

Ye take him out upo the green,
And get him saddled and bridled seen.

Get ane for you, anither for me,
And lat us ride out ower the lee.

Ye do you to my mother's coffer,
And out of it ye'll take my tocher.

Therein are sixty thousand pounds,
Which all to me by right belongs.

He's done him to her father's stable,
Where steeds stood baith wicht and able.

Then he strake ane upon the back,
The swiftest gae his head a wap.

He's taen him out upo the green,
And got him saddled and bridled seen.

Ane for him, and another for her,
To carry them baith wi might and virr.

He's done him to her mother's coffer,
And there he's taen his lover's tocher;

Wherein were sixty thousand pound,
Which all to her by right belongd.

When they had ridden about six mile,
His true love then began to fail.

O wae's me, said that gay ladye,
I fear my back will gang in three!

O gin I had but a gude midwife,
Here this day to save my life,

And ease me o my misery,
O dear, how happy I woud be!

My love, we're far frae ony town,
There is nae midwife to be foun.

But if ye'll be content wi me,
I'll do for you what man can dee.

For no, for no, this maunna be,
Wi a sigh, replied this gay ladye.

When I endure my grief and pain,
My companie ye maun refrain.

Ye'll take your arrow and your bow,
And ye will hunt the deer and roe.

Be sure ye touch not the white hynde,
For she is o the woman kind.

He took sic pleasure in deer and roe,
Till he forgot his gay ladye.

Till by it came that milk-white hynde,
And then he mind on his ladye syne.

He hasted him to yon greenwood tree,
For to relieve his gay ladye;

But found his ladye lying dead,
Likeways her young son at her head.

syne afterwards

His mother lay ower her castle wa,
  And she beheld baith dale and down;
And she beheld young Leesome Brand,
  As he came riding to the town.

Get minstrels for to play, she said,
  And dancers to dance in my room;
For here comes my son, Leesome Brand,
  And he comes merrilie to the town.

Seek nae minstrels to play, mother,
  Nor dancers to dance in your room;
But tho your son comes, Leesome Brand,
  Yet he comes sorry to the town.

O I hae lost my gowden knife;
I rather had lost my ain sweet life!

And I hae lost a better thing,
The gilded sheath that it was in.

Are there nae gowdsmiths here in Fife,
Can make to you anither knife?

Are there nae sheath-makers in the land,
Can make a sheath to Leesome Brand?

There are nae gowdsmiths here in Fife,
Can make me sic a gowden knife;

Nor nae sheath-makers in the land,
Can make to me a sheath again.

There ne'er was man in Scotland born,
Ordaind to be so much forlorn.

I 've lost my ladye I lovd sae dear,
Likeways the son she did me bear.

Put in your hand at my bed head,
  There ye'll find a gude grey horn;
In it three draps o' Saint Paul's ain blude,
  That hae been there sin he was born.

Drap twa o them o your ladye,
  And ane upo your little young son;
Then as lively they will be
  As the first night ye brought them hame.

He put his hand at her bed head,
  And there he found a gude grey horn,
Wi three draps o' Saint Paul's ain blude,
  That had been there sin he was born.

Then he drappd twa on his ladye,
  And ane o them on his young son,
And now they do as lively be,
  As the first day he brought them hame.

53

THE CLERK'S TWA SONS O OWSENFORD

O I will sing to you a sang,
  But oh my heart is sair!
The clerk's twa sons in Owsenford
  Has to learn some unco lair.

They hadna been in fair Parish
  A twelvemonth an a day,
Till the clerk's twa sons o Owsenford
  Wi the mayor's twa daughters lay.

O word's gaen to the mighty mayor,
  As he saild on the sea,
That the clerk's twa sons o Owsenford
  Wi his twa daughters lay.

If they hae lain wi my twa daughters,
  Meg an Marjorie,
The morn, or I taste meat or drink,
  They shall be hangit hie.

O word's gaen to the clerk himself,
  As he sat drinkin wine,
That his twa sons in fair Parish
  Were bound in prison strong.

Then up and spak the clerk's ladye,
  And she spak powrfully:
O tak with ye a purse of gold,
  Or take with ye three,
And if ye canna get William,
  Bring Andrew hame to me.

unco unknown, strange   *lair* learning

O lye ye here for owsen, dear sons,
    Or lie ye here for kye?
Or what is it that ye lie for,
    Sae sair bound as ye lie?

We lie not here for owsen, dear father,
    Nor yet lie here for kye,
But it's for a little o dear bought love
    Sae sair bound as we lie.

O he's gane to the mighty mayor,
    And he spoke powerfully:
Will ye grant me my twa sons' lives,
    Either for gold or fee?
Or will ye be sae gude a man
    As grant them baith to me?

I'll no grant ye yere twa sons' lives,
    Neither for gold or fee,
Nor will I be sae gude a man
    As gie them back to thee;
Before the morn at twelve o'clock
    Ye'll see them hangit hie.

Up an spak his twa daughters,
    An they spak powrfully:
Will ye grant us our twa loves' lives,
    Either for gold or fee?
Or will ye be sae gude a man
    As grant them baith to me.

I'll no grant ye yere twa loves' lives,
    Neither for gold or fee,
Nor will I be sae gude a man
    As grant their lives to thee;
Before the morn at twelve o'clock
    Ye'll see them hangit hie.

owsen oxen

O he's taen out these proper youths,
    And hangd them on a tree,
And he's bidden the clerk o Owsenford
    Gang hame to his ladie.

His lady sits on yon castle-wa,
    Beholding dale an doun,
And there she saw her ain gude lord
    Come walkin to the toun.

Ye're welcome, welcome, my ain gude lord,
    Ye're welcome hame to me;
But where away are my twa sons?
    Ye should hae brought them wi ye.

It's I've putten them to a deeper lair,
    An to a higher schule;
Yere ain twa sons ill no be here
    Till the hallow days o Yule.

O sorrow, sorrow come mak my bed,
    An dool come lay me doon!
For I'll neither eat nor drink,
    Nor set a fit on ground.

hallow holy

54

JOHNY COCK

Johny he has risen up i' the morn,
  Calls for water to wash his hands;
But little knew he that his bloody hounds
  Were bound in iron bands, bands,
  Were bound in iron bands.

Johny's mother has gotten word o that,
  And care-bed she has taen:
O Johny, for my benison,
  I beg you'l stay at hame;
For the wine so red, and the well baken bread,
  My Johny shall want nane.

There are seven forsters at Pickeram Side,
  At Pickeram where they dwell,
And for a drop of thy heart's bluid
  They wad ride the fords of hell.

Johny he's gotten word of that,
  And he's turnd wondrous keen;
He's put off the red scarlett,
  And he's put on the Lincolm green.

With a sheaf of arrows by his side,
  And a bent bow in his hand,
He's mounted on a prancing steed,
  And he has ridden fast oer the strand.

He's up i Braidhouplee, and down i Bradyslee,
  And up under a buss o broom,
And there he found a good dun deer,
  Feeding in a buss of ling.

---

care-bed sick-bed   *buss* bush
forsters foresters

Johny shot, and the dun deer lap,
  And she lap wondrous wide,
Until they came to the wan water,
  And he stemd her of her pride.

He 'as taen out the little pen-knife,
  'Twas full three quarters long,
And he has taen out of that dun deer
  The liver bot and the tongue.

They eat of the flesh, and they drank of the blood,
  And the blood it was so sweet,
Which caused Johny and his bloody hounds
  To fall in a deep sleep.

By then came an old palmer,
  And an ill death may he die!
For he's away to Pickram Side,
  As fast as he can drie.

What news, what news? says the Seven Forsters,
  What news have ye brought to me?
I have noe news, the palmer said,
  But what I saw with my eye.

High up i Bradyslee, low down i Bradisslee,
  And under a buss of scroggs,
O there I spied a well-wight man,
  Sleeping among his dogs.

His coat it was of light Lincolm,
  And his breeches of the same,
His shoes of the American leather,
  And gold buckles tying them.

lap leapt
stemd her of her pride stopped
  her pride of life
bot and and also

palmer wanderer, beggar
drie manage
scroggs blackthorn

Up bespake the Seven Forsters,
  Up bespake they ane and a':
O that is Johny o Cockleys Well,
  And near him we will draw.

O the first y stroke that they gae him,
  They struck him off by the knee;
Then up bespake his sister's son:
  O the next'll gar him die!

O some they count ye well-wight men,
  But I do count ye nane;
For you might well ha wakend me,
  And askd gin I wad be taen.

The wildest wolf in aw this wood
  Wad not ha done so by me;
She'd ha wet her foot ith wan water,
  And sprinkled it oer my brae,
And if that wad not ha wakend me,
  She wad ha gone and let me be.

O bows of yew, if ye be true,
  In London where ye were bought,
Fingers five, get up belive,
  Manhuid shall fail me nought.

He has killd the Seven Forsters,
  He has killd them all but ane,
And that wan scarce to Pickeram Side,
  To carry the bode-words hame.

Is there never a boy in a' this wood
  That will tell what I can say;
That will go to Cockleys Well,
  Tell my mither to fetch me away?

well-wight very sturdy *gin* if
the firsty the one first *brae* brow
gar make *bode-words* tidings

There was a boy into that wood,
  That carried the tidings away,
And mony ae was the well-wight man
  At the fetching o Johny away.

mony ae many a one

55

JELLON GRAME

O Jellon Grame sat in Silver Wood,
   He whistled and he sang,
And he has calld his little foot-page
   His errand for to gang.

Win up, my bonny boy, he says,
   As quick as e'er you may;
For ye maun gang for Lillie Flower
   Before the break of day.

The boy he's buckled his belt about
   And thro the green-wood ran,
And he came to the ladie's bower-door
   Before the day did dawn.

O sleep ye or wake ye, Lillie Flower?
   The red sun's i the rain:
I sleep not aft, I wake right aft;
   Wha 's that that kens my name?

Ye are bidden come to Silver Wood,
   But I fear you'll never win hame;
Ye are bidden come to Silver Wood
   And speak wi Jellon Grame.

O I will gang to Silver Wood
   Though I shoud never win hame;
For the thing I most desire on earth
   Is to speak wi Jellon Grame.

She had na ridden a mile, a mile,
   A mile but barely three,
Ere she came to a new made grave
   Beneath a green oak tree.

O then up started Jellon Grame
    Out of a bush hard bye:
Light down, light down now, Lillie Flower,
    For it's here that ye maun ly.

She lighted aff her milk-white steed
    And knelt upon her knee:
O mercy, mercy, Jellon Grame,
    For I'm nae prepar'd to die.

Your bairn that stirs between my sides
    Maun shortly see the light;
But to see it weltring in my blude
    Woud be a piteous sight.

O shoud I spare your life, he says,
    Until that bairn be born,
I ken fu well your stern father
    Would hang me on the morn.

O spare my life now, Jellon Grame,
    My father ye neer need dread;
I'll keep my bairn i the good green wood
    Or wi it I'll beg my bread.

He took nae pity on that ladie
    Tho she for life did pray,
But pierced her thro the fair body
    As at his feet she lay.

He felt nae pity for that ladie
    Tho she was lying dead,
But he felt some for the bonny boy
    Lay weltring in her blude.

Up has he taen that bonny boy,
    Gien him to nurices nine,
Three to wake and three to sleep
    And three to go between.

And he's brought up that bonny boy,
    Calld him his sister's son;
He thought nae man would eer find out
    The deed that he had done.

But it sae fell out upon a time,
    As a hunting they did gae,
That they rested them in Silver Wood
    Upon a summer-day.

Then out it spake that bonny boy
    While the tear stood in his eye:
O tell me this now, Jellon Grame,
    And I pray you dinna lie:

The reason that my mother dear
    Does never take me hame?
To keep me still in banishment
    Is baith a sin and shame.

You wonder that your mother dear
    Does never send for thee:
Lo, there's the place I slew thy mother
    Beneath that green oak tree.

Wi that the boy has bent his bow
    (It was baith stout and lang),
And through and thro him Jellon Grame
    He's gard an arrow gang.

Says, Lye you thare now, Jellon Grame,
    My mellison you wi;
The place my mother lies buried in
    Is far too good for thee.

gard made   *mellison* malison, curse

56

KINMONT WILLIE

O have ye na heard o the fause Sakelde?
 O have ye na heard o the keen Lord Scroope?
How they hae taen bauld Kinmont Willie,
 On Haribee to hang him up?

Had Willie had but twenty men,
 But twenty men as stout as he,
Fause Sakelde had never the Kinmont taen
 Wi eight score in his cumpanie.

They band his legs beneath the steed,
 They tied his hands behind his back;
They guarded him, fivesome on each side,
 And they brought him ower the Liddel-rack.

They led him thro the Liddel-rack
 And also thro the Carlisle sands;
They brought him to Carlisle castell
 To be at my Lord Scroope's commands.

My hands are tied but my tongue is free,
 And whae will dare this deed avow?
Or answer by the border law?
 Or answer to the bauld Buccleuch?

Now haud thy tongue, thou rank reiver,
 There's never a Scot shall set ye free;
Before ye cross my castle yate
 I trow ye shall take farewell o me.

rack ford   *yate* gate
reiver robber

Fear na ye that, my lord, quo Willie;
    By the faith o my bodie, Lord Scroope, he said,
I never yet lodged in a hostelrie
    But I paid my lawing before I gaed.

Now word is gane to the bauld Keeper
    In Branksome Ha where that he lay,
That Lord Scroope has taen the Kinmont Willie
    Between the hours of night and day.

He has taen the table wi his hand,
    He garrd the red wine spring on hie:
Now Christ's curse on my head, he said,
    But avenged of Lord Scroope I'll be:

O is my basnet a widow's curch?
    Or my lance a wand of the willow-tree?
Or my arm a ladye's lilye hand?
    That an English lord should lightly me.

And have they taen him, Kinmont Willie,
    Against the truce of Border tide,
And forgotten that the bauld Buccleuch
    Is keeper here on the Scottish side?

And have they een taen him, Kinmont Willie,
    Withouten either dread or fear,
And forgotten that the bauld Buccleuch
    Can back a steed or shake a spear?

O were there war between the lands,
    As well I wot that there is none,
I would slight Carlisle castell high
    Tho it were builded of marble stone.

lawing bill   *curch* kerchief
garrd made   *wand* branch
basnet light helmet   *lightly* slight

I would set that castell in a low
    And sloken it with English blood;
There 's nevir a man in Cumberland
    Should ken where Carlisle castell stood.

But since nae war's between the lands
    And there is peace, and peace should be,
I'll neither harm English lad or lass
    And yet the Kinmont freed shall be.

He has calld him forty marchmen bauld,
    I trow they were of his ain name
    Except Sir Gilbert Elliot, calld
The Laird of Stobs, I mean the same.

He has calld him forty marchmen bauld,
    Were kinsmen to the bauld Buccleuch,
With spur on heel, and splent on spauld,
    And gleuves of green, and feathers blue.

There were five and five before them a'
    Wi hunting horns and bugles bright;
And five and five came wi Buccleuch
    Like Warden's men, arrayed for fight.

And five and five like a mason gang
    That carried the ladders lang and hie,
And five and five like broken men;
    And so they reached the Woodhouselee.

And as we crossd the Bateable Land,
    When to the English side we held,
The first o men that we met wi,
    Whae sould it be but fause Sakelde!

low blaze
sloken extinguish
marchmen men of the march (the
  border)
splent on spauld plate-armour on
  shoulder

Bateable Land land in debate
  between Scotland and England,
  between Scots Dyke and Solway
  Firth

Where be ye gaun, ye hunters keen,
  Quo fause Sakelde, Come tell to me:
We go to hunt an English stag,
  Has trespassed on the Scots countrie.

Where be ye gaun, ye marshal men,
  Quo fause Sakelde, Come tell me true:
We go to catch a rank reiver,
  Has broken faith wi the bauld Buccleuch.

Where are ye gaun, ye mason lads,
  Wi a' your ladders lang and hie?
We gang to herry a corbie's nest
  That wons not far frae Woodhouselee.

Where be ye gaun, ye broken men,
  Quo fause Sakelde, Come tell to me:
Now Dickie of Dryhope led that band,
  And the nevir a word o lear had he.

Why trespass ye on the English side?
  Row-footed outlaws, stand, quo he;
The nevir a word had Dickie to say,
  Sae he thrust the lance thro his fause bodie.

Then on we held for Carlisle toun
  And at Staneshaw-bank the Eden we crossd;
The water was great and meikle of spait,
  But the nevir a horse nor man we lost.

And when we reachd the Staneshaw-bank
  The wind was rising loud and hie;
And there the laird garrd leave our steeds
  For fear that they should stamp and nie.

marshal martial	*lear* learning
corbie raven	*garrd leave* caused (us) to leave
wons lives	

And when we left the Staneshaw-bank
  The wind began full loud to blaw,
But 't was wind and weet and fire and sleet
  When we came beneath the castel-wa.

We crept on knees and held our breath
  Till we placed the ladders against the wa,
And saw ready was Buccleuch himsell
  To mount the first before us a'.

He has taen the watchman by the throat,
  He flung him down upon the lead:
Had there not been peace between our lands
  Upon the other side thou hadst gaed.

Now sound out, trumpets, quo Buccleuch,
  Let's waken Lord Scroope right merrilie!
Then loud the Warden's trumpets blew,
  O whae dare meddle wi me?

Then speedilie to wark we gaed
  And raised the slogan ane and a',
And cut a hole thro a sheet of lead,
  And so we wan to the castel ha.

They thought King James and a' his men
  Had won the house wi bow and speir;
It was but twenty Scots and ten
  That put a thousand in sic a stear.

Wi coulters and wi forehammers
  We garrd the bars bang merrilie,
Untill we cam to the inner prison
  Where Willie o Kinmont he did lie.

And when we cam to the lower prison
  Where Willie o Kinmont he did lie:
O sleep ye, wake ye, Kinmont Willie,
  Upon the morn that thou's to die?

stear stir   *forehammers* sledgehammers

O I sleep saft and I wake aft,
  It's lang since sleeping was fleyd frae me;
Gie my service back to my wyfe and bairns
  And a' gude fellows that speer for me.

Then Red Rowan has hente him up,
  The starkest man in Teviotdale;
Abide, abide now, Red Rowan,
  Till of my Lord Scroope I take farewell.

Farewell, farewell, my gude Lord Scroope;
  My gude Lord Scroope, farewell, he cried:
I'll pay you for my lodging maill
  When first we meet on the border side.

Then shoulder high with shout and cry
  We bore him down the ladder lang;
At every stride Red Rowan made
  I wot the Kinmont's airns playd clang.

O mony a time, quo Kinmont Willie,
  I have ridden horse baith wild and wood;
But a rougher beast than Red Rowan
  I ween my legs have neer bestrode.

And mony a time, quo Kinmont Willie,
  I've pricked a horse out oure the furs:
But since the day I backed a steed
  I nevir wore sic cumbrous spurs.

We scarce had won the Staneshaw-bank
  When a' the Carlisle bells were rung,
And a thousand men in horse and foot
  Cam wi the keen Lord Scroope along.

fleyd frightened   *lodging maill* rent
speer enquire   *pricked* spurred
hente taken   *furs* furrows
starkest strongest

Buccleuch has turned to Eden Water
    Even where it flowd frae bank to brim,
And he has plunged in wi a' his band
    And safely swam them thro the stream.

He turned him on the other side
    And at Lord Scroope his glove flung he:
If ye like na my visit in merry England,
    In fair Scotland come visit me!

All sore astonished stood Lord Scroope,
    He stood as still as rock of stane;
He scarcely dared to trew his eyes
    When thro the water they had gane:

He is either himsell a devil frae hell,
    Or else his mother a witch maun be;
I wad na have ridden that wan water
    For a' the gowd in Christentie.

trew believe (trow)

BONNIE GEORGE CAMPBELL

Hie upon Hielands and laigh upon Tay
Bonnie George Campbell rode out on a day.
He saddled, he bridled, and gallant rode he,
And hame cam his guid horse, but never cam he.

Out cam his mother dear greeting fu' sair,
And out cam his bonnie bryde riving her hair.
My meadow lies green and my corn is unshorn,
My barn is to build and my baby's unborn.

Saddled and bridled and booted rode he,
A plume in his helmet, a sword at his knee.
But toom cam his saddle all bloody to see;
Oh hame cam his guid horse, but never cam he.

greeting crying   *toom* empty

BROWN ROBIN

The king but an his nobles a'
    Sat birling at the wine;
The king but an his nobles a'
    Sat birling at the wine;
He would ha nane but his ae daughter
    To wait on them at dine.

She's served them butt, she's servd them ben,
    Intill a gown of green,
But her ee was ay on Brown Robin,
    That stood low under the rain.

She's doen her to her bigly bowr,
    As fast as she could gang,
An there she's drawn her shot-window,
    An she's harped an she sang.

There sits a bird i my father's garden,
    An O but she sings sweet!
I hope to live an see the day
    Whan wi my love I'll meet.

O gin that ye like me as well
    As your tongue tells to me,
What hour o the night, my lady bright,
    At your bowr sal I be?

Whan my father an gay Gilbert
    Are baith set at the wine,
O ready, ready I will be
    To lat my true-love in.

but an and also   *butt, ben* in kitchen, in parlour
birling drinking   *bigly* fine, pleasant
ae only   *shot-window* hinged window
        which opens and shuts

O she has birld her father's porter
   Wi strong beer an wi wine,
Untill he was as beastly drunk
   As ony wild-wood swine:
She's stown the keys o her father's yates
   An latten her true-love in.

Whan night was gane, an day was come,
   An the sun shone on their feet,
Then out it spake him Brown Robin,
   I'll be discoverd yet.

Then out it spake that gay lady:
   My love, ye need na doubt;
For wi ae wile I've got you in,
   Wi anither I'll bring you out.

She's taen her to her father's cellar,
   As fast as she can fare;
She's drawn a cup o the gude red wine,
   Hung't low down by her gare;
An she met wi her father dear
   Just coming down the stair.

I woud na gi that cup, daughter,
   That ye hold i your han
For a' the wines in my cellar,
   An gantrees whare they stan.

O wae be to your wine, father,
   That ever't came oer the sea;
'T 'is pitten my head in sick a steer
   I my bowr I canna be.

stown stolen   *gare* skirt
yates gates   *gantrees* barrel-stands
ae one   *steer* stir

Gang out, gang out, my daughter dear,
    Gang out an tack the air;
Gang out an walk i the good green wood,
    An a' your marys fair.

Then out it spake the proud porter –
    Our lady wishd him shame –
We'll send the marys to the wood,
    But we'll keep our lady at hame.

There's thirty marys i my bowr,
    There's thirty o them an three;
But there's nae ane amo them a'
    Kens what flowr gains for me.

She's doen her to her bigly bowr,
    As fast as she could gang,
An she has dresst him Brown Robin
    Like ony bowr-woman.

The gown she pat upon her love
    Was o the dainty green,
His hose was o the saft, saft silk
    His shoon o the cordwain fine.

She's pitten his bow in her bosom,
    His arrow in her sleeve,
His sturdy bran her body next,
    Because he was her love.

Then she is unto her bowr-door,
    As fast as she could gang;
But out it spake the proud porter –
    Our lady wishd him shame –
We'll count our marys to the wood,
    An we'll count them back again.

marys maids
wishd him shame wished him to
  the devil
Kens Knows

gains for me suits me
doen her taken herself
bran sword

The firsten mary she sent out
   Was Brown Robin by name;
Then out it spake the king himsel,
   This is a sturdy dame.

O she went out in a May morning,
   In a May morning so gay,
But she came never back again,
   Her auld father to see.

59

BONNY BARBARA ALLAN

It was in and about the Martinmas time,
  When the green leaves were a falling,
That Sir John Graeme in the West Country
  Fell in love with Barbara Allan.

He sent his man down through the town,
  To the place where she was dwelling,
O haste, and come to my master dear,
  Gin ye be Barbara Allan.

O hooly, hooly rose she up,
  To the place where he was lying,
And when she drew the curtain by,
  Young man, I think you're dying.

O it's I'm sick, and very very sick,
  And 'tis a' for Barbara Allan,
O the better for me ye's never be,
  Tho your heart's blood were a-spilling.

O dinna ye mind, young man, said she,
  When ye was in the tavern a-drinking,
That ye made the healths gae round and round,
  And slighted Barbara Allan?

He turnd his face unto the wall,
  And death was with him dealing;
Adieu, adieu, my dear friends all,
  And be kind to Barbara Allan.

hooly gently

And slowly, slowly raise she up,
  And slowly, slowly left him;
And sighing, said, she coud not stay,
  Since death of life had reft him.

She had not gane a mile but twa,
  When she heard the dead-bell ringing,
And every jow that the dead-bell gied,
  It cry'd, Woe to Barbara Allan.

O mother, mother, make my bed,
  O make it saft and narrow,
Since my love died for me to-day,
  I'll die for him to-morrow.

jow stroke

60

YOUNG JOHNSTONE

Young Johnstone and the young Col'nel
   Sat drinking at the wine;
O gin ye wad marry my sister
   It's I wad marry thine.

I wadna marry your sister
   For a' your houses and land,
But I'll keep her for my leman
   When I come oer the strand.

I wadna marry your sister
   For a' your gowd so gay,
But I'll keep her for my leman
   When I come by the way.

Young Johnstone had a nut brown sword
   Hung low down by his gair,
And he ritted it through the young Col'nel,
   That word he ne'er spak mair.

But he's awa to his sister's bower,
   He's tirled at the pin;
Whare hae ye been, my dear brither,
   Sae late a coming in?
I hae been at the school, sister,
   Learning young clerks to sing.

I've dreamed a dreary dream this night,
   I wish it may be for good;
They were seeking you with hawks and hounds
   And the young Col'nel was dead.

leman lover   *ritted* ripped
strand stream, or ground   *tirled at the pin* rattled at the pin
gair gown   (of the door)

Hawks and hounds they may seek me,
    As I trow well they be;
For I have killed the young Col'nel
    And thy own true love was he.

If ye hae killed the young Col'nel
    O dule and wae is me;
But I wish ye may be hanged on a hie gallows
    And hae nae power to flee.

And he's awa to his true love's bower,
    He's tirled at the pin;
Whar hae ye been, my dear Johnstone,
    Sae late a coming in?
It's I hae been at the school, he says,
    Learning young clerks to sing.

I have dreamed a dreary dream, she says,
    I wish it may be for good;
They were seeking you with hawks and hounds
    And the young Col'nel was dead.

Hawks and hounds they may seek me,
    As I trow well they be;
For I hae killed the young Col'nel
    And thy ae brother was he.

If ye hae killed the young Col'nel
    O dule and wae is me;
But I care the less for the young Col'nel
    If thy ain body be free.

Come in, come in, my dear Johnstone,
    Come in and take a sleep;
And I will go to my casement
    And carefully I will thee keep.

ae only

He had not weel been in her bower door,
   No not for half an hour,
When four and twenty belted knights
   Came riding to the bower.

Well may you sit and see, Lady,
   Well may you sit and say;
Did you not see a bloody squire
   Come riding by this way?

What colour were his hawks? she says,
   What colour were his hounds?
What colour was the gallant steed
   That bore him from the bounds?

Bloody, bloody were his hawks
   And bloody were his hounds,
But milk-white was the gallant steed
   That bore him from the bounds.

Yes, bloody, bloody were his hawks
   And bloody were his hounds,
But milk-white was the gallant steed
   That bore him from the bounds.

Light down, light down now, gentlemen,
   And take some bread and wine;
And the steed be swift that he rides on,
   He's past the brig o' Lyne.

We thank you for your bread, fair Lady,
   We thank you for your wine;
But I wad gie thrice three thousand pound
   That bloody knight was taen.

brig bridge

Lie still, lie still, my dear Johnstone,
  Lie still and take a sleep;
For thy enemies are past and gone
  And carefully I will thee keep.

But young Johnstone had a little wee sword
  Hung low down by his gair,
And he stabbed it in fair Annet's breast,
  A deep wound and a sair.

What aileth thee now, dear Johnstone?
  What aileth thee at me?
Hast thou not got my father's gold
  Bot and my mither's fee?

Ohon, alas, my lady gay,
  To come sae hastilie!
I thought it was my deadly foe
  Ye had trysted into me.

Now live, now live, my dear ladye,
  Now live but half an hour;
And there's no a leech in a' Scotland
  But shall be in thy bower.

How can I live, how shall I live?
  Young Johnstone, do not you see
The red, red drops o my bonny heart's blood
  Rin trinkling down my knee?

But take thy harp into thy hand
  And harp out owre yon plain,
And neer think mair on thy true love
  Than if she had never been.

He hadna weel been out o the stable
  And on his saddle set,
Till four and twenty broad arrows
  Were thrilling in his heart.

trysted enticed, lured   *thrilling in* piercing

MARY HAMILTON

Word's gane to the kitchen,
    And word's gane to the ha,
That Marie Hamilton gangs wi bairn
    To the hichest Stewart of a'.

He's courted her in the kitchen,
    He's courted her in the ha,
He's courted her in the laigh cellar,
    And that was warst of a'.

She's tyed it in her apron
    And she's thrown it in the sea;
Says, Sink ye, swim ye, bonny wee babe!
    You'l neer get mair o me.

Down then cam the auld queen,
    Goud tassels tying her hair:
O Marie, where's the bonny wee babe
    That I heard greet sae sair?

There never was a babe intill my room,
    As little designs to be;
It was but a touch o my sair side,
    Come oer my fair bodie.

O Marie, put on your robes o black,
    O else your robes o brown,
For ye maun gang wi me the night,
    To see fair Edinbro town.

laigh low   *As little designs to be*
greet cry   as little as there will be

I winna put on my robes o black,
  Nor yet my robes o brown;
But I'll put on my robes o white,
  To shine through Edinbro town.

When she gaed up the Cannogate,
  She laughd loud laughters three;
But whan she cam down the Cannogate
  The tear blinded her ee.

When she gaed up the Parliament stair,
  The heel cam aff her shee;
And lang or she cam down again
  She was condemnd to dee.

When she cam down the Cannogate,
  The Cannogate sae free,
Many a ladie lookd oer her window,
  Weeping for this ladie.

Ye need nae weep for me, she says,
  Ye need nae weep for me;
For had I not slain mine own sweet babe,
  This death I wadna dee.

Bring me a bottle of wine, she says,
  The best that eer ye hae,
That I may drink to my weil-wishers,
  And they may drink to me.

Here's a health to the jolly sailors,
  That sail upon the main;
Let them never let on to my father and mother
  But what I'm coming hame.

shee shoe

Here's a health to the jolly sailors,
  That sail upon the sea;
Let them never let on to my father and mother
  That I came here to dee.

Oh little did my mother think,
  The day she cradled me,
What lands I was to travel through,
  What death I was to dee.

Oh little did my father think,
  The day he held up me,
What lands I was to travel through,
  What death I was to dee.

Last night I washd the queen's feet,
  And gently laid her down;
And a' the thanks I've gotten the nicht
  To be hangd in Edinbro town!

Last nicht there was four Maries,
  The nicht there'l be but three;
There was Marie Seton, and Marie Beton,
  And Marie Carmichael, and me.

Maries maids-of-honour

62

RARE WILLIE DROWNED IN YARROW

Willy's rare, and Willy's fair,
  And Willy's wondrous bony,
And Willy heght to marry me,
  Gin eer he marryd ony.

Yestreen I made my bed fu brade,
  The night I'll make it narrow,
For a' the live-long winter's night
  I lie twind of my marrow.

O came you by yon water-side?
  Pu'd you the rose or lilly?
Or came you by yon meadow green?
  Or saw you my sweet Willy?

She sought him east, she sought him west,
  She sought him brade and narrow,
Sine in the clifting of a craig
  She found him drownd in Yarrow.

heght promised
Gin If
twind of deprived of

marrow mate
Sine Then
clifting cleft

EDWARD

Why dois your brand sae drap wi bluid,
    Edward, Edward,
Why dois your brand sae drap wi bluid,
 And why sae sad gang yee O?
O I hae killed my hauke sae guid,
    Mither, mither,
O I hae killed my hauke sae guid,
 And I had nae mair bot hee O.

Your haukis bluid was nevir sae reid,
    Edward, Edward,
Your haukis bluid was nevir sae reid,
 My deir son I tell thee O.
O I hae killed my reid-roan steid,
    Mither, mither,
O I hae killed my reid-roan steid,
 That erst was sae fair an frie O.

Your steid was auld, and ye hae gat mair,
    Edward, Edward,
Your steid was auld, and ye hae gat mair,
 Sum other dule ye drie O.
O I hae killed my fadir deir,
    Mither, mither,
O I hae killed my fadir deir,
 Alas, and wae is mee O!

And whatten penance wul ye drie for that,
    Edward, Edward?
And whatten penance will ye drie for that?
 My deir son, now tell me O.

drie suffer

Ile set my feit in yonder boat,
           Mither, mither,
Ile set my feit in yonder boat,
  And Ile fare ovir the sea O.

And what wul ye doe wi your towirs and your ha,
           Edward, Edward?
And what wul ye doe wi your towirs and your ha,
  That were sae fair to see O?
Ile let thame stand tul they doun fa,
           Mither, mither,
Ile let thame stand tul they doun fa,
  For here nevir mair maun I bee O.

And what wul ye leive to your bairns and your wife,
           Edward, Edward?
And what wul ye leive to your bairns and your wife,
  Whan ye gang ovir the sea O?
The warldis room, late them beg thrae life,
           Mither, mither,
The warldis room, late them beg thrae life,
  For thame nevir mair wul I see O.

And what wul ye leive to your ain mither deir,
           Edward, Edward?
And what wul ye leive to your ain mither deir?
  My deir son, now tell me O.
The curse of hell frae me sall ye beir,
           Mither, mither,
The curse of hell frae me sall ye beir,
  Sic counseils ye gave to me O.

64

LAMKIN

It's Lamkin was a mason good
  As ever built wi stane;
He built Lord Wearie's castle,
  But payment got he nane.

O pay me, Lord Wearie,
  Come, pay me my fee:
I canna pay you, Lamkin,
  For I maun gang oer the sea.

O pay me now, Lord Wearie,
  Come, pay me out o hand:
I canna pay you, Lamkin,
  Unless I sell my land.

O gin ye winna pay me,
  I here sall mak a vow,
Before that ye come hame again,
  Ye sall hae cause to rue.

Lord Wearie got a bonny ship,
  To sail the saut sea faem;
Bade his lady weel the castle keep,
  Ay till he should come hame.

But the nourice was a fause limmer
  As eer hung on a tree;
She laid a plot wi Lamkin,
  Whan her lord was oer the sea.

limmer creature

She laid a plot wi Lamkin,
　When the servants were awa,
Loot him in at a little shot-window,
　And brought him to the ha.

O whare's a' the men o this house,
　That ca me Lamkin?
They're at the barn-well thrashing;
　'T will be lang ere they come in.

And whare's the women o this house,
　That ca me Lamkin?
They're at the far well washing;
　'T will be lang ere they come in.

And whare's the bairns o this house,
　That ca me Lamkin?
They're at the school reading;
　'T will be night or they come hame.

O whare's the lady o this house,
　That ca's me Lamkin?
She's up in her bower sewing,
　But we soon can bring her down.

Then Lamkin's tane a sharp knife,
　That hang down by his gaire,
And he has gien the bonny babe
　A deep wound and a sair.

Then Lamkin he rocked,
　And the fause nourice sang,
Till frae ilkae bore o the cradle
　The red blood out sprang.

shot-window hinged window　　*well* spring, stream
　which opens and shuts　　　*gaire* gown
barn-well stream or spring by a　*bore* crevice
　barn

Then out it spak the lady,
  As she stood on the stair:
What ails my bairn, nourice,
  That he's greeting sae sair?

O still my bairn, nourice,
  O still him wi the pap!
He winna still, lady,
  For this nor for that.

O still my bairn, nourice,
  O still him wi the wand!
He winna still, lady,
  For a' his father's land.

O still my bairn, nourice,
  O still him wi the bell!
He winna still, lady,
  Till ye come down yoursel.

O the firsten step she steppit,
  She steppit on a stane;
But the neisten step she steppit,
  She met him Lamkin.

O mercy, mercy, Lamkin,
  Hae mercy upon me!
Though you've taen my young son's life,
  Ye may let mysel be.

O sall I kill her, nourice,
  Or sall I lat her be?
O kill her, kill her, Lamkin,
  For she neer was good to me.

O scour the bason, nourice,
    And mak it fair and clean,
For to keep this lady's heart's blood,
    For she's come o noble kin.

There need nae bason, Lamkin,
    Lat it run through the floor;
What better is the heart's blood
    O the rich than o the poor?

But ere three months were at an end,
    Lord Wearie came again;
But dowie, dowie was his heart
    When first he came hame.

O wha's blood is this, he says,
    That lies in the chamer?
It is your lady's heart's blood;
    'Tis as clear as the lamer.

And wha's blood is this, he says,
    That lies in my ha?
It is your young son's heart's blood;
    'T is the clearest ava.

O sweetly sang the black-bird
    That sat upon the tree;
But sairer grat Lamkin,
    When he was condemnd to die.

And bonny sang the mavis,
    Out o the thorny brake;
But sairer grat the nourice,
    When she was tied to the stake.

dowie sad   *ava* of all
lamer amber   *grat* cried

65

JAMES HARRIS
(THE DEMON LOVER)

O where have you been, my long, long love,
    This long seven years and mair?
O I'm come to seek my former vows
    Ye granted me before.

O hold your tongue of your former vows,
    For they will breed sad strife;
O hold your tongue of your former vows,
    For I am become a wife.

He turned him right and round about,
    And the tear blinded his ee:
I wad never hae trodden on Irish ground,
    If it had not been for thee.

I might hae had a king's daughter,
    Far, far beyond the sea;
I might have had a king's daughter,
    Had it not been for love o thee.

If ye might have had a king's daughter,
    Yer sel ye had to blame;
Ye might have taken the king's daughter,
    For ye kend that I was nane.

If I was to leave my husband dear,
    And my two babes also,
O what have you to take me to,
    If with you I should go?

I hae seven ships upon the sea –
    The eighth brought me to land –
With four-and-twenty bold mariners,
    And music on every hand.

She has taken up her two little babes,
  Kissd them baith cheek and chin:
O fair ye weel, my ain two babes,
  For I'll never see you again.

She set her foot upon the ship,
  No mariners could she behold;
But the sails were o the taffetie,
  And the masts o the beaten gold.

They had not sailed a league, a league,
  A league but barely three,
When dismal grew his countenance,
  And drumlie grew his ee.

They had not sailed a league, a league,
  A league but barely three,
Until she espied his cloven foot,
  And she wept right bitterlie.

O hold your tongue of your weeping, says he,
  Of your weeping now let me be;
I will shew you how lilies grow
  On the banks of Italy.

O what hills are yon, yon pleasant hills,
  That the sun shines sweetly on?
O yon are the hills of heaven, he said,
  Where you will never win.

O whaten mountain is yon, she said,
  All so dreary wi frost and snow?
O yon is the mountain of hell, he cried
  Where you and I will go.

He strack the tap-mast wi his hand,
  The fore-mast wi his knee,
And he brake that gallant ship in twain,
  And sank her in the sea.

drumlie gloomy

66

SIR PATRICK SPENS

The king sits in Dumferling toune,
    Drinking the blude-reid wine:
O whar will I get guid sailor,
    To sail this schip of mine?

Up and spak an eldern knicht,
    Sat at the kings richt kne:
Sir Patrick Spence is the best sailor
    That sails upon the se.

The king has written a braid letter,
    And signed wi his hand,
And sent it to Sir Patrick Spence,
    Was walking on the sand.

The first line that Sir Patrick red,
    A loud lauch lauched he;
The next line that Sir Patrick red,
    The teir blinded his ee.

O wha is this has done this deid,
    This ill deid don to me,
To send me out this time o the yeir,
    To sail upon the se?

Mak hast, mak hast, my mirry men all,
    Our guid schip sails the morne:
O say na sae, my master deir,
    For I feir a deadlie storme.

braid long

Late late yestreen I saw the new moone,
  Wi the auld moone in hir arme,
And I feir, I feir, my deir master,
  That we will cum to harme.

O our Scots nobles were richt laith
  To weet their cork-heild schoone;
Bot lang owre a' the play wer playd,
  Thair hats they swam aboone.

O lang, lang, may their ladies sit,
  Wi thair fans into their hand,
Or eir they se Sir Patrick Spence
  Cum sailing to the land.

O lang, lang, may the ladies stand,
  Wi thair gold kems in their hair,
Waiting for their ain deir lords,
  For they'll se thame na mair.

Have owre, have owre to Aberdour,
  It's fifty fadom deip,
And thair lies guid Sir Patrick Spence,
  Wi the Scots lords at his feit.

laith loath   *Have owre* Half over
aboone above (them)

67

JAMIE TELFER OF THE FAIR DODHEAD

It fell about the Martinmas tyde
  Whan our Border steeds get corn and hay,
The Captain of Bewcastle hath bound him to ryde
  And he's ower to Tividale to drive a prey.

The first ae guide that they met wi,
  It was high up in Hardhaughswire;
The second guide that they met wi,
  It was laigh down in Borthwick water.

What tidings, what tidings, my trusty guide?
  Nae tidings, nae tidings I hae to thee;
But gin ye'll gae to the Fair Dodhead
  Mony a cow's cauf I'll let thee see.

And whan they cam to the Fair Dodhead
  Right hastily they clam the peel;
They loosed the kye out, ane and a',
  And ranshakled the house right weel.

Now Jamie Telfer's heart was sair,
  The tear aye rowing in his ee;
He pled wi the Captain to hae his gear
  Or else revenged he wad be.

The Captain turned him round and leugh,
  Said, Man, there's naething in thy house
But ae auld sword without a sheath
  That hardly now wad fell a mouse.

clam the peel climbed the stockade   *rowing* rolling
  (pale, palisade)   *gear* cattle

The sun was na up but the moon was down,
  It was the gryming of a new fa'n snaw;
Jamie Telfer has run ten myles a-foot
  Between the Dodhead and the Stobs's Ha.

And whan he cam to the fair tower yate
  He shouted loud and cried weel hie,
Till out bespak auld Gibby Elliot:
  Whae's this that brings the fray to me?

It's I, Jamie Telfer o the Fair Dodhead,
  And a harried man I think I be;
There's naething left at the Fair Dodhead
  But a waeful wife and bairnies three.

Gae seek your succour at Branksome Ha
  For succour ye'se get nane frae me;
Gae seek your succour where ye paid black-mail
  For, man, ye neer paid money to me.

Jamie has turned him round about,
  I wat the tear blinded his ee:
I'll neer pay mail to Elliott again,
  And the Fair Dodhead I'll never see.

My hounds may a' rin masterless,
  My hawks may fly frae tree to tree,
My lord may grip my vassal lands
  For there again maun I never be.

He has turned him to the Tiviot side
  Een as fast as he could drie,
Till he cam to the Coultart Cleugh,
  And there he shouted baith loud and hie.

gryming sprinkling   *black-mail* protection money
yate gate   *grip* seize
weel hie very loud   *drie* manage

214

Then up bespak him auld Jock Grieve:
  Whae's this that brings the fray to me?
It's I, Jamie Telfer o the Fair Dodhead,
  A harried man I trow I be.

There's naething left in the Fair Dodhead
  But a greeting wife and bairnies three;
And sax poor ca's stand in the sta
  A' routing loud for their minnie.

Alack a wae! quo auld Jock Grieve,
  Alack, my heart is sair for thee;
For I was married on the elder sister
  And you on the youngest of a' the three.

Then he has taen out a bonny black,
  Was right weel fed wi corn and hay,
And he's set Jamie Telfer on his back
  To the Catslockhill to tak the fray.

And whan he cam to the Catslockhill
  He shouted loud and cried weel hie,
Till out and spak him William's Wat:
  O whae's this brings the fray to me?

It's I, Jamie Telfer o the Fair Dodhead,
  A harried man I think I be;
The Captain o Bewcastle has driven my gear;
  For God's sake rise and succour me.

Alas for wae! quo William's Wat,
  Alack, for thee my heart is sair;
I never cam by the Fair Dodhead
  That ever I fand thy basket bare.

greeting crying	*routing* lowing
ca's calves	*minnie* mother

He's set his twa sons on coal-black steeds,
  Himsel upon a freckled gray,
And they are on wi Jamie Telfer
  To Branksome Ha to tak the fray.

And whan they cam to Branksome Ha
  They shouted a' baith loud and hie,
Till up and spak him auld Buccleuch:
  Said, Whae's this brings the fray to me?

It's I, Jamie Telfer o the Fair Dodhead,
  And a harried man I think I be;
There's nought left in the Fair Dodhead
  But a greeting wife and bairnies three.

Alack for wae! quo the gude auld lord,
  And ever my heart is wae for thee;
But fye, gar cry on Willie my son,
  And see that he cum to me speedilie.

Gar warn the water, braid and wide;
  Gar warn it sune and hastilie:
They that winna ride for Telfer's kye,
  Let them never look in the face o me.

Warn Wat o Harden and his sons,
  Wi them will Borthwick water ride;
Warn Gaudilands and Allanhaugh
  And Gilmanscleugh and Commonside;

Ride by the gate at Priesthaughswire
  And warn the Currors o the Lee;
As ye cum down the Hermitage Slack
  Warn doughty Willie o Gorrinberry.

gar cry go and cry   *warn the water* warn the
                                     riverside people

The Scotts they rade, the Scotts they ran,
    Sae starkly and sae steadilie,
And aye the ower-word o the thrang
    Was, Rise for Branksome readilie!

The gear was driven the Frostylee up,
    Frae the Frostylee unto the plain,
Whan Willie has lookd his men before
    And saw the kye right fast driving.

Whae drives thir kye, can Willie say,
    To make an outspeckle o me?
It's I, the Captain o Bewcastle, Willie;
    I winna layne my name for thee.

O will ye let Telfer's kye gae back?
    Or will ye do aught for regard o me?
Or by the faith of my body, quo Willie Scott,
    I'se ware my dame's cauf's skin on thee.

I winna let the kye gae back
    Neither for thy love nor yet thy fear;
But I will drive Jamie Telfer's kye
    In spite of every Scott that's here.

Set on them, lads, quo Willie than;
    Fye, lads, set on them cruellie;
For ere they win to the Ritterford
    Mony a toom saddle there sall be!

Then till't they gaed wi heart and hand,
    The blows fell thick as bickering hail;
And mony a horse ran masterless
    And mony a comely cheek was pale.

starkly strongly
ower-word burden, refrain
outspeckle fool, laughing stock
layne conceal
ware use

my dame's cauf's skin my
    mother's calf hide (whip)
toom empty
till't to it

But Willie was stricken ower the head
  And through the knapscap the sword has gane;
And Harden grat for very rage
  Whan Willie on the grund lay slane.

But he's taen aff his gude steel cap
  And thrice he's waved it in the air;
The Dinlay snaw was neer mair white
  Nor the lyart locks of Harden's hair.

Revenge, revenge, auld Wat can cry:
  Fye, lads, lay on them cruellie;
We'll neer see Tiviot side again
  Or Willie's death revenged sall be.

O mony a horse ran masterless,
  The splintered lances flew on hie;
But or they wan to the Kershope ford
  The Scotts had gotten the victory.

John o Brigham there was slane
  And John o Barlow, as I hear say,
And thirty mae o the Captain's men
  Lay bleeding on the grund that day.

The Captain was run through the thick of the thigh
  And broken was his right leg-bane;
If he had lived this hundred years
  He had never been loved by woman again.

Hae back thy kye, the Captain said;
  Dear kye, I trow, to some they be;
For gin I suld live a hundred years
  There will neer fair lady smile on me.

knapscap head-piece   lyart grizzled
grat cried   Or Before

218

Then word is gane to the Captain's bride
  Even in the bower where that she lay,
That her lord was prisoner in enemy's land
  Since into Tividale he had led the way.

I wad lourd have had a winding-sheet
  And helped to put it ower his head,
Ere he had been disgraced by the border Scot
  Whan he ower Liddel his men did lead.

There was a wild gallant amang us a',
  His name was Watty wi the Wudspurs,
Cried, On for his house in Stanegirthside
  If ony man will ride with us!

Whan they cam to the Stanegirthside
  They dang wi trees and burst the door;
They loosed out a' the Captain's kye
  And set them forth our lads before.

There was an auld wyfe ayont the fire,
  A wee bit o the Captain's kin:
Whae dar loose out the Captain's kye,
  Or answer to him and his men?

It's I, Watty Wudspurs, loose the kye,
  I winna layne my name frae thee;
And I will loose out the Captain's kye
  In scorn of a' his men and he.

Whan they cam to the Fair Dodhead
  They were a wellcum sight to see;
For instead of his ain ten milk-kye
  Jamie Telfer has gotten thirty and three.

---

wad lourd would rather *dang* banged, battered
Wudspurs mad, angry, spurs, hot *layne* lie about
spurs

And he has paid the rescue shot
    Baith wi gowd and white monie;
And at the burial o Willie Scott
    I wat was mony a weeping ee.

68

ROBIN HOOD AND ALLEN A DALE

Come listen to me, you gallants so free,
  All you that loves mirth for to hear,
And I will you tell of a bold outlaw,
  That lived in Nottinghamshire,
  That lived in Nottinghamshire.

As Robin Hood in the forrest stood,
  All under the green-wood tree,
There was he ware of a brave young man,
  As fine as fine might be.

The youngster was clothed in scarlet red,
  In scarlet fine and gay,
And he did frisk it over the plain,
  And chanted a roundelay.

As Robin Hood next morning stood,
  Amongst the leaves so gay,
There did he espy the same young man
  Come drooping along the way.

The scarlet he wore the day before,
  It was clean cast away;
And every step he fetcht a sigh,
  Alack and a well a day.

Then stepped forth brave Little John,
  And Nick the miller's son,
Which made the young man bend his bow,
  When as he see them come.

Stand off, stand off, the young man said,
  What is your will with me?
You must come before our master straight,
  Under yon green-wood tree.

And when he came bold Robin before,
   Robin askt him courteously,
O hast thou any money to spare
   For my merry men and me?

I have no money, the young man said,
   But five shillings and a ring;
And that I have kept this seven long years,
   To have it at my wedding.

Yesterday I should have married a maid,
   But she is now from me tane,
And chosen to be an old knights delight,
   Whereby my poor heart is slain.

What is thy name? then said Robin Hood,
   Come tell me, without any fail.
By the faith of my body, then said the young man,
   My name it is Allen a Dale.

What wilt thou give me, said Robin Hood,
   In ready gold or fee,
To help thee to thy true-love again,
   And deliver her unto thee?

I have no money, then quoth the young man,
   No ready gold nor fee,
But I will swear upon a book
   Thy true servant for to be.

How many miles is it to thy true-love?
   Come tell me without any guile.
By the faith of my body, then said the young man,
   It is but five little mile.

Then Robin he hasted over the plain,
   He did neither stint nor lin,
Until he came into the church
   Where Allen should keep his wedding.

stint nor lin stop nor desist

What dost thou do here? the bishop he said,
    I prethee now tell to me:
I am a bold harper, quoth Robin Hood,
    And the best in the north countrey.

O welcome, O welcome, the bishop he said.
    That musick best pleaseth me.
You shall have no musick, quoth Robin Hood,
    Till the bride and the bridegroom I see.

With that came in a wealthy knight,
    Which was both grave and old.
And after him a finikin lass,
    Did shine like glistering gold.

This is no fit match, quoth bold Robin Hood,
    That you do seem to make here;
For since we are come unto the church,
    The bride she shall chuse her own dear.

Then Robin Hood put his horn to his mouth,
    And blew blasts two or three,
When four and twenty bowmen bold
    Came leaping over the lee.

And when they came into the church-yard,
    Marching all on a row,
The first man was Allen a Dale,
    To give bold Robin his bow.

This is thy true-love, Robin he said;
    Young Allen, as I hear say,
And you shall be married at this same time,
    Before we depart away.

That shall not be, the bishop he said,
    For thy word shall not stand;
They shall be three times askt in the church,
    As the law is of our land.

Robin Hood pulled off the bishops coat,
    And put it upon Little John;
By the faith of my body, then Robin said,
    This cloath doth make thee a man.

When Little John went into the quire,
    The people began for to laugh;
He askt them seven times in the church,
    Least three times should not be enough.

Who gives me this maid, then said Little John;
    Quoth Robin, That do I,
And he that doth take her from Allen a Dale
    Full dearly he shall her buy.

And thus having ended this merry wedding,
    The bride lookt as fresh as a queen,
And so they returned to the merry green wood,
    Amongst the leaves so green.

69

ROBIN HOOD AND THE SHERIFF

Robin Hood's to Nottinghame gane,
  Wi a linkie down and a day,
And there he met wi an auld woman,
  Coming weeping alang the highway.

Weep ye for any of my gold, auld woman?
  Or weep ye for my fee?
Or weep ye for any warld's gear
  This day I can grant to thee?

I weep not for your gold, kind sir,
  I weep not for your fee;
But I weep for my three braw sons,
  This day condemned to die.

O have they parishes burned? he said,
  Or have they ministers slain?
Or have they forced maidens against their will?
  Or wi other men's wives hae they lain?

They have not parishes burned, kind sir,
  They have not ministers slain;
They neer forced a maid against her will,
  Nor wi no man's wife hae they lain.

O what hae they done then? quo Robin Hood,
  I pray thee tell unto me:
O they killed the king's fallow deer,
  And this day are condemned to die.

O have you mind, old mother, he said,
  Since you made my merry men to dine?
And for to repay it back unto thee
  Is come in a very good time.

Sae Robin Hood's to Nottinghame gane,
   With a linkie down and a day,
And there he met an old beggar man,
   Coming creeping along the high way.

What news, what news, old father? he said,
   What news hast thou for me?
There's three merry men, quo the poor auld man,
   This day condemned to die.

Will you change your apparel wi me, old father?
   Will you change your apparel for mine?
And twenty broad shillings I'll gie ye to the boot,
   To drink gude beer or wine.

Thine is of the scarlet fine,
   And mine is baith ragged and torn;
Sae never let a young supple youth
   Laugh a gude auld man to scorn.

Change your apparel wi me, old churl,
   And quickly change it for mine,
And thirty broad shillings I'll gie to the boot,
   To drink gude beer or wine.

When Robin put on the auld man's hat,
   It was weary high in the crown;
By the hand of my body, quo Robin Hood,
   I am lang whan I loot down.

Whan Robin put on the auld man's cloak,
   There was mony a pock therein;
A pock for meal, and a pock for maut,
   And a pock for groats and corn,
And a little wee pockie that hung by his side
   That he put in his bugle-horn.

loot bend

Sae Robin Hood's to Nottinghame gane,
  Wi a linkie down and a day,
And there he met wi the high sheriff,
  Coming riding alang the high way.

O save you, O save you, high sheriff, he said,
  And weel saved mote you be!
And what will you gie to the silly auld man
  Your hangman for to be?

Thirteen pence, the sheriff replied,
  That is the hangman's fee,
But an the claiths of the three young men
  This day condemned to die.

I never hanged a man in a' my life,
  And intend not to begin;
But ever I hang a man in my life,
  High sheriff, thou's be the ane.

But I have a horn in my pocket,
  I gat it frae Robin Hood,
And gif I tak out my little horn,
  For thee it will no blaw gude.

Blaw, blaw, bauld beggar, he said,
  Blaw, and fear nae doubt;
I wish you may gie sic a blast
  Till your eyne loup out.

Then Robin he gave a skip,
  And he skipped frae a stick till a stane;
By the hand of my body, quo the high sheriff,
  You are a supple auld man.

Then Robin set his horn to his mouth,
  And he blew baith loud and shrill,
Till sixty-four of bold Robin's men
  Cam marching down the green hill.

But an And also   *loup* jump

What men are these, quo the high sheriff,
   That comes sae merrily?
They are my men, quo Robin Hood,
   And they'll pay a visit to thee.

They tack the gallows out of the glen,
   And they set it in a slap;
They hanged the sheriff upon it,
   And his best men at his back.

They took the gallows out o the slap,
   And they set it back in the glen,
And they hanged the sheriff upon it,
   Let the three young men gae hame.

slap muddy place

70

ROBIN HOOD AND THE BISHOP
OF HEREFORD

Some they will talk of bold Robin Hood,
  And some of barons bold,
But I'll tell you how he servd the Bishop of Hereford,
  When he robbd him of his gold.

As it befel in merry Barnsdale,
  And under the green-wood tree,
The Bishop of Hereford was to come by,
  With all his company.

Come, kill a venson, said bold Robin Hood,
  Come, kill me a good fat deer;
The Bishop of Hereford is to dine with me to-day,
  And he shall pay well for his cheer.

We'll kill a fat venison, said bold Robin Hood,
  And dress it by the highway-side;
And we will watch the Bishop narrowly,
  Lest some other way he should ride.

Robin Hood dressd himself in shepherd's attire,
  With six of his men also;
And, when the Bishop of Hereford came by,
  They about the fire did go.

O what is the matter? then said the Bishop,
  Or for whom do you make this a-do?
Or why do you kill the king's venson,
  When your company is so few?

We are shepherds, said bold Robin Hood,
  And we keep sheep all the year,
And we are disposed to be merry this day,
  And to kill of the king's fat deer.

You are brave fellows! said the Bishop,
  And the king of your doings shall know;
Therefore make haste and come along with me,
  For before the king you shall go.

O pardon, O pardon, said bold Robin Hood,
  O pardon, I thee pray!
For it becomes not your lordship's coat
  To take so many lives away.

No pardon, no pardon, says the Bishop,
  No pardon I thee owe;
Therefore make haste, and come along with me,
  For before the king you shall go.

Then Robin set his back against a tree,
  And his foot against a thorn,
And from underneath his shepherd's coat
  He pulld out a bugle-horn.

He put the little end to his mouth,
  And a loud blast did he blow,
Till threescore and ten of bold Robin's men
  Came running all on a row;

All making obeysance to bold Robin Hood;
  'T was a comely sight for to see:
What is the matter, master, said Little John,
  That you blow so hastily?

O here is the Bishop of Hereford,
  And no pardon we shall have:
Cut off his head, master, said Little John,
  And throw him into his grave.

O pardon, O pardon, said the Bishop,
  O pardon, I thee pray!
For if I had known it had been you,
  I'd have gone some other way.

No pardon, no pardon, said Robin Hood,
 No pardon I thee owe;
Therefore make haste and come along with me,
 For to merry Barnsdale you shall go.

Then Robin he took the Bishop by the hand,
 And led him to merry Barnsdale;
He made him to stay and sup with him that night,
 And to drink wine, beer, and ale.

Call in the reckoning, said the Bishop,
 For methinks it grows wondrous high:
Lend me your purse, Bishop, said Little John,
 And I'll tell you bye and bye.

Then Little John took the bishop's cloak,
 And spread it upon the ground,
And out of the bishop's portmantua
 He told three hundred pound.

Here's money enough, master, said Little John,
 And a comely sight 'tis to see;
It makes me in charity with the Bishop,
 Tho he heartily loveth not me.

Robin Hood took the Bishop by the hand,
 And he caused the music to play,
And he made the Bishop to dance in his boots,
 And glad he could so get away.

71

CHEVY CHASE
(THE HUNTING OF THE CHEVIOT)

God prosper long our noble king,
  Our liffes and saftyes all!
A woefull hunting once there did
  In Chevy Chase befall.

To drive the deere with hound and horne
  Erle Pearcy took the way:
The child may rue that is unborne
  The hunting of that day!

The stout Erle of Northumberland
  A vow to God did make
His pleasure in the Scottish woods
  Three sommers days to take,

The cheefest harts in Chevy Chase
  To kill and beare away:
These tydings to Erle Douglas came
  In Scottland where he lay.

Who sent Erle Pearcy present word
  He wold prevent his sport;
The English erle, not fearing that,
  Did to the woods resort,

With fifteen hundred bowmen bold,
  All chosen men of might,
Who knew ffull well in time of neede
  To ayme their shafts arright.

The gallant greyhounds swiftly ran
  To chase the fallow deere;
On Munday they began to hunt,
  Ere daylight did appeare.

And long before high noone they had
   A hundred fat buckes slaine;
Then having dined, the drovyers went
   To rouze the deare againe.

The bowmen mustered on the hills,
   Well able to endure;
Theire backsids all with speciall care
   That day were guarded sure.

The hounds ran swiftly through the woods
   The nimble deere to take,
That with their cryes the hills and dales
   An eccho shrill did make.

Lord Pearcy to the querry went
   To view the tender deere;
Quoth he, Erle Douglas promised once
   This day to meete me here;

But if I thought he wold not come,
   Noe longer wold I stay.
With that a brave younge gentlman
   Thus to the erle did say:

Loe, yonder doth Erle Douglas come,
   Hys men in armour bright;
Full twenty hundred Scottish speres
   All marching in our sight.

All men of pleasant Tivydale,
   Fast by the river Tweede.
O ceaze your sportts! Erle Pearcy said,
   And take your bowes with speede.

And now with me, my countrymen,
   Your courage forth advance!
For there was never champion yett,
   In Scotland nor in Ffrance,

querry quarry (the dead deer)

That ever did on horsbacke come,
  But, if my hap it were,
I durst encounter man for man,
  With him to breake a spere.

Erle Douglas on his milk-white steede,
  Most like a baron bold,
Rode formost of his company,
  Whose armor shone like gold.

Shew me, sayd hee, whose men you bee
  That hunt so boldly heere,
That without my consent doe chase
  And kill my fallow deere.

The first man that did answer make
  Was noble Pearcy hee;
Who sayd, Wee list not to declare
  Nor shew whose men wee bee;

Yett wee will spend our deerest blood
  Thy cheefest harts to slay.
Then Douglas swore a solempne oathe,
  And thus in rage did say:

Ere thus I will outbraved bee,
  One of us tow shall dye;
I know thee well, an erle thou art;
  Lord Pearcy, soe am I.

But trust me, Pearcye, pittye it were,
  And great offence, to kill
Then any of these our guiltlesse men,
  For they have done none ill.

Let thou and I the battell trye,
  And set our men aside:
Accurst bee he! Erle Pearcye sayd,
  By whome it is denyed.

Then stept a gallant squire forth –
　　Witherington was his name –
Who said, I wold not have it told
　　To Henery our king, for shame,

That ere my captaine fought on foote,
　　And I stand looking on.
You bee two Erles, quoth Witheringhton,
　　And I a squier alone;

I'le doe the best that doe I may,
　　While I have power to stand;
While I have power to weeld my sword,
　　I'le fight with hart and hand.

Our English archers bent their bowes;
　　Their harts were good and trew;
Att the first flight of arrowes sent,
　　Full foure score Scotts they slew.

To drive the deere with hound and horne,
　　Dauglas bade on the bent;
Two captaines moved with mickle might,
　　Their speres to shivers went.

They closed full fast on every side,
　　Noe slackness there was found,
But many a gallant gentleman
　　Lay gasping on the ground.

O Christ! it was great greeve to see
　　How eche man chose his spere,
And how the blood out of their brests
　　Did gush like water cleare.

At last these two stout erles did meet,
　　Like captaines of great might;
Like lyons woode they layd on lode;
　　They made a cruell fight.

---

bade on the bent stayed on the field　　*layd on lode*
woode maddened　　　　　　　　　　　　delivered blows

They fought untill they both did sweat,
    With swords of tempered steele,
Till blood downe their cheekes like raine
    The trickling downe did feele.

O yeeld thee, Pearcye! Douglas sayd,
    And in faith I will thee bringe
Where thou shall high advanced bee
    By James our Scottish king.

Thy ransome I will freely give,
    And this report of thee,
Thou art the most couragious knight
    That ever I did see.

Noe, Douglas! quoth Erle Percy then,
    Thy profer I doe scorne;
I will not yeelde to any Scott
    That ever yett was borne!

With that there came an arrow keene,
    Out of an English bow,
Which stroke Erle Douglas on the brest
    A deepe and deadlye blow.

Who never sayd more words than these:
    Fight on, my merry men all!
For why, my life is att an end,
    Lord Pearcy sees my fall.

Then leaving liffe, Erle Pearcy tooke
    The dead man by the hand;
Who said, Erle Dowglas, for thy life,
    Wold I had lost my hand;

O Christ! my verry hart doth bleed
    For sorrow for thy sake,
For sure, a more redoubted knight
    Mischance could never take.

A knight amongst the Scotts there was
   Which saw Erle Douglas dye,
Who streight in hart did vow revenge
   Upon the Lord Pearcye.

Sir Hugh Mountgomerye was he called,
   Who, with a spere full bright,
Well mounted on a gallant steed,
   Ran feircly through the fight,

And past the English archers all,
   Without all dread or feare,
And through Erle Percyes body then
   He thrust his hatfull spere.

With such a vehement force and might
   His body he did gore,
The staff ran through the other side
   A large cloth-yard and more.

Thus did both those nobles dye,
   Whose courage none cold staine;
An English archer then perceived
   The noble erle was slaine.

He had a good bow in his hand,
   Made of a trusty tree;
An arrow of a cloth-yard long
   To the hard head haled hee.

Against Sir Hugh Mountgomerye
   His shaft full right he sett;
The grey-goose winge that was there-on
   In his harts bloode was wett.

This fight from breake of day did last
   Till setting of the sun,
For when they rung the evening-bell
   The battele scarse was done.

With stout Erle Percy there was slaine
 Sir John of Egerton,
Sir Robert Harcliffe and Sir William,
 Sir James, that bold barron.

And with Sir George and Sir James,
 Both knights of good account,
Good Sir Raphe Rebbye there was slaine,
 Whose prowesse did surmount.

For Witherington needs must I wayle
 As one in dolefull dumpes,
For when his leggs were smitten of,
 He fought upon his stumpes.

And with Erle Dowglas there was slaine
 Sir Hugh Mountgomerye,
And Sir Charles Morrell, that from feelde
 One foote wold never flee;

Sir Roger Hever of Harcliffe tow,
 His sisters sonne was hee;
Sir David Lambwell, well esteemed,
 But saved he cold not bee.

And the Lord Maxwell, in like case,
 With Douglas he did dye;
Of twenty hundred Scottish speeres,
 Scarce fifty-five did flye.

Of fifteen hundred Englishmen
 Went home but fifty-three;
The rest in Chevy Chase were slaine,
 Under the greenwoode tree.

Next day did many widdowes come
 Their husbands to bewayle;
They washt their wounds in brinish teares,
 But all wold not prevayle.

Theyr bodyes, bathed in purple blood,
    They bore with them away;
They kist them dead a thousand times
    Ere they were cladd in clay.

The newes was brought to Eddenborrow,
    Where Scottlands king did rayne,
That brave Erle Douglas soddainlye
    Was with an arrow slaine.

O heavy newes! King James can say;
    Scottland may wittenesse bee
I have not any captaine more
    Of such account as hee.

Like tydings to King Henery came,
    Within as short a space,
That Pearcy of Northumberland
    Was slaine in Chevy Chase.

Now God be with him! said our king,
    Sith it will noe better bee;
I trust I have within my realme
    Five hundred as good as hee.

Yett shall not Scotts nor Scotland say
    But I will vengeance take,
And be revenged on them all
    For brave Erle Percyes sake.

This vow the king did well performe
    After on Humble-downe;
In one day fifty knights were slayne,
    With lords of great renowne.

And of the rest of small account,
    Did many hundreds dye:
Thus endeth the hunting in Chevy Chase,
    Made by the Erle Pearcye.

God save our king, and blesse this land
With plentye, ioy, and peace,
And grant hencforth that foule debate
Twixt noble men may ceaze!

72

QUEEN ELENOR'S CONFESSION

Queen Elenor was a sick woman,
    And afraid that she should dye;
Then she sent for two fryars of France,
    For to speak with them speedily.

The King calld down his nobles all,
    By one, by two, and by three,
And sent away for Earl Martial,
    For to speak with him speedily.

When that he came before the King,
    He fell on his bended knee;
A boon, a boon! our gracious king,
    That you sent so hastily.

I'll pawn my living and my lands,
    My septer and my crown,
That whatever Queen Elenor says,
    I will not write it down.

Do you put on one fryar's coat,
    And I'll put on another,
And we will to Queen Elenor go,
    One fryar like another.

Thus both attired then they go;
    When they came to Whitehall,
The bells they did ring, and the quiristers sing,
    And the torches did light them all.

When that they came before the Queen,
    They fell on their bended knee:
A boon, a boon! our gracious queen,
    That you sent so hastily.

Are you two fryars of France? she said,
  Which I suppose you be;
But if you are two English fryars,
  Then hanged shall you be.

We are two fryars of France, they said,
  As you suppose we be;
We have not been at any mass
  Since we came from the sea.

The first vile thing that ere I did
  I will to you unfold;
Earl Martial had my maidenhead,
  Underneath this cloath of gold.

That is a vile sin, then said the king,
  God may forgive it thee!
Amen! Amen! quoth Earl Martial,
  With a heavy heart then spoke he.

The next vile thing that ere I did
  To you I'll not deny;
I made a box of poyson strong,
  To poyson King Henry.

That is a vile sin, then said the King,
  God may forgive it thee!
Amen! Amen! quoth Earl Martial,
  And I wish it so may be.

The next vile thing that ere I did
  To you I will discover;
I poysoned Fair Rosamond,
  All in fair Woodstock bower.

That is a vile sin, then said the King,
  God may forgive it thee!
Amen! Amen! quoth Earl Martial,
  And I wish it so may be.

Do you see yonders little boy,
  A tossing of that ball?
That is Earl Martial's eldest son,
  And I love him the best of all.

Do you see yonders little boy,
  A catching of the ball?
That is King Henry's son, she said,
  And I love him the worst of all.

His head is like unto a bull,
  His nose is like a boar;
No matter for that, King Henry said,
  I love him the better therefore.

The King pulld of his fryar's coat,
  And appeard all in red;
She shriekd and she cry'd, she wrong her hands,
  And said she was betrayd.

The King lookd over his left shoulder,
  And a grim look looked he,
And said, Earl Martial, but for my oath,
  Then hanged shouldst thou be.

73

KING EDWARD THE FOURTH AND A
TANNER OF TAMWORTH

In summer time, when leaves grew green,
  And birds were singing on every tree,
King Edward would a hunting ride,
  Some pastime for to see.

Our king he would a hunting ride,
  By eight a clock of the day,
And well was he ware of a bold tanner,
  Came riding on the way.

A good russet coat the tanner had on,
  Fast buttoned under his chin,
And under him a good cow-hide,
  And a mare of four shilling.

Now stand you here, my good lords all,
  Under this trusty tree,
And I will wend to yonder fellow,
  To know from whence came he.

God speed, God speed, then said our king;
  Thou art welcome, good fellow, quoth he;
Which is the way to Drayton Basset
  I pray thee shew to me.

The ready way to Drayton Basset,
  From this place as thou dost stand,
The next pair of gallows thou comst to
  Thou must turn up on thy right hand.

That is not the way, then said our king,
  The ready way I pray thee shew me;
Whether thou be thief or true man, quoth the tanner,
  I'm weary of thy company.

Away, with a vengeance, quoth the tanner,
   I hold thee out of thy wit,
For all this day have I ridden and gone,
   And I am fasting yet.

Go with me to Drayton Basset, said our king,
   No daintyes we will lack;
We'l have meat and drink of the best,
   And I will pay the shot.

Godamercy for nothing, said the tanner,
   Thou shalt pay for no dinner of mine;
I have more groats and nobles in my purse
   Then thou hast pence in thine.

God save your goods, then said the king,
   And send them well to thee!
Be thou thief or true man, quoth the tanner,
   I am weary of thy company.

Away, with a vengeance, quoth the tanner,
   Of thee I stand in fear;
The aparrell thou wearst on thy back
   May seem a good lord to wear.

I never stole them, said our king,
   I swear to thee by the rood;
Thou art some ruffian of the country,
   Thou rid'st in the midst of thy good.

What news dost thou hear? then said our king,
   I pray what news do you hear?
I hear no news, answered the tanner,
   But that cow-hides be dear.

Cow-hides? cow-hides? then said our king,
   I marvell what they be;
Why, art thou a fool? quoth the tanner,
   Look, I have one under me.

Yet one thing now I would thee pray,
   So that thou wouldst not be strange;
If thy mare be better than my steed,
   I pray thee let us change.

But if you needs with me will change,
   As change full well may ye,
By the faith of my body, quoth the tanner,
   I look to have boot of thee.

What boot wilt thou ask? then said our king,
   What boot dost thou ask on this ground?
No pence nor half-pence, said the tanner,
   But a noble in gold so round.

Here's twenty good groats, then said the king,
   So well paid see you be;
I love thee better then I did before,
   I thought thou hadst nere a peny.

But if so be we needs must change,
   As change thou must abide,
Though thou hast gotten Brock my mare,
   Thou shalt not have my cow-hide.

The tanner took the good cow-hide,
   That of the cow was hilt,
And threw it upon the king's saddle,
   That was so fairly guilt.

Now help me, help me, quoth the tanner,
   Full quickly that I were gone,
For when I come home to Gillian my wife
   She'l say I'm a gentleman.

The king took the tanner by the leg,
   He girded a fart so round;
You'r very homely, said the king,
   Were I aware, I'd laid you o th' ground.

boot profit

But when the tanner was in the king's saddle
  Astonëd then he was;
He knew not the stirrops that he did wear,
  Whether they were gold or brass.

But when the steed saw the black cow-tale wag,
  For and the black cow-horn,
The steed began to run away,
  As the divel the tanner had born.

Untill he came unto a nook,
  A little beside an ash;
The steed gave the tanner such a fall
  His neck was almost brast.

Take thy horse again, with a vengeance, he said,
  With me he shall not abide;
It is no marvell, said the king, and laught,
  He knew not your cow-hide.

But if that we needs now must change,
  As change that well we mought,
I'le swear to you plain, if you have your mare,
  I look to have some boot.

What boot will you ask? quoth the tanner,
  What boot will you ask on this ground?
No pence nor half-pence, said our king,
  But a noble in gold so round.

Here's twenty good groats, said the tanner,
  And twenty more I have of thine;
I have ten groats more in my purse,
  We'l drink five of them at the wine.

The king set a bugle-horne to his mouth,
  That blew both loud and shrill,
And five hundred lords and knights
  Came riding over a hill.

boot profit

Away, with a vengeance, quoth the tanner,
  With thee I'le no longer abide;
Thou art a strong thief, yonder be thy fellows,
  They will steal away my cow-hide.

No, I protest, then said our king,
  For so it may not be;
They be the lords of Drayton Basset,
  Come out of the North Country.

But when they came before the king
  Full low they fell on their knee;
The tanner had rather then a thousand pound
  He had been out of his company.

A coller! a coller! then said the king,
  A coller! then did he cry;
Then would he have given a thousand pound
  He had not been so nigh.

A coller? a coller? then quoth the tanner,
  It is a thing which will breed sorrow;
For after a coller commeth a halter,
  And I shall be hanged tomorrow.

No, do not fear, the king did say;
  For pastime thou hast shown me,
No coller nor halter thou shalt have,
  But I will give thee a fee.

For Plompton Park I will give thee,
  With tenements three beside,
Which is worth three hundred pound a year,
  To maintain thy good cow-hide.

Godamercy, Godamercy, quoth the tanner;
  For this good deed thou hast done,
If ever thou comest to merry Tamworth,
  Thou shalt have clouting-leather for thy shone.

clouting-leather mending leather

74

THE GREAT SILKIE OF SULE SKERRY

An eartly nourris sits and sings,
   And aye she sings, Ba, lily wean,
Little ken I my bairnis father,
   Far less the land that he staps in.

Then ane arose at her bed-fit,
   An a grumly guest I'm sure was he:
Here am I, thy bairnis father,
   Although that I be not comelie.

I am a man, upo the lan,
   An I am a silkie in the sea,
And when I'm far and far frae lan,
   My dwelling is in Sule Skerrie.

It was na weel, quo the maiden fair,
   It was na weel, indeed, quo she,
That the Great Silkie of Sule Skerrie
   Suld hae come and aught a bairn to me.

Now he has taen a purse of goud,
   And he has pat it upo her knee,
Sayin, Gie to me my little young son,
   An tak thee up thy nourris-fee.

An it sall come to pass on a simmer's day,
   When the sin shines het on evera stane,
That I will tak my little young son,
   An teach him for to swim the faem.

Silkie Seal
Sule Skerry 'seal skerry', skerry or
  reef in the Atlantic west of
  Orkney

lily wean lovely little one
grumly fierce-looking
aught a bairn to me had a child by
  me

An thu sall marry a proud gunner,
  An a proud gunner I'm sure he'll be,
An the very first schot that ere he schoots,
  He'll schoot baith my young son and me.

75

SEALCHIE SONG

(Another Version)

I heard a mither baing her bairn
An ay she rockit an she sang
She took sae hard upon the verse
Till the heart within her body rang.

O row cradle an go cradle
An ay sleep thou my bairn within.
O little ken I my bairn's faither
Or yet the land that he liggs in.

O up then spake a grimly ghost
A aye sae laigh at her bed's feet
O here am I thy bairns faither
Although I'm nae thy luve sae sweet.

Jo Immrannoe it is my name,
Jo Immrannoe they do ca me,
An my lands they lie baith braid an wide
Amang the rocks o Sule Skerry.

An foster weel my young young son
An for a twalmont an a day
An when the twalmonts fairly done
I'll come an pay the nourice's fee.

But how shall I my young son ken
An how shall I my young son know?
'Mang a' the selkies i Sule Skerry
He will be midmost amang them a'.

baing singing a lullaby to   *selkies* Seals

My husband is a proud gunner
An aye a proud gunner is he
An the first shot that he will fire
Will be at my young son an thee.

I fear nae livin proud gunner
I fear nae mortal man, quo he,
For pouther winna burn i saut
 Sae I an thy young son'll gae free.

O when that weary twalmont gaed
He cam to pay the nourice fee.
He had ae coffer fu o gowd
An anither fu o white money.

Upo the Skerry is thy young son,
Upo the Skerry lieth he.
Sin thou wilt see they ain young son
Now is the time to speak wi he.

The gunner lay ahind a rock,
Ahind a tangie rock lay he
An the very first shot the gunner loot
It strack his wife aboon the bree.

Jo Immrannoe an his young son
Wi heavy hearts took tae the sea.
Let a' that live on mortal lird
Neer mell wi selchies o the sea.

pouther powder	*loot* let off, fired
ae one	*lird* ground, land
white money silver	*mell* couple
tangie covered with sea weed	

2

LATER BALLADS,
ENGLISH, SCOTCH, IRISH,
AUSTRALIAN AND AMERICAN

76

THE DEATH OF ADMIRAL BENBOW

Come all you sailors bold,
  Lend an ear,
Come all you sailors bold,
  Lend an ear:
'Tis of our Admiral's fame,
Brave Benbow called by name,
How he fought on the main
  You shall hear.

Brave Benbow he set sail
  For to fight,
Brave Benbow he set sail
  For to fight:
Brave Benbow he set sail,
With a fine and pleasant gale,
But his captains they turned tail
  In a fight.

Says Kirkby unto Wade,
  I will run,
Says Kirkby unto Wade,
  I will run:
I value not disgrace,
Nor the losing of my place,
My foes I will not face
  With a gun.

'Twas the *Ruby* and *Noah's Ark*
  Fought the French,
'Twas the *Ruby* and *Noah's Ark*
  Fought the French:
And there was ten in all,
Poor souls they fought them all,
They recked them not at all
  Nor their noise.

It was our Admiral's lot,
  With a chain-shot,
It was our Admiral's lot,
  With a chain-shot:
Our Admiral lost his legs,
And to his men he begs,
Fight on, my boys, he says,
  'Tis my lot.

While the surgeon dressed his wounds,
  Thus he said,
While the surgeon dressed his wounds,
  Thus he said,
Let my cradle now in haste
On the quarter-deck be placed,
That the Frenchmen I may face,
  Till I'm dead.

And there bold Benbow lay,
  Crying out,
And there bold Benbow lay,
  Crying out,
O let us tack once more,
We'll drive them to the shore,
As our fathers did before
  Long ago.

77

THE VALIANT SEAMAN'S HAPPY RETURN
TO HIS LOVE, AFTER A
LONG SEVEN YEARS' ABSENCE

When Sol did cast no light,
  Being darken'd over,
And the dark time of night
  Did the skies cover,
Running a river by
  There were ships sailing,
A maid most fair I spy'd,
  Crying and wailing.

Unto this maid I stept,
  Asking what griev'd her,
She answer'd me and wept,
  Fates had deceiv'd her:
My love is prest, quoth she,
  To cross the ocean,
Proud waves to make the ship
  Ever in motion.

We lov'd seven years and more,
  Both being sure,
But I am left on shore,
  Grief to endure.
He promis'd back to turn,
  If life was spar'd him,
With grief I dayly mourn,
  Death hath debar'd him.

Straight a brisk lad she spy'd,
  Made her admire,
A present she receiv'd,
  Pleas'd her desire.

Is my love safe, quoth she,
  Will he come near me,
The young man answer made,
  Virgin pray hear me.

Under one banner bright,
  For England's glory,
Your love and I did fight,
  Mark well my story;
By an unhappy shot,
  We two were parted,
His deaths wound then he got,
  Though valiant-hearted.

All this I witness can,
  For I stood by him,
For courage I must say,
  None did out-vye him;
He still would foremost be,
  Striving for honour;
But fortune is a whore,
  Vengeance upon her.

But e're he was quite dead,
  Or his heart broken,
To me these words he said,
  Pray give this token
To my love, for there is
  Then she none fairer,
Tell her she must be kind
  And love the bearer.

Intomb'd he now doth lye,
  In stately manner,
'Cause he fought valiantly,
  For love and honour:
That right he had in you,
  To me he gave it:
Now since it is my due,
  Pray let me have it.

She raging flung away,
   Like one distracted,
Not knowing what to say,
   Nor what she acted:
To last she curst her fate,
   And shew'd her anger,
Saying, friend you come too late,
   I'le have no stranger.

To your own house return,
   I am best pleased,
Here for my love to mourn,
   Since he's deceased:
In sable weeds I'le go,
   Let who will jear me;
Since death has serv'd me so,
   None shall come near me.

The chast Penelope
   Mourn'd for Ulisses,
I have more grief then she,
   Rob'd of my blisses:
I'le ne'er love man again,
   Therefore pray hear me;
I'le slight you with disdain,
   If you come near me.

I know he lov'd me well
   For when we parted,
None did in grief excell,
   Both were true-hearted.
Those promises we made,
   Ne'r shall be broken;
Those words that then he said,
   Ne'r shall be spoken.

He hearing what she said,
   Made his love stronger,
Off his disguise he laid,
   And staid no longer:

When her dear love she knew,
    In wanton fashion,
Into his arms she flew,
    Such is loves passion.

He ask'd her how she lik'd
    His counterfeiting,
Whether she was well pleas'd
    With such like greeting:
You are well vers'd, quoth she,
    In several speeches,
Could you coyn money so,
    You might get riches.

O happy gale of wind,
    That waft thee over,
May Heaven preserve that ship,
    That brought my lover;
Come kiss me now my sweet,
    True love's no slander;
Thou shalt my Hero be,
    I thy Leander.

Dido of Carthage Queen
    Lov'd stout Aeneas,
But my true love is found
    More true then he was:
Venus ne'r fonder was
    Of young Adonis,
Then I will be of thee,
    Since thy love known is.

Then hand in hand they walk,
    With mirth and pleasure,
They laugh, they kiss, they talk,
    Love knows no measure;
Now both do sit and sing,
    But she sings clearest;
Like nightingale in spring,
    Welcome my dearest.

TEACH THE ROVER

Will you hear of a bloody Battle,
  Lately fought upon the Seas,
It will make your Ears to rattle,
  And your Admiration cease;
Have you heard of Teach the Rover,
  And his Knavery on the Main;
How of Gold he was a Lover,
  How he lov'd an ill-got Gain.

When the Act of Grace appeared,
  Captain Teach with all his men,
Unto Carolina steered,
  Where they kindly us'd him then;
There he marry'd to a Lady,
  And gave her five hundred Pound,
But to her he prov'd unsteady,
  For he soon march'd off the Ground.

And returned, as I tell you,
  To his Robbery as before,
Burning, sinking Ships of value,
  Filling them with Purple Gore;
When he was at Carolina,
  There the Governor did send,
To the Governor of Virginia,
  That he might assistance lend.

Then the Man-of-War's Commander,
  Two small Sloops he fitted out,
Fifty Men he put on board, Sir,
  Who resolv'd to stand it out:
The Lieutenant he commanded
  Both the Sloops, and you shall hear,
How before he landed,
  He suppress'd them without fear.

Valiant Maynard as he sailed,
　　Soon the Pirate did espy,
With his Trumpet he then hailed,
　　And to him they did reply:
'Captain Teach is our Commander,'
　　Maynard said, 'he is the Man,
Whom I am resolv'd to hang, Sir,
　　Let him do the best he can.'

Teach replyed unto Maynard,
　　'Sir, no Quarter you shall see,
But be hang'd on the Mainyard,
　　You and all your Company';
Maynard said, 'I none desire,
　　Of such knaves as thee and thine,
None I'll give.' Teach replied,
　　'My Boys, give me a Glass of Wine.'

He took the glass and drank Damnation,
　　Unto Maynard and his Crew,
To himself and Generation,
　　Then the Glass away he threw;
Brave Maynard was resolv'd to have him,
　　Tho' he'd Cannons nine or ten;
Teach a broadside quickly gave him,
　　Killing sixteen valiant Men.

Maynard boarded him, and to it
　　They fell with Sword and Pistol too;
They had Courage, and did show it,
　　Killing of the Pirate's Crew.
Teach and Maynard on the Quarter,
　　Fought it out most manfully,
Maynard's Sword did cut him shorter,
　　Losing his head, he there did die.

Every sailor fought while he, Sir,
　　Power had to wield the Sword,
Not a coward could you see, Sir,
　　Fear was driven from aboard;

Wounded Men on both Sides fell, Sir,
   'Twas a doleful Sight to see,
Nothing could their Courage quell, Sir,
   O, they fought courageously.

When the bloody Fight was over,
   We're informed by a Letter writ,
Teach's Head was made a Cover,
   To the Jack Staff of the Ship:
Thus they sailed to Virginia,
   And when they the Story told,
How they kill'd the Pirates many,
   They'd Applause from young and old.

Jack Staff staff on prow or bowsprit for carrying a ship's
   jack or national flag

79

THE SALCOMBE SEAMAN'S FLAUNT
TO THE PROUD PIRATE

A lofty ship from Salcombe came,
 Blow high, blow low, and so sailed we;
She had golden trucks that shone like flame,
 On the bonny coasts of Barbary.

'Masthead, masthead,' the captains hail,
 Blow high, blow low, and so sailed we;
'Look out and round; d' ye see a sail?'
 On the bonny coasts of Barbary.

'There's a ship what looms like Beachy Head,'
 Blow high, blow low, and so sailed we;
'Her banner aloft it blows out red,'
 On the bonny coasts of Barbary.

'Oh, ship ahoy, and where do you steer?'
 Blow high, blow low, and so sailed we;
'Are you man-of-war, or privateer?'
 On the bonny coasts of Barbary.

'I am neither one of the two,' said she,
 Blow high, blow low, and so sailed we;
'I'm a pirate, looking for my fee,'
 On the bonny coasts of Barbary.

'I'm a jolly pirate, out for gold':
 Blow high, blow low, and so sailed we;
'I will rummage through your after hold,'
 On the bonny coasts of Barbary.

The grumbling guns they flashed and roared,
 Blow high, blow low, and so sailed we;
Till the pirate's masts went overboard,
 On the bonny coasts of Barbary.

They fired shot till the pirate's deck,
　　Blow high, blow low, and so sailed we;
Was blood and spars and broken wreck,
　　On the bonny coasts of Barbary.

'O do not haul the red flag down,'
　　Blow high, blow low, and so sailed we;
'O keep all fast until we drown,'
　　On the bonny coasts of Barbary.

They called for cans of wine, and drank,
　　Blow high, blow low, and so sailed we;
They sang their songs until she sank,
　　On the bonny coasts of Barbary.

Now let us brew good cans of flip,
　　Blow high, blow low, and so sailed we;
And drink a bowl to the Salcombe ship,
　　On the bonny coasts of Barbary.

And drink a bowl to the lad of fame,
　　Blow high, blow low, and so sailed we;
Who put the pirate ship to shame,
　　On the bonny coasts of Barbary.

flip beer mixed with spirits and sugar and heated with hot iron

80

CAPTAIN ROBERT KIDD

You captains bold and brave, hear our cries, hear our cries,
You captains bold and brave, hear our cries,
You captains brave and bold, though you seem uncontrolled,
Don't for the sake of gold lose your souls, lose your souls.
Don't for the sake of gold lose your souls.

My name was Robert Kidd, when I sailed, when I sailed.
My name was Robert Kidd, when I sailed,
My name was Robert Kidd, God's laws I did forbid,
And so wickedly I did, when I sailed.

My parents taught me well, when I sailed, when I sailed,
My parents taught me well, when I sailed,
My parents taught me well to shun the gates of hell,
But against them I rebelled when I sailed.

I cursed my father dear when I sailed, when I sailed,
I cursed my father dear when I sailed,
I cursed my father dear and her that did me bear,
And so wickedly did swear when I sailed.

I made a solemn vow when I sailed, when I sailed,
I made a solemn vow when I sailed,
I made a solemn vow to God I would not bow,
Nor myself one prayer allow, as I sailed.

I'd a Bible in my hand when I sailed, when I sailed,
I'd a Bible in my hand when I sailed,
I'd a Bible in my hand by my father's great command,
And sunk it in the sand when I sailed.

I murdered William Moore, as I sailed, as I sailed,
I murdered William Moore, as I sailed,
I murdered William Moore, and left him in his gore,
Nor many leagues from shore, as I sailed.

And being cruel still, as I sailed, as I sailed,
And being cruel still, as I sailed,
And being cruel still, my gunner I did kill,
And his precious blood did spill, as I sailed.

My mate was sick and died, as I sailed, as I sailed,
My mate was sick and died as I sailed,
My mate was sick and died, which me much terrified,
When he called me to his bedside, as I sailed,

And unto me did say, 'See me die, see me die,'
And unto me did say, 'See me die,'
And unto me did say, 'Take warning now by me,
There comes a reckoning day, you must die.

'You cannot then withstand, when you die, when you die,
You cannot then withstand when you die,
You cannot then withstand the judgment of God's hand,
But bound then in iron bands you must die.'

I was sick and nigh to death, as I sailed, as I sailed,
I was sick and nigh to death, as I sailed,
I was sick and nigh to death, and I vowed at every breath,
To walk in wisdom's ways as I sailed.

I thought I was undone, as I sailed, as I sailed,
I thought I was undone as I sailed,
I thought I was undone and my wicked glass had run,
But health did soon return, as I sailed.

My repentance lasted not, as I sailed, as I sailed,
My repentance lasted not, as I sailed,
My repentance lasted not, my vows I soon forgot,
Damnation's my just lot, as I sailed.

I steered from sound to sound, as I sailed, as I sailed,
I steered from sound to sound, as I sailed,
I steered from sound to sound, and many ships I found,
And most of them I burned, as I sailed.

I spied three ships from France as I sailed, as I sailed,
I spied three ships from France, as I sailed,
I spied three ships from France, to them I did advance,
I took them all by chance, as I sailed.

I spied three ships of Spain as I sailed, as I sailed,
I spied three ships of Spain, as I sailed,
I spied three ships of Spain, I fixed on them amain,
Till most of them were slain, as I sailed.

I'd ninety bars of gold as I sailed, as I sailed,
I'd ninety bars of gold as I sailed,
I'd ninety bars of gold and dollars manifold,
With riches uncontrolled, as I sailed.

Then fourteen ships I saw, as I sailed, as I sailed,
Then fourteen ships I saw, as I sailed,
Then fourteen ships I saw, and brave men they were,
Ah! they were too much for me, as I sailed.

Thus being o'ertaken at last, I must die, I must die,
Thus being o'ertaken at last, I must die,
Thus being o'ertaken at last, and into prison cast,
And sentence being passed, I must die.

Farewell, the raging sea, I must die, I must die,
Farewell, the raging sea, I must die,
Farewell, the raging main, to Turkey, France, and Spain,
I ne're shall see you again, I must die.

To Newgate now I'm cast, and must die, and must die,
To Newgate now I'm cast, and must die,
To Newgate now I'm cast, with a sad and heavy heart,
To receive my just desert, I must die.

To Execution Dock I must go, must go,
To Execution Dock I must go,
To Execution Dock will many thousands flock,
But I must bear the shock, I must die.

Come all you young and old, see me die, see me die,
Come all you young and old, see me die,
Come all you young and old, you're welcome to my gold,
For by it I've lost my soul, and must die.

Take warning now by me, for I must die, for I must die,
Take warning now by me, for I must die,
Take warning now by me, and shun bad company,
Lest you come to hell with me, for I must die,
Lest you come to hell with me, for I must die.

81

THE GREENLAND WHALE

'Twas in the year of forty-nine,
  On March, the twentieth day,
Our gallant ship her anchor weigh'd,
  And to the sea she bore away,
    Brave boys,
And to the sea she bore away.
    With a fa la la la la la la
    Fa la la la la la la
    Fa la la fa la la
    Fa la la la la.

Old Blowhard was our captain's name,
  Our ship the *Lion* bold,
And we were bound to the North Country
  To face the frost and the cold.

And when we came to that cold country
  Where the ice and the snow do lie,
Where there's ice and snow, and the great whales blow,
  And the daylight does not die,

Our mate went up to the topmast head
  With a spyglass in his hand.
A whale, a whale, a whale, he cries,
  And she spouts at every span,

Up jumped old Blowhard on the deck,
  And a clever little man was he –
Overhaul, overhaul, let your main-tackle fall,
  And launch your boat to sea.

We struck that fish and away she flew
    With a flourish of her tail,
But oh! and alas! we lost one man
    And we did not catch that whale.

Now when the news to our captain came
    He called up all his crew,
And for the losing of that man
    He down his colours drew,

Says he, My men, be not dismayed
    At the losing of one man,
For Providence will have his will,
    Let man do what he can.

Now the losing of that prentice boy
    It grieved our captain sore,
But the losing of that great big whale
    It grieved him a damned sight more,
        Brave boys,
    It grieved him a damned sight more.
        With a fa la la la la la la
        Fa la la la la la la
        Fa la la fa la la
        Fa la la la la.

82

THE BLYTHSOME BRIDAL

Fy let us a to the bridal,
  For there will be lilting there,
For Jock's to be married to Maggie,
  The lass wi the gowden hair.
And there will be langkail and porridge,
  And bannocks of barley-meal,
And there will be good sawt herring,
  To relish a cogue of good ale.
    Fy let us, etc.

And there will be Sawney the soutar,
  And Will wi the meikle mou:
And there will be Tam the blutter,
  With Andrew the tinkler I trow;
And there will be bow'd-legged Robie,
  With thumbless Katie's goodman;
And there will be blue-cheeked Dowbie,
  And Lawrie the laird of the land.
    Fy let us, etc.

And there will be sowlibber Patie,
  And plucky-fac'd Wat i th' mill,
Capper-nos'd Francie, and Gibbie
  That wons in the how o the hill;
And there will be Alaster Sibbie,
  Wha in wi black Bessie did mool,
With snivling Lilly, and Tibby,
  The lass that stands oft on the stool.
    Fy let us, etc.

langkail cabbage cooked with the leaves whole	*plucky* pimply
cogue wooden cup	*capper* copper
soutar cobbler	*wons* dwells
blutter gabbler	*how* hollow
sowlibber sow gelder	*mool* make love
	stool stool of repentance in the kirk

And Madge that was buckled to Stennie,
    And coft him grey breeks to his arse,
Wha after was hangit for stealing,
    Great mercy it happen'd nae warse;
And there will be gleed Georgy Janners,
    And Kirsh wi the lily-white leg,
Who gade to the south for manners,
    And bang'd up her wame in Mons Meg.
        Fy let us, etc.

And there will be Juden Maclourie,
    And blinkin daft Barbara Macleg,
Wi flea-lugged sharney-fac'd Lawrie,
    And shangy-mou'd halucket Meg,
And there will be happer-arsed Nansy,
    And fairy-fac'd Flowrie by name,
Muck Madie, and fat-hippet Grisy,
    The lass with the gowden wame.
        Fy let us, etc.

And there will be girn-again Gibby,
    Wi his glaiket wife Jenny Bell,
And measly-shin'd Mungo Macapie,
    The lad that was skipper himsel:
There lads, and lasses in pearlings,
    Will feast i the heart of the ha,
On sybows, and risarts, and carlings,
    That are baith sodden and raw.
        Fy let us, etc.

buckled married
coft bought
gleed squinting
wame belly
Mons Meg cannon at Edinburgh
    Castle
lugged eared
sharney-fac'd cowpat-faced
shangy-mou'd with a mouth like
    a cleft stick

halucket giddy
happer hopper
girn grin
glaiket flighty
measly-shin'd spotty-legged
pearlings laced-edged gowns
sybows chives
risarts radishes
carlings parched pease
sodden boiled

273

And there will be fadges and brochen,
  With fouth of good gabbocks of skate,
Powsoudie, and drammock, and crowdie,
  And caller nowtfeet in a plate.
And there will be partens and buckies,
  And whytens and spaldings enew,
And singit sheepheads, and a haggies,
  And scadlips to sup till ye spue.
    Fy let us, etc.

And there will be lapper'd-milk kebbucks,
  And sowens, and farles, and baps,
With swats, and well-scraped paunches,
  And brandy in stoups and in caps:
And there will be mealkail and castocks,
  And skink to sup till ye rive:
And roasts to roast on a brander
  Of flowks that were taken alive.
    Fy let us, etc.

Scrapt haddocks, wilks, dulse and tangles,
  And a mill of good snishing to prie;

fadges rolls
brochen oatmeal with butter, honey and water
fouth plenty
gabbocks mouthfuls
powsoudie sheep's head soup
drammock, crowdie oatmeal and water
caller fresh
nowtfeet cow's feet
partens crabs
buckies whelks
whytens whitings
spaldings dried fish
scadlips hot barley broth (scald lips)
lapper'd curdled

kebbucks cheeses
sowens fermented sour oatmeal
farles oatcakes
baps yeast rolls
swats small ale
caps drinking bowls
mealkail cabbage and oatmeal soup
castocks cabbage stalks
skink beef and vegetable soup
rive burst
brander gridiron
flowks flatfish
dulse edible seaweed
tangles another edible seaweed
snishing snuff
prie try

When weary with eating, and drinking,
We'll rise up and dance till we die.
They fy let us a to the bridal,
For there will be lilting there,
For Jock's to be married to Maggie,
The lass wi the gowden hair.

FRANCIS SEMPILL (?)

83

THE FOGGY DEW

When I was a batchelor early and young,
  I followed the weaving trade,
And all the harm ever I done,
  Was courting a servant maid.
I courted her the summer season,
  And part of the winter too,
And many a night I rolled her in my arms,
  All over the Foggy dew.

One night as I lay on my bed,
  As I laid fast asleep,
There came a pretty fair maid,
  And most bitterly did weep.
She wept she mourned she tore her hair,
  Crying, alas what shall I do,
This night I'm resolved to come to bed with you
  For fear of the Foggy dew.

It was in the first part of the night,
  We both did sport and play,
And in the latter part of the night,
  She slept in my arms till day.
When broad day-light did appear,
  She cried I am undone,
Hold your tongue you foolish girl,
  The Foggy dew is gone.

Suppose that we should have a child,
  It would cause us to smile,
Suppose that we should have another
  It would make us laugh awhile.
Suppose that we should have another,
  And another one too,
Would make you leave off your foolish tricks
  And think no more of the Foggy dew.

I love this young girl dearly,
    I loved her as my life,
Took this girl and married her,
    And made her my lawful wife.
Never told her of her faults,
    Nor never intend to do,
But every time she winks or smiles,
    She thinks of the Foggy dew.

THE MILLER'S DAUGHTER

The young man and the miller's lass they set out on the hill,
Hey, with a gay and a grinding O.
They took a sack of corn and they went to grind the mill.
And the mill turns about with a grinding O.

The young man barred the door and the maiden she did sigh,
Hey, with a gay and a grinding O.
And then it came into her head that with him she would lie,
And the mill turns about with a grinding O.

She has cast off her petticoat and so she has her gown,
Hey, with a gay and a grinding O.
And all upon the running corn she straightway did lay down.
And the mill turns about with a grinding O.

So up then starts the young man and run from mill to town,
Hey, with a gay and a grinding O.
And there he spied the miller all a-walking up and down.
And the mill turns about with a grinding O.

O I have served you seven long year and never sought a fee,
Hey, with a gay and a grinding O.
And I will serve you seven more if you'll keep your lass from
me.
And the mill turns about with a grinding O.

THE WEDNESBURY COCKING

At Wednesbury there was a cocking,
  A match between Newton and Scroggins;
The colliers and nailers left work,
  And all to old Spittle's went jogging.
To see this noble sport,
  Many noblemen resorted;
And though they'd but little money,
  Yet that little they freely sported.

There was Jeffery and Colborn from Hampton,
  And Dusty from Bilston was there;
Plummery he came from Darlaston,
  And he was as rude as a bear.
There was old Will from Walsall,
  And Smacker from Westbromwich come;
Blind Robin he came from Rowley,
  And staggering he went home.

Ralph Moody came hobbling along,
  As though he some cripple were mocking,
To join in the blackguard throng,
  That met at Wednesbury cocking.
He borrowed a trifle of Doll,
  To back old Taverner's grey;
He laid fourpence-halfpenny to fourpence,
  He lost and went broken away.

But soon he returned to the pit,
  For he'd borrowed a trifle more money,
And ventured another large bet,
  Along with blubbermouth Coney.

When Coney demanded his money,
  As is common on all such occasions,
He cried: 'Rot thee, if thee don't hold thy rattle,
  I'll pay thee as Paul paid the Ephesians.'

Scroggins' breeches were made of nankeen,
  And worn very thin in the groin,
When he stooped to handle his cock,
  His buttocks burst out behind!
Besides, his shirt tail was beshet,
  Which caused among them much laughter,
Scroggins turned around in a pet,
  And cried: 'Damn ye all, what's the matter?'

The morning's sport being over,
  Old Spittle a dinner proclaimed,
Each man he should dine for a groat,
  If he grumbled he ought to be maimed.
For there was plenty of beef,
  But Spittle he swore by his troth
That never a man should dine
  Till he'd ate his noggin of broth.

The beef it was old and tough,
  Of a bull that was baited to death,
Barney Hyde got a lump in his throat,
  That had like to have stopped his breath;
The company all fell in confusion,
  At seeing poor Barney Hyde choke,
So they took him into the kitchen,
  And held him over the smoke.

They held him so close to the fire,
  He frizzled just like a beefsteak,
They then threw him down on the floor,
  Which had like to have broken his neck.
One gave him a kick in the stomach,
  Another a clout on the brow,

His wife said: 'Throw him into the stable,
  And he'll be better just now.'

Then they all returned to the pit,
  And the fighting went forward again;
Six battles were fought on each side,
  And the next was to decide the main.
For these were two famous cocks
  As ever this country bred,
Scroggins' a duck-winged black,
  And Newton's a shift-winged red.

The conflict was hard on both sides,
  Till Brassy's shift-winged was choked;
The colliers were tarnationly vexed,
  And the nailers were sorely provoked.
Peter Stevens he swore a great oath
  That Scroggins had played his cock foul;
Scroggins gave him a kick on the head,
  And cried: 'Yea, God damn thy soul!'

The company then fell in discord,
  A bold, bold fight did ensue;
Kick, bludgeon and bite was the word,
  Till the Walsall men all were subdued.
Ralph Moody bit off a man's nose,
  And wished that he could have him slain,
So they trampled both cocks to death,
  And they made a draw of the main.

The cock-pit was near to the church,
  An ornament unto the town;
On one side an old coal pit,
  The other well gorsed around.
Peter Hadley peeped through the gorse,
  In order to see the cocks fight;
Spittle jobbed out his eye with a fork,
  And said: 'Rot thee, it served thee right!'

Some people may think this strange,
　Who Wednesbury Town never knew;
But those who have ever been there,
　Won't have the least doubt it is true;
For they are so savage by nature,
　And guilty of deeds the most shocking;
Jack Baker he whacked his own father,
　And thus ended Wednesbury Cocking.

86

THE BOLD TROOPER

In fair London city a woman did dwell,
For style and for beauty no one could excel,
For style and for beauty no one could excel,
And her husband he was a bold trooper.
Ti-in-the-ti-i, talorum-la-li,
And her husband he was a bold trooper.

There was an old tailor who lived there close by,
And on this 'ere woman he casted his eye,
Ten guineas I'll give you this night for to lie,
If your husband is out upon duty.

The bargain was made and they both went to bed,
They hadn't been there long till they fell fast asleep,
Then, hide me! oh! hide me! the tailor he said,
For I hear the bold knock of the trooper.

There's a three-cornered cupboard behind the room door,
And there I will hide you so safe and secure,
And there I will hide you so safe and secure,
If you've heard the bold knock of the trooper.

She goes down the stairs for to welcome him in,
For your kisses and compliments I don't care a pin,
For your kisses and compliments I don't care a pin,
Come, light me a fire, said the trooper.

Dear husband, dear husband, there's no firestuff,
We'll both go to bed and we'll feel warm enough,
We'll both go to bed and we'll feel warm enough,
No! come light me a fire, said the trooper.

There's a three-cornered cupboard behind the room door,
And that I will burn so certain and sure,
And that I will burn so certain and sure,
So, come light me a fire, said the trooper.

Dear husband, dear husband, that's not my desire,
For to burn a good cupboard to light you a fire,
For in it I keep a game-cock I admire,
Then I'll scare your game-cock, said the trooper,

He goes up the stairs and he opens the door,
And there sat the tailor so safe and so sure,
He give the cupboard a knock to the middle of the floor,
Is this your game-cock? said the trooper.

He put his hand in his pocket and pulled out his shears,
And off on the table he cut his two ears,
Saying, for my night's lodging I've paid very dear,
And away ran the poor croppy tailor.

SIR MARMADUKE

i

Sir Marmaduke was a hearty knight;
    Good man! Old man!
He's painted standing bolt upright,
  With his hose rolled over his knee;
His periwig's as white as chalk,
And on his fist he holds a hawk;
    And he looks like the head
  Of an ancient family.

ii

His dining-room was long and wide;
    Good man! Old man!
His spaniels lay by the fireside;
  And in other parts, d'ye see,
Cross-bows, tobacco-pipes, old hats,
A saddle, his wife, and a litter of cats;
    And he looked like the head
  Of an ancient family.

iii

He never turned the poor from his gate;
    Good man! Old man!
But was always ready to break the pate
  Of his country's enemy.
What knight could do a better thing
Than serve the poor and fight for his king?
    And so may every head
  Of an ancient family.

GEORGE COLMAN THE YOUNGER

UNFORTUNATE MISS BAILEY

i

A captain bold in Halifax, that dwelt in country quarters,
Seduced a maid who hanged herself one morning in her
    garters:
His wicked conscience smited him: he lost his stomach daily;
He took to drinking ratafia, and thought upon Miss Bailey.
        Oh, Miss Bailey! unfortunate Miss Bailey!

ii

One night betimes he went to rest, for he had caught a fever.
Says he, 'I am a handsome man, but I'm a gay deceiver.'
His candle just at twelve o'clock began to burn quite palely;
A ghost stepped up to his bedside, and said, 'Behold Miss
    Bailey!'
        Oh, Miss Bailey! unfortunate Miss Bailey!

iii

'Avaunt, Miss Bailey!' then he cried. 'Your face looks white
    and mealy!'
'Dear Captain Smith,' the ghost replied, 'you've used me
    ungenteelly.
The crowner's quest goes hard with me because I've acted
    frailly,
And Parson Biggs won't bury me, though I am dead Miss
    Bailey.'
        Oh, Miss Bailey! unfortunate Miss Bailey!

iv

'Dear corpse,' says he, 'since you and I accounts must once
    for all close,
I've got a one-pound note in my regimental small-clothes;

'Twill bribe the sexton for your grave.' The ghost then
  vanished gaily,
Crying, 'Bless you, wicked Captain Smith! remember poor
  Miss Bailey.'
        Oh, Miss Bailey! unfortunate Miss Bailey!

GEORGE COLMAN THE YOUNGER

THE FRIAR OF RUBYGILL

It was a friar of orders free,
A friar of Rubygill:
At the greenwood-tree a vow made he,
But he kept it very ill:
A vow made he of chastity,
But he kept it very ill.

He kept it, perchance, in the conscious shade
Of the bounds of the forest wherein it was made:
But he roamed where he listed, as free as the wind,
And he left his good vow in the forest behind:
For its woods out of sight were his vow out of mind,
With the friar of Rubygill.

In lonely hut himself he shut,
The friar of Rubygill;
Where the ghostly elf absolved himself,
To follow his own good will:
And he had no lack of canary sack,
To keep his conscience still,

And a damsel well knew, when at lonely midnight
It gleamed on the waters, his signal-lamp light:
'Over, over!' she warbled with nightingale throat,
And the friar sprang forth at the magical note,
And she crossed the dark stream in his trim ferry-boat,
With the friar of Rubygill.

THOMAS LOVE PEACOCK

A MERRY JEST OF ROBIN HOOD

Bold Robin has robed him in ghostly attire,
And forth he is gone like a holy friar,
   Singing, hey down, ho down, down, derry down:
And of two grey friars he soon was aware,
Regaling themselves with dainty fair,
   All on the fallen leaves so brown.

'Good morrow, good brothers,' said bold Robin Hood.
'And what make you in good greenwood,
   Singing, hey down, ho down, down, derry down!
Now give me, I pray you, wine and food;
For none can I find in the good greenwood,
   All on the fallen leaves so brown.'

'Good brother,' they said, 'we would give you full fain,
But we have no more than enough for twain,
   Singing, hey down, ho down, down, derry down.'
'Then give me some money,' said bold Robin Hood,
'For none can I find in the good greenwood,
   All on the fallen leaves so brown.'

'No money have we, good brother,' said they:
'Then,' said he, 'we three for money will pray:
   Singing, hey down, ho down, down, derry down:
And whatever shall come at the end of our prayer,
We three holy friars will piously share,
   All on the fallen leaves so brown.'

'We will not pray with thee, good brother. God wot:
For truly, good brother, thou pleases us not,
   Singing, hey down, ho down, down, derry down':
Then up they both started from Robin to run,
But down on their knees Robin pulled them each one,
   All on the fallen leaves so brown.

The grey friars prayed with a doleful face,
But bold Robin prayed with a right merry grace,
　　Singing, hey down, ho down, down, derry down:
And when they had prayed, their portmanteau he took,
And from it a hundred good angels he shook,
　　All on the fallen leaves so brown.

'The saints,' said bold Robin, 'have hearkened our prayer,
And here's a good angel apiece for your share;
If more you would have, you must win ere you wear;
　　Singing, hey down, ho down, down, derry down':
Then he blew his good horn with a musical cheer,
And fifty green bowmen came trooping full near,
And away the grey friars they bounded like deer,
　　All on the fallen leaves so brown.

THOMAS LOVE PEACOCK

91

THE COW ATE THE PIPER

In the year ninety-eight, when our troubles were great,
It was treason to be a Milesian.
I can never forget the big black whiskered set
That history tells us were Hessians.
In them heart breaking times we had all sorts of crimes,
As murder never was rifer.
On the hill of Glencree not an acre from me,
Lived bould Denny Byrne, the piper.

Neither wedding nor wake was worth an old shake,
If Denny was not first invited,
For at emptying kegs or squeezing the bags
He astonished as well as delighted.
In such times poor Denny could not earn a penny,
Martial law had a sting like a viper –
It kept Denny within till his bones and his skin
Were a-grin through the rags of the piper.

'Twas one heavenly night, with the moon shining bright,
Coming home from the fair of Rathangan,
He happened to see, from the branch of a tree,
The corpse of a Hessian there hanging;
Says Denny, 'These rogues have fine boots, I've no brogues,'
He laid on the heels such a griper,
They were so gallus tight, and he pulled with such might,
Legs and boots came away with the piper.

So he tucked up the legs and he took to his pegs,
Till he came to Tim Kavanagh's cabin,
'By the powers,' says Tim, 'I can't let you in,
You'll be shot if you stop out there rappin'.'

Milesian Irishman (descendant of   *Hessians* mercenaries from Hesse
the legendary King of Milesius)   *gallus* very

He went round to the shed, where the cow was in bed,
With a wisp he began for to wipe her –
They lay down together on the seven foot feather,
And the cow fell a-hugging the piper.

The daylight soon dawned, Denny got up and yawned,
Then he dragged on the boots of the Hessian:
The legs, by the law! he threw them on the straw,
And he gave them leg-bail on his mission.
When Tim's breakfast was done he sent out his son
To make Denny lep like a lamp-lighter –
When two legs there he saw, he roared like a daw
　'Oh! daddy, de cow eat de piper.'

'Sweet bad luck to the baste, she'd a musical taste,'
Says Tim, 'to go eat such a chanter,
Here Pádraic, avic, take this lump of a stick,
Drive her up to Glenealy, I'll cant her.'
Mrs Kavanagh bawled – the neighbours were called,
They began for to humbug and jibe her,
To the churchyard she walks with the legs in a box,
Crying out, 'We'll be hanged for the piper.'

The cow then was drove just a mile or two off,
To a fair by the side of Glenealy,
And the crathur was sold for four guineas in gold
To the clerk of the parish, Tim Daly.
They went into a tent, and the luck-penny spent,
(For the clerk was a woeful old swiper),
Who the divil was there, playing the Rakes of Kildare,
But their friend, Denny Byrne, the piper.

Then Tim gave a bolt like a half-broken colt,
At the piper he gazed like a gommach;
Says he, 'By the powers, I thought these eight hours,

daw fool, loony   *luck-penny* part of a price
cant auction   returned for luck
                           gommach idiot

You were playing in Dhrimindhu's stomach.'
But Denny observed how the Hessian was served,
So they all wished Nick's cure to the viper,
And for grá that they met, their whistles they wet,
And like devils they danced round the piper.

grá love

YOUNG MOLLY BÁN

Come all you young fellows that follow the gun,
Beware of goin' a-shootin' by the late setting sun.
It might happen to anyone as it happened to me,
To shoot your own true love in-under a tree.

She was going to her uncle's, when the shower it came on,
She went under a bush, the rain for to shun.
With her apron all around her, I took her for a swan
And I levelled my gun and I shot Molly Bán.

I ran to her uncle's in haste and great fear,
Saying Uncle, dear Uncle, I've shot Molly dear.
With her apron all around her I took her for a swan,
But oh and alas! it was my Molly Bán.

I shot my own true love – alas I'm undone,
While she was in the shade by the setting of the sun;
If I thought she was there I'd caress her tenderly,
And soon I'd get married to my own dear Molly.

My curses on you, Toby, that lent me your gun
To go out a-shooting by the late setting sun,
I rubbed her fair temples and found she was dead;
A fountain of tears for my Molly I shed.

Up comes my father and his locks they were grey,
Stay in your own country and don't run away,
Stay in your own country till your trial comes on,
And I'll see you set free by the laws of the land.

Oh the maids of this country they will all be very glad
When they hear the sad news that my Molly is dead.
Take them all in their hundreds, set them all in a row,
Molly Bán she shone above them like a mountain of snow.

Molly Bán fair Molly

ARTHUR McBRIDE

I once knew a fellow named Arthur McBride,
And he and I rambled down by the sea-side,
A-looking for pleasure or what might betide,
And the weather was pleasant and charming.

So gaily and gallant we went on our tramp,
And we met Sergeant Harper and Corporal Cramp,
And the little wee fellow who roused up the camp
With his row-de-dow-dow in the morning.

Good morning, young fellows, the sergeant he cried.
And the same to you, sergeant, was all our reply.
There was nothing more spoken, we made to pass by,
And continue our walk in the morning.

Well now, my fine fellows, if you will enlist,
A guinea in gold I will slap in your fist,
And a crown in the bargain to kick up the dust
And drink the Queen's health in the morning.

Oh no, mister sergeant, we aren't for sale,
We'll make no such bargain, and your bribe won't avail.
We're not tired of our country, and don't care to sail,
Though your offer is pleasant and charming.

If we were such fools as to take your advance,
It's right bloody slender would be our poor chance,
For the Queen wouldn't scruple to send us to France
And get us all shot in the morning.

Ha now, you young blackguards, if you say one more word,
I swear by the herrins, I'll draw out my sword
And run through your bodies as my strength may afford.
So now, you young buggers, take warning.

Well, we beat that bold drummer as flat as a shoe,
And we make a football of his row-de-dow-do,
And as for the others we knocked out the two.
Oh, we were the boys in that morning.

We took the old weapons that hung by their side
And flung them as far as we could in the tide.
May the devil go with you, says Arthur McBride,
For delaying our walk this fine morning.

94

JOHNNY, I HARDLY KNEW YE

While going the road to sweet Athy,
    Hurroo! Hurroo!
While going the road to sweet Athy,
    Hurroo! Hurroo!
While going the road to sweet Athy,
A stick in my hand and a drop in my eye,
A doleful damsel I heard cry:
  Och, Johnny, I hardly knew ye!
    With drums and guns and guns and drums,
      The enemy nearly slew ye!
      My darling dear, you look so queer,
    Och, Johnny, I hardly knew ye!

'Where are your eyes that looked so mild?
    Hurroo! Hurroo!
Where are your eyes that looked so mild?
    Hurroo! Hurroo!
Where are your eyes that looked so mild
When my poor heart you first beguiled?
Why did you run from me and the child?
  Och, Johnny, I hardly knew ye!

'Where are the legs with which you run?
    Hurroo! Hurroo!
Where are the legs with which you run?
    Hurroo! Hurroo!
Where are the legs with which you run,
When you went to carry a gun? –
Indeed your dancing days are done!
  Och, Johnny, I hardly knew ye!

'It grieved my heart to see you sail,
    Hurroo! Hurroo!
It grieved my heart to see you sail,
    Hurroo! Hurroo!

It grieved my heart to see you sail,
Though from my heart you took leg bail, –
Like a cod you're doubled up head and tail,
   Och, Johnny, I hardly knew ye!

'You haven't an arm and you haven't a leg,
      Hurroo! Hurroo!
You haven't an arm and you haven't a leg,
      Hurroo! Hurroo!
You haven't an arm and you haven't a leg,
You're an eyeless, noseless, chickenless egg:
You'll have to be put in a bowl to beg,
   Och, Johnny, I hardly knew ye!

'I'm happy for to see you home,
      Hurroo! Hurroo!
I'm happy for to see you home,
      Hurroo! Hurroo!
I'm happy for to see you home,
All from the island of Sulloon,
So low in flesh, so high in bone,
   Och, Johnny, I hardly knew ye!

'But sad as it is to see you so,
      Hurroo! Hurroo!
But sad as it is to see you so,
      Hurroo! Hurroo!
But sad as it is to see you so,
And to think of you now as an object of woe,
Your Peggy'll still keep ye on as her beau.
   Och, Johnny, I hardly knew ye!'
      With drums and guns and guns and drums,
         The enemy nearly slew ye,
         My darling dear, you look so queer,
      Och, Johnny, I hardly knew ye!

95

THE NIGHT BEFORE LARRY
WAS STRETCHED

The night before Larry was stretched,
  The boys they all paid him a visit;
A bait in their sacks, too, they fetched;
  They sweated their duds till they riz it,
For Larry was ever the lad
  When a boy was condemned to the squeezer,
Would fence all the duds that he had
  To help a poor friend to a sneezer,
     And warm his gob 'fore he died.

The boys they came crowding in fast,
  They drew all their stools round about him,
Six glims round his trap-case were placed,
  He couldn't be well waked without 'em.
When one of us asked could he die
  Without having duly repented?
Says Larry, 'That's all in my eye;
  And first by the clergy invented,
     To get a fat bit for themselves.'

'I'm sorry, dear Larry,' says I,
  'To see you in this situation,
And blister my limbs if I lie,
  I'd as lieve it had been my own station.'
'Ochone! it's all over,' says he,
  'For the neckcloth I'll be forced to put on,

bait refreshment
sweated their duds pawned their
  clothes
sneezer strong drink

gob mouth
glims candles
trap-case coffin
waked given a wake

And by this time to-morrow you'll see
    Your poor Larry as dead as a mutton,
        Because, why, his courage was good.

'And I'll be cut up like a pie,
    And my nob from my body be parted.'
'You're in the wrong box, then,' says I,
    'For blast me if they're so hard-hearted:
A chalk on the back of your neck
    Is all that Jack Ketch dares to give you;
Then mind not such trifles a feck,
    For why should the likes of them grieve you?
        And now, boys, come tip us the deck.'

The cards being called for, they played
    Till Larry found one of them cheated;
A dart at his napper he made
    (The boy being easily heated):
'O, by the hokey, you thief,
    I'll scuttle your nob with my daddle!
You cheat me because I'm in grief,
    But soon I'll demolish your noddle,
        And leave you your claret to drink.'

Then the clergy came in with his book,
    He spoke him so smooth and so civil;
Larry tipped him a Kilmainham look,
    And pitched his big wig to the devil.
Then sighing he threw back his head
    To get a sweet drop of the bottle,
And pitiful sighing he said,
    'O the hemp will be soon round my throttle,
        And choke my poor windpipe to death.

chalk scratch
Jack Ketch i.e. the hangman
tip us the deck give us the pack
    (of cards)
napper head

scuttle your nob break your head
daddle fist
claret blood
Kilmainham look (he is in
    Kilmainhan Gaol in Dublin)

300

'Though sure it's the best way to die,
  O the devil a better a-livin'!
For when the gallows is high
  Your journey is shorter to heaven.
But what harasses Larry the most,
  And makes his poor soul melancholy,
Is that he thinks of the time when his ghost
  Will come in a sheet to sweet Molly.
    O sure it will kill her alive!'

So moving these last words he spoke,
  We all vented our tears in a shower.
For my part, I thought my heart broke,
  To see him cut down like a flower.
On his travels we watched him next day;
  O the throttler, I thought I could kill him.
But Larry not one word did say,
  Nor changed till he came to 'King William',
    Then, musha his colour grew white.

When he came to the nubbing chit,
  He was tucked up so neat and so pretty,
The rumbler jogged off from his feet,
  And he died with his face to the city.
He kicked, too – but that was all pride,
  For soon you might see 'twas all over.
Soon after the noose was untied,
  And at darkee we waked him in clover,
    And sent him to take a ground sweat.

nubbing chit 'hanging thing', i.e.   *in clover* in comfort
  gallows   *to take a ground sweat* to take a
rumbler cart   grave, to be buried
darkee night

96

JIM JONES AT BOTANY BAY

O listen for a moment, lads,
  And hear me tell my tale,
How o'er the sea from England's shore
  I was compelled to sail.

The jury says, He's guilty, sir,
  And says the judge, says he,
For life, Jim Jones, I'm sending you
  Across the stormy sea.

And take my tip before you ship
  To join the Iron Gang,
Don't be too gay at Botany Bay,
  Or else you'll surely hang.

Or else you'll hang, he says, says he,
  And after that, Jim Jones,
High up upon the gallows tree
  The crows will peck your bones.

You'll have no chance for mischief then,
  Remember what I say,
They'll flog the poaching out of you
  Out there at Botany Bay.

The winds blew high upon the sea,
  And pirates came along,
But the soldiers on our convict ship
  Were full five hundred strong.

They opened fire and somehow drove
  That pirate ship away.
I'd rather have joined that pirate ship
  Than come to Botany Bay.

For night and day the irons clang,
  And like poor galley slaves
We toil and toil, and when we die
  Must fill dishonoured graves.

But bye and bye I'll break my chains,
  Into the bush I'll go
And join the brave bushrangers there –
  Jack Donohoo and Co.

And some black night when everything
  Is silent in the town
I'll kill the tyrants, one and all,
  And shoot the floggers down.

I'll give the law a little shock,
  Remember what I say,
They'll yet regret they sent Jim Jones
  In chains to Botany Bay.

97

THE WILD COLONIAL BOY

'Tis of a wild Colonial boy, Jack Doolan was his name,
Of poor but honest parents he was born in Castlemaine.
He was his father's only hope, his mother's only joy,
And dearly did his parents love the wild Colonial boy.
Chorus:
Come, all my hearties, we'll roam the mountains high,
Together we will plunder, together we will die.
We'll wander over valleys, and gallop over plains,
And we'll scorn to live in slavery, bound down with iron
chains.

He was scarcely sixteen years of age when he left his father's
home,
And through Australia's sunny clime a bushranger did roam.
He robbed those wealthy squatters, their stock he did destroy,
And a terror to Australia was the wild Colonial boy.

In sixty-one this daring youth commenced his wild career,
With a heart that knew no danger, no foeman did he fear.
He stuck up the Beechworth mail-coach, and robbed Judge
MacEvoy,
Who trembled, and gave up his gold to the wild Colonial boy.

He bade the judge 'Good morning', and told him to beware,
That he'd never rob a hearty chap that acted on the square,
And never to rob a mother of her son and only joy,
Or else you may turn outlaw, like the wild Colonial boy.

One day as he was riding the mountain-side along,
A-listening to the little birds, their pleasant laughing song,
Three mounted troopers rode along – Kelly, Davies, and
FitzRoy –
They thought that they would capture him, the wild Colonial
boy.

'Surrender now, Jack Doolan, you see there's three to one.
Surrender now, Jack Doolan, you daring highwayman.'
He drew a pistol from his belt, and shook the little toy.
'I'll fight, but not surrender,' said the wild Colonial boy.

He fired at Trooper Kelly and brought him to the ground,
And in return from Davis received a mortal wound.
All shattered through the jaws he lay still firing at FitzRoy,
And that's the way they captured him – the wild Colonial boy.

98

THE BANKS OF THE CONDAMINE

Oh, hark the dogs are barking, love,
I can no longer stay.
The men are all gone mustering
And it is nearly day,
And I must be off by the morning light
Before the sun doth shine
To meet the Sydney shearers
On the banks of the Condamine.

Oh, Willie, dearest Willie,
I'll go along with you,
I'll cut off all my auburn fringe
And be a shearer, too,
I'll cook and count your tally, love,
While ringer-o you shine,
And I'll wash your greasy moleskins
On the banks of the Condamine.

Oh, Nancy, dearest Nancy,
With me you cannot go,
The squatters have given orders, love,
No woman should do so;
Your delicate constitution
Is not equal unto mine
To stand the constant tigering
On the banks of the Condamine.

Oh, Willie, dearest Willie,
Then stay back home with me,
We'll take up a selection
And a farmer's wife I'll be.

ringer highest-scoring shearer in
  the shed
squatters owners of sheep stations

selection land selected under the
  Australian Land Law

I'll help you husk the corn, love,
And cook your meals so fine
You'll forget the ram-stag mutton
On the banks of the Condamine.

Oh, Nancy, dearest Nancy,
Please do not hold me back,
Down there the boys are waiting,
And I must be on the track;
So here's a good-bye kiss, love,
Back home here I'll incline
When we've shore the last of the jumbucks
On the banks of the Condamine.

ram-stag mutton mutton from old ewes past breeding ('ram-struck')

jumbucks sheep

99

BOLD JACK DONOHUE

Attend ye valiant highwaymen and outlaws of disdain,
Who've cause to live in slavery, or wear the ball and chain,
Attention pay to what I say, and value it if you do,
While I relate the matchless fate of Bold Jack Donohue.

Then come, my hearties, we'll roam the mountains high,
Together we will plunder, together we will die,
We'll roam the wild Blue Mountains and scour the Bathurst
*   plains,*
For we scorn to live in slavery, bound down in iron chains.

This bold undaunted highwayman, as you shall understand,
Was banished for his natural life from Erin's happy land,
In Dublin town of high renown, where his first breath he
    drew,
The deeds of honour title him the Bold Jack Donohue.

He'd not been longer than twelve months upon the Australian
    shore
When he turned to the highway, as many had done before,
MacNamara and Underwood, Walmsley and Webber, too,
They were the chief associates of Bold Jack Donohue.

Now Donohue was taken, in the middle of his prime,
And sentenced to be hung all for an out-daring crime;
But when they came to Sydney Jail they learnt his derring-do,
For when they came to call the roll, they missed Bold Donohue.

When he effected his escape he took to the highway,
Where tyrants did not dare to walk the road by night or day,
Every morning in the newspapers, there was published
    something new,
Concerning that brave hero called the Bold Jack Donohue.

As Donohue was cruising out one September afternoon,
Not thinking that the pains of death would overtake him
soon,
The horse police they did appear, all horrors to subdue,
And in quick time they did advance to take Bold Donohue.

Said Donohue to his comrades: 'If you prove true to me,
This day we'll fight with all our might and gain our liberty,
We've got courage stout and bold and Irish blood so true,
So this day we'll fight with all our might,' cried Bold Jack
Donohue.

'Oh, no!' cried cowardly Walmsley, 'to that we'll not agree,
Don't you see there's eight or nine of them, it's time for us to
flee,
And if we stay 'twill be too late, and the battle we'll surely
rue.'
'Then begone from me, ye cowardly dogs!' cried Bold Jack
Donohue.

'If you had but proved true to me, I would record your name,
But people they will look on you with scorn and bitter
shame;
For to hang upon the gallows tree I ne'er intend to do,
So this day I'll fight with all my might,' cried Bold Jack
Donohue.

'It never shall be said that Jack Donohue, the brave,
Should yield unto that alien crew, or live to be a slave,
I'd rather range the mountains like a wolf or kangaroo
Than work one hour for your government men,' cried Bold
Jack Donohue.

Said the sergeant to Jack Donohue, 'Discharge your carabine;
Do you intend to fight with us, or unto us resign?'
'Resign to you, ye cowardly dogs! I'll ne'er for mercy sue,
But this day I'll fight for liberty!' cried Bold Jack Donohue.

The sergeant and the corporal their men they did divide,
Some they placed behind him and more then by his side,
The sergeant and the corporal in front they fired too,
'Til at length a fatal ball spelt 'Death' for Donohue.

Nine rounds he fought with the horse police until a powder
ball
It struck the throat of Donohue, which caused him for to fall;
In closing of his sparkling eyes he bid the world adieu:
Saying: 'Good people all, pray for the soul of Bold Jack
Donohue.'

The like of Bold Jack Donohue was not in this country,
For maintaining of the people's laws he fought so manfully;
He was chased about by hundreds – by police and soldiers,
too –
The Nepean knew the courage brave of Bold Jack Donohue.

There were Freney, Grant, bold Robin Hood, Brennan and
O'Hare –
With Donohue the highwayman none of them could
compare –
And of his sad and mournful fate I've told it plain and true,
May the Lord have mercy on the soul of Bold Jack Donohue.

Then come, my hearties, we'll roam the mountains high,
Together we will plunder, together we will die,
We'll roam the wild Blue Mountains and scour the Bathurst
plains,
For we scorn to live in slavery, bound down in iron chains.

The Nepean   river in New South Wales

100

LOWLANDS AWAY

Lowlands, Lowlands, away, my John,
Lowlands away I heard them say,
My Lowlands away.

I dreamed a dream the other night,
Lowlands, Lowlands, away, my John,
My love she came dressed all in white,
My Lowlands away.

I dreamed my love came in my sleep,
Lowlands, Lowlands, away, my John,
Her cheeks were wet, her eyes did weep,
My Lowlands away.

She came to me as my best bride,
Lowlands, Lowlands, away, my John,
All dressed in white like some fair bride,
My Lowlands away.

And bravely in her bosom fair,
Lowlands, Lowlands, away, my John,
A red, red rose did my love wear,
My Lowlands away.

She made no sound, no word she said,
Lowlands, Lowlands, away, my John,
And then I knew my love was dead,
My Lowlands away.

I bound the weeper round my head,
Lowlands, Lowlands, away, my John,
For now I knew my love was dead,
My Lowlands away.

weeper black mourning band worn round the hat

She waved her hand, she said goodbye,
  Lowlands, Lowlands, away, my John,
I wiped the tear from out my eye,
  My Lowlands away.

And then awoke to hear the cry,
  Lowlands, Lowlands, away, my John,
Oh, watch on deck, oh, watch ahoy,
  My Lowlands away.

101

MARY ARNOLD THE FEMALE MONSTER

Of all the tales was ever told,
I now will you impart,
That cannot fail to terror strike,
To every human heart.
The deeds of Mary Arnold,
Who does in a jail deplore,
Oh! such a dreadful tale as this,
Was never told before.
This wretched woman's dreadful deed,
Does every one affright.
With black beetles in walnut shells
She deprived her child of sight.

Now think you, tender parents,
What must this monster feel,
The heart within her breast must ten
Times harder be than steel.
The dreadful crime she did commit
Does all the world surprise,
Black beetles placed in walnut shells
Bound round her infant's eyes.

The beetles in a walnut shell
This monster she did place,
This dreadful deed, as you may read,
All history does disgrace,
The walnut shell, and beetles,
With a bandage she bound tight,
Around her infant's tender eyes,
To take away its sight.

A lady saw this monster
In the street when passing by,

And she was struck with terror
For to hear the infant cry.
The infant's face she swore to see,
Which filled her with surprise,
To see the fatal bandage,
Tied round the infant's eyes.

With speed she called an officer,
Oh! shocking to relate,
Who beheld the deed, and took the wretch
Before the Magistrate.
Who committed her for trial,
Which did the wretch displease,
And she's now transported ten long years,
Across the briny seas.

Is there another in the world,
Could plan such wicked deed,
No one upon this earth before,
Of such did ever see.
To take away her infant's sight,
'Tis horrible to tell,
Binding black beetles round its eyes
Placed in walnut shells.

102

THE WORKHOUSE BOY

The cloth was laid in the Vorkhouse hall,
The great-coats hung on the white-wash'd wall,
The paupers all were blithe and gay,
Keeping their Christmas holiday,
When the Master he cried with a roguish leer,
'You'll all get fat on your Christmas cheer!'
When one by his looks did seem to say,
'I'll have some more soup on this Christmas-day.'
    Oh the Poor Vorkhouse Boy.

At length, all on us to bed vos sent,
The boy vos missing – in search ve vent.
Ve sought him above, ve sought him below,
Ve sought him with faces of grief and woe,
Ve sought him that hour, ve sought him that night,
Ve sought him in fear, and ve sought him in fright,
Ven a young pauper cried 'I knows ve shall
Get jolly vell vopt for losing our pal.'
    Oh the Poor Vorkhouse Boy.

Ve sought in each corner, each crevice ve knew
Ve sought down the yard, ve sought up the flue,
Ve sought in each kettle, each saucepan, each pot,
In the water-butt look'd, but found him not.
And veeks roll'd on; – ve vere all of us told
That somebody said, he'd been burk'd and sold.
Ven our master goes out, the Parishioners vild
Cry 'There goes the cove that burk'd the poor child.'
    Oh the Poor Vorkhouse Boy.

At length the soup copper repairs did need,
The Coppersmith came, and there he seed,
A dollop of bones lay a-grizzling there,
In the leg of the breeches the poor boy did vear!

To gain his fill the boy did stoop,
And dreadful to tell, he was boil'd in the soup!
And ve all of us say, and ve say it sincere,
That he was push'd in there by an overseer.
  Oh the Poor Vorkhouse Boy.

103

GENTLE ALICE BROWN

It was a robber's daughter, and her name was Alice Brown,
Her father was the terror of a small Italian town;
Her mother was a foolish, weak, but amiable old thing;
But it isn't of her parents that I'm going for to sing.

As Alice was a-sitting at her window-sill one day,
A beautiful young gentleman he chanced to pass that way;
She cast her eyes upon him, and he looked so good and true,
That she thought, 'I could be happy with a gentleman like
   you!'

And every morning passed her house that cream of gentlemen,
She knew she might expect him at a quarter unto ten;
A sorter in the Custom-house, it was his daily road
(The Custom-house was fifteen minutes' walk from her
   abode).

But Alice was a pious girl, who knew it wasn't wise
To look at strange young sorters with expressive purple eyes;
So she sought the village priest to whom her family confessed,
The priest by whom their little sins were carefully assessed.

'Oh, holy father,' Alice said, ''t would grieve you, would it
   not,
To discover that I was a most disreputable lot?
Of all unhappy sinners I'm the most unhappy one!'
The padre said, 'Whatever have you been and gone and
   done?'

'I have helped mamma to steal a little kiddy from its dad,
I've assisted dear papa in cutting up a little lad,
I've planned a little burglary and forged a little cheque,
And slain a little baby for the coral on its neck!'

The worthy pastor heaved a sigh, and dropped a silent tear,
And said, 'You mustn't judge yourself too heavily, my dear:
It's wrong to murder babies, little corals for to fleece;
But sins like these one expiates at half-a-crown apiece.

'Girls will be girls – you're very young, and flighty in your
  mind;
Old heads upon young shoulders we must not expect to find:
We mustn't be too hard upon these little girlish tricks –
Let's see – five crimes at half-a-crown – exactly twelve-and-
  six.'

'Oh, father,' little Alice cried, 'your kindness makes me weep,
You do these little things for me so singularly cheap –
Your thoughtful liberality I never can forget;
But, oh! there is another crime I haven't mentioned yet!

'A pleasant-looking gentleman, with pretty purple eyes
I've noticed at my window, as I've sat a-catching flies;
He passes by it every day as certain as can be –
I blush to say I've winked at him, and he has winked at me!'

'For shame!' said Father Paul, 'my erring daughter! On my
  word
This is the most distressing news that I have ever heard.
Why, naughty girl, your excellent papa has pledged your
  hand
To a promising young robber, the lieutenant of his band!

'This dreadful piece of news will pain your worthy parents
  so!
They are the most remunerative customers I know;
For many many years they've kept starvation from my doors:
I never knew so criminal a family as yours!

'The common country folk in this insipid neighbourhood
Have nothing to confess, they're so ridiculously good;
And if you marry any one respectable at all,
Why, you'll reform, and what will then become of Father
  Paul?'

The worthy priest, he up and drew his cowl upon his crown,
And started off in haste to tell the news to Robber Brown –
To tell him how his daughter, who was now for marriage fit,
Had winked upon a sorter, who reciprocated it.

Good Robber Brown he muffled up his anger pretty well:
He said, 'I have a notion, and that notion I will tell;
I will nab this gay young sorter, terrify him into fits,
And get my gentle wife to chop him into little bits.

'I've studied human nature, and I know a thing or two:
Though a girl may fondly love a living gent, as many do –
A feeling of disgust upon her senses there will fall
When she looks upon his body chopped particularly small.'

He traced that gallant sorter to a still suburban square;
He watched his opportunity, and seized him unaware;
He took a life-preserver and he hit him on the head,
And Mrs Brown dissected him before she went to bed.

And pretty little Alice grew more settled in her mind,
She never more was guilty of a weakness of the kind,
Until at length good Robber Brown bestowed her pretty hand
On the promising young robber, the lieutenant of his band.

W. S. GILBERT

104

THE LAMBTON WORM

One Sunday mornin' Lambton went
A-fishin' in the Wear;
An' catched a fish upon he's heuk,
He thowt leuk't varry queer,
But whatt'n a kind ov fish it was
Young Lambton cuddent tell
He waddn't fash te carry'd hyem,
So he hoyed it in a well.

> *Whisht! lads, haad yor gobs,*
> *An' Aa'll tell ye aall an aaful story,*
> *Whisht! lads, haad yor gobs,*
> *An' Aa'll tell ye 'boot the worm.*

Noo Lambton felt inclined te gan
An' fight i' foreign wars.
He joined a troop ov Knights that cared
For nowther woonds nor scars,
An' off he went te Palestine
Where queer things him befel,
An varry seun forgat aboot
The queer worm i' the well.

But the worm got fat an' growed an' growed.
An' growed an aaful size;
He'd greet big teeth, a greet big gob,
An' greet big goggle eyes.
An' when at neets he craaled aboot
Te pick up bits o' news,
If he felt dry upon the road,
He milked a dozen coos.

fash bother   *hoyed* threw
hyem home   *haad yor gobs* shut your mouths

This feorful worm would often feed
On caalves an' lambs an' sheep,
An' swally little bairns alive
When they laid doon te sleep.
An' when he'd eaten aall he cud
An' he had had he's fill,
He craaled away an' lapped he's tail
Ten times roond Pensher Hill.

The news of this myest aaful worm
An' his queer gannins on
Seun crossed the seas, gat te the ears
Ov brave an' bowld Sor John.
So hyem he cam an' catched the beast
An' cut 'im in twe haalves,
An' that seun stopped he's eatin' bairns
An' sheep an' lambs an' caalves.

So noo ye knaa hoo aall the foaks
On byeth sides ov the Wear
Lost lots o' sheep an' lots o' sleep
An' leeved i' mortal feor.
So let's hev one te brave Sor John
That kept the bairns frae harm,
Saved coos an' caalves by myekin' haalves
O' the famis Lambton Worm.

Noo, lads, Aa'll haad me gob,
That's aall Aa knaa aboot the story
Ov Sor John's clivvor job
Wi' the aaful Lambton Worm.

Pensher Hill Penshaw, hill above the Wear, Co. Durham, near
Lambton Castle

105

THE YARN OF THE *NANCY BELL*

'Twas on the shores that round our coast
　From Deal to Ramsgate span,
That I found alone on a piece of stone
　An elderly naval man.

His hair was weedy, his beard was long,
　And weedy and long was he,
And I heard this wight on the shore recite,
　In a singular minor key:

'Oh, I am a cook and a captain bold,
　And the mate of the *Nancy* brig,
And a bo'sun tight, and a midshipmite,
　And the crew of the captain's gig.'

And he shook his fists and he tore his hair,
　Till I really felt afraid,
For I couldn't help thinking the man had been drinking,
　And so I simply said:

'Oh, elderly man, it's little I know
　Of the duties of men of the sea,
And I'll eat my hand if I understand
　However you can be

'At once a cook, and a captain bold,
　And the mate of the *Nancy* brig,
And a bo'sun tight, and a midshipmite,
　And the crew of the captain's gig.'

Then he gave a hitch to his trousers, which
　Is a trick all seamen larn,
And having got rid of a thumping quid,
　He spun this painful yarn:

'"Twas in the good ship *Nancy Bell*
  That we sailed to the Indian Sea,
And there on a reef we come to grief,
  Which has often occurred to me.

'And pretty nigh all the crew was drowned
  (There was seventy-seven o' soul),
And only ten of the *Nancy*'s men
  Said "Here!" to the muster-roll.

'There was me and the cook and the captain bold,
  And the mate of the *Nancy* brig,
And the bo'sun tight, and a midshipmite,
  And the crew of the captain's gig.

'For a month we'd neither wittles nor drink,
  Till a-hungry we did feel,
So we drawed a lot, and, accordin' shot
  The captain for our meal.

'The next lot fell to the *Nancy*'s mate,
  And a delicate dish he made;
Then our appetite with the midshipmite
  We seven survivors stayed.

'And then we murdered the bo'sun tight,
  And he much resembled pig;
Then we wittled free, did the cook and me,
  On the crew of the captain's gig.

'Then only the cook and me was left,
  And the delicate question, "Which
Of us two goes to the kettle?" arose,
  And we argued it out as sich.

'For I loved that cook as a brother, I did,
  And the cook he worshipped me;
But we'd both be blowed if we'd either be stowed
  In the other chap's hold, you see.

' "I'll be eat if you dines off me," says Tom;
  "Yes, that," says I, "you'll be, –
"I'm boiled if I die, my friend," quoth I;
  And "Exactly so," quoth he.

'Says he, "Dear James, to murder me
  Were a foolish thing to do,
For don't you see that you can't cook *me*,
  While I can – and will – cook *you*!"

'So he boils the water, and takes the salt
  And the pepper in portions true
(Which he never forgot), and some chopped shalot,
  And some sage and parsley too.

' "Come here," says he, with a proper pride,
  Which his smiling features tell,
"'Twill soothing be if I let you see
  How extremely nice you'll smell."

'And he stirred it round and round and round,
  And he sniffed at the foaming froth;
When I ups with his heels, and smothers his squeals
  In the scum of the boiling broth.

'And I eat that cook in a week or less,
  And – as I eating be
The last of his chops, why, I almost drops,
  For a wessel in sight I see!

                    *

'And I never larf, and I never smile,
  And I never lark nor play,
But sit and croak, and a single joke
  I have – which is to say:

' "Oh, I am a cook and a captain bold,
  And the mate of the *Nancy* brig,
And a bo'sun tight, and a midshipmite,
  And the crew of the captain's gig!" '

W. S. GILBERT

106

THE WIDOW'S PARTY

'Where have you been this while away,
        Johnnie, Johnnie?'
Out with the rest on a picnic lay,
        Johnnie, my Johnnie, aha!
They called us out of the barrack-yard
To Gawd knows where from Gosport Hard,
And you can't refuse when you get the card,
        And the Widow gives the party.
        (*Bugle*: Ta – rara – ra-ra-rara!)

'What did you get to eat and drink,
        Johnnie, Johnnie?'
Standing water as thick as ink,
        Johnnie, my Johnnie, aha!
A bit o' beef that were three year stored,
A bit of mutton as tough as a board,
And a fowl we killed with a sergeant's sword,
        When the Widow give the party.

'What did you do for knives and forks,
        Johnnie, Johnnie?'
We carries 'em with us wherever we walks,
        Johnnie, my Johnnie, aha!
And some was sliced and some was halved,
And some was crimped and some was carved,
And some was gutted and some was starved,
        When the Widow give the party.

'What ha' you done with half your mess,
        Johnnie, Johnnie?'
They couldn't do more and they wouldn't do less,
        Johnnie, my Johnnie, aha!
They ate their whack and they drank their fill,

And I think the rations has made them ill,
For half my comp'ny's lying still
    Where the Widow give the party.

'How did you get away – away,
    Johnnie, Johnnie?'
On the broad o' my back at the end o' the day,
    Johnnie, my Johnnie, aha!
I comed away like a bleedin' toff,
For I got four niggers to carry me off,
As I lay in the bight of a canvas trough,
    When the Widow give the party.

'What was the end of all the show,
    Johnnie, Johnnie?'
Ask my Colonel, for I don't know,
    Johnnie, my Johnnie, aha!
We broke a King and we built a road –
A court-house stands where the Reg'ment goed.
And the river's clean where the raw blood flowed,
    When the Widow give the party.
     (*Bugle*: Ta – rara – ra-ra-rara!)

RUDYARD KIPLING

107

DANNY DEEVER

'What are the bugles blowin' for?' said Files-on-Parade.
'To turn you out, to turn you out,' the Colour-Sergeant said.
'What makes you look so white, so white?' said Files-on-
    Parade.
'I'm dreadin' what I've got to watch,' the Colour-Sergeant
    said.
  For they're hangin' Danny Deever, you can hear the Dead
    March play,
  The Regiment's in 'ollow square – they're hangin' him
    to-day;
  They've taken of his buttons off an' cut his stripes away,
  An' they're hangin' Danny Deever in the mornin'.

'What makes the rear-rank breathe so 'ard?' said Files-on-
    Parade.
'It's bitter cold, it's bitter cold,' the Colour-Sergeant said.
'What makes that front-rank man fall down?' said Files-on-
    Parade.
'A touch o' sun, a touch o' sun,' the Colour-Sergeant said.
  They are hangin' Danny Deever, they are marchin' of 'im
    round,
  They 'ave 'alted Danny Deever by 'is coffin on the ground;
  An' 'e'll swing in 'arf a minute for a sneakin' shootin'
    hound –
  O they're hangin' Danny Deever in the mornin'!

''Is cot was right-'and cot to mine,' said Files-on-Parade.
''E's sleepin' out an' far to-night,' the Colour-Sergeant said.
'I've drunk 'is beer a score o' times,' said Files-on-Parade.
''E's drinkin' bitter beer alone,' the Colour-Sergeant said.
  They are hangin' Danny Deever, you must mark 'im to 'is
    place,
  For 'e shot a comrade sleepin' – you must look 'im in the
    face;

Nine 'undred of 'is county an' the Regiment's disgrace,
While they're hangin' Danny Deever in the mornin'.

'What's that so black agin the sun?' said Files-on-Parade.
'It's Danny fightin' 'ard for life,' the Colour-Sergeant said.
'What's that that whimpers over'ead?' said Files-on-Parade.
'It's Danny's soul that's passin' now,' the Colour-Sergeant
    said.
  For they're done with Danny Deever, you can 'ear the
      quickstep play,
  The Regiment's in column, an' they're marchin' us away;
  Ho! the young recruits are shakin', an' they'll want their
      beer to-day,
  After hangin' Danny Deever in the mornin'!

RUDYARD KIPLING

108

SHE WAS POOR, BUT SHE WAS HONEST

She was poor, but she was honest,
    Victim of the squire's whim.
First he loved her, then he left her,
    And she lost her honest name.

Then she ran away to London,
    For to hide her grief and shame,
There she met another squire,
    And she lost her name again.

See her riding in her carriage,
    In the Park and all so gay,
All the nibs and nobby persons
    Come to pass the time of day,

See the little old-world village
    Where her aged parents live,
Drinking the champagne she sends them,
    But they never can forgive.

In the rich man's arms she flutters,
    Like a bird with broken wing,
First he loved her, then he left her,
    And she hasn't got a ring.

See him in the splendid mansion,
    Entertaining with the best,
While the girl that he has ruined,
    Entertains a sordid guest.

See him in the House of Commons,
    Making laws to put down crime,
While the victim of his passions
    Trails her way through mud and slime.

Standing on the bridge at midnight,
  She says: Farewell, blighted Love.
There's a scream, a splash – Good Heavens!
  What is she a-doing of?

Then they drag her from the river,
  Water from her clothes they wrang,
For they thought that she was drownded,
  But the corpse got up and sang:

It's the same the whole world over,
  It's the poor that gets the blame,
It's the rich that get the pleasure.
  Isn't it a blooming shame?

109

JOHN HENRY

John Henry was a li'l baby, uh-huh,
Sittin' on his mama's knee, oh, yeah,
Said: 'De Big Bend Tunnel on de C. & O. road
Gonna cause de death of me,
Lawd, Lawd, gonna cause de death of me.'

John Henry, he had a woman,
Her name was Mary Magdalene,
She would go to de tunnel and sing for John,
Jes' to hear John Henry's hammer ring,
Lawd, Lawd, jes' to hear John Henry's hammer ring.

John Henry had a li'l woman,
Her name was Lucy Ann,
John Henry took sick an' had to go to bed,
Lucy Ann drove steel like a man,
Lawd, Lawd, Lucy Ann drove steel like a man.

Cap'n says to John Henry,
'Gonna bring me a steam drill 'round,
Gonna take dat steam drill out on de job,
Gonna whop dat steel on down,
Lawd, Lawd, gonna whop dat steel on down.'

John Henry tol' his cap'n,
Lightnin' was in his eye:
'Cap'n, bet yo' las' red cent on me,
Fo' I'll beat it to de bottom or I'll die,
Lawd, Lawd, I'll beat it to de bottom or I'll die.'

Sun shine hot an' burnin',
Wer'n't no breeze a-tall,
Sweat ran down like water down a hill,
Dat day John Henry let his hammer fall,
Lawd, Lawd, dat day John Henry let his hammer fall.

John Henry went to de tunnel,
An' dey put him in de lead to drive;
De rock so tall an' John Henry so small,
Dat he lied down his hammer an' he cried,
Lawd, Lawd, dat he lied down his hammer an' he cried.

John Henry started on de right hand,
De steam drill started on de lef' –
'Before I'd let dis steam drill beat me down,
I'd hammer my fool self to death,
Lawd, Lawd, I'd hammer my fool self to death.'

White man tol' John Henry,
'Nigger, damn yo' soul,
You might beat dis steam an' drill of mine,
When de rocks in dis mountain turn to gol',
Lawd, Lawd, when de rocks in dis mountain turn to gol'.'

John Henry said to his shaker,
'Nigger, why don' you sing?
I'm throwin' twelve poun's from my hips on down,
Jes' listen to de col' steel ring,
Lawd, Lawd, jes' listen to de col' steel ring.'

Oh, de captain said to John Henry,
'I b'lieve this mountain's sinkin' in.'
John Henry said to his captain, oh my!
'Ain' nothin' but my hammer suckin' win',
Lawd, Lawd, ain' nothin' but my hammer suckin' win'.'

John Henry tol' his shaker,
'Shaker, you better pray,
For, if I miss dis six-foot steel,
Tomorrow'll be yo' buryin' day,
Lawd, Lawd, tomorrow'll be yo' buryin' day.'

John Henry tol' his captain,
'Looka yonder what I see —
Yo' drill's done broke an' yo' hole's done choke,
An' you cain' drive steel like me,
Lawd, Lawd, an' you cain' drive steel like me.'

De man dat invented de steam drill,
Thought he was mighty fine.
John Henry drove his fifteen feet,
An' de steam drill only made nine,
Lawd, Lawd, an' de steam drill only made nine.

De hammer dat John Henry swung,
It weighed over nine pound;
He broke a rib in his lef'-han' side,
An' his intrels fell on de groun',
Lawd, Lawd, an' his intrels fell on de groun'.

John Henry was hammerin' on de mountain,
An' his hammer was strikin' fire,
He drove so hard till he broke his pore heart,
An' he lied down his hammer an' he died,
Lawd, Lawd, he lied down his hammer an' he died.

All de womens in de Wes',
When dey heared of John Henry's death,
Stood in de rain, flagged de eas'-boun' train,
Goin' where John Henry fell dead,
Lawd, Lawd, goin' where John Henry fell dead.

John Henry's lil mother,
She was all dressed in red,
She jumped in bed, covered up her head,
Said she didn' know her son was dead,
Lawd, Lawd, didn' know her son was dead.

John Henry had a pretty lil woman,
An' de dress she wo' was blue,
An' de las' words she said to him:
'John Henry, I've been true to you,
Lawd, Lawd, John Henry, I've been true to you.'

'Oh, who's gonna show yo' lil feetses,
An' who's gonna glub yo' han's,
An' who's gonna kiss yo' rosy, rosy lips,
An' who's gonna be yo' man,
Lawd, Lawd, an' who's gonna be yo' man?'

'Oh, my mama's gonna show my lil feetses,
An' my papa's gonna glub my lil han's,
An' my sister's gonna kiss my rosy, rosy lips,
An' I don' need no man,
Lawd, Lawd, an' I don' need no man.'

Dey took John Henry to de graveyard,
An' dey buried him in de san',
An' every locomotive come roarin' by,
Says, 'Dere lays a steel-drivin' man,
Lawd, Lawd, dere lays a steel-drivin' man.'

glub glove

THE BUFFALO SKINNERS

Come all you jolly cowboys and listen to my song,
There are not many verses, it will not detain you long;
It's concerning some young fellows who did agree to go
And spend one summer pleasantly on the range of the buffalo.

It happened in Jacksboro in the spring of seventy-three,
A man by the name of Crego came stepping up to me,
Saying, 'How do you do, young fellow, and how would you
    like to go
And spend one summer pleasantly on the range of the buffalo?'

'It's me being out of employment,' this to Crego I did say,
'This going out on the buffalo range depends upon the pay.
But if you will pay good wages and transportation too,
I think, sir, I will go with you to the range of the buffalo.'

'Yes, I will pay good wages, give transportation too,
Provided you will go with me and stay the summer through;
But if you should grow homesick, come back to Jacksboro,
I won't pay transportation from the range of the buffalo.'

It's now our outfit was complete – seven able-bodied men,
With navy six and needle gun – our troubles did begin;
Our way it was a pleasant one, the route we had to go,
Until we crossed Pease River on the range of the buffalo.

It's now we've crossed Pease River, our troubles have begun.
The first damned tail I went to rip, Christ! how I cut my
    thumb!
While skinning the damned old stinkers our lives wasn't a
    show,
For the Indians watched to pick us off while skinning the
    buffalo.

six and needle gun the Dreyse rifle

He fed us on such sorry chuck I wished myself most dead,
It was old jerked beef, croton coffee, and sour bread.
Pease River's as salty as hell fire, the water I could never go —
Oh, God! I wished I had never come to the range of the
    buffalo.

Our meat it was buffalo rump and iron wedge bread,
And all we had to sleep on was a buffalo robe for a bed;
The fleas and graybacks worked on us, O boys, it was not
    slow,
I'll tell you there's no worse hell on earth than the range of
    the buffalo.

Our hearts were cased with buffalo hocks, our souls were
    cased with steel,
And the hardships of that summer would nearly make us reel.
While skinning the damned old stinkers our lives they had no
    show,
For the Indians waited to pick us off on the hills of Mexico.

The season being near over, old Crego he did say
The crowd had been extravagant, was in debt to him that day,
We coaxed him and we begged him and still it was no go —
We left old Crego's bones to bleach on the range of the
    buffalo.

Oh, it's now we've crossed Pease River and homeward we
    are bound,
No more in that hell-fired country shall ever we be found.
Go home to our wives and sweethearts, tell others not to go,
For God's forsaken the buffalo range and the damned old
    buffalo.

> *jerked beef* beef cut in strips and   *graybacks* lice
>   sun-dried
> *croton coffee* ? coffee as nasty as
>   croton oil

THE COWBOY'S LAMENT

As I walked out in the streets of Laredo,
As I walked out in Laredo one day,
I spied a poor cowboy wrapped up in white linen,
Wrapped up in white linen as cold as the clay.

Oh beat the drum slowly and play the fife lowly,
Play the Dead March as you carry me along;
Take me to the green valley, there lay the sod o'er me,
For I'm a young cowboy and I know I've done wrong.

I see by your outfit that you are a cowboy –
These words he did say as I boldly stepped by.
Come sit down beside me and hear my sad story,
I am shot in the breast and I know I must die.

Let sixteen gamblers come handle my coffin,
Let sixteen cowboys come sing me a song.
Take me to the graveyard and lay the sod o'er me,
For I'm a poor cowboy and I know I've done wrong.

My friends and relations they live in the Nation,
They know not where their boy has gone.
I first came to Texas and hired to a ranchman.
Oh I'm a young cowboy and I know I've done wrong.

It was once in the saddle I used to go dashing,
It was once in the saddle I used to go gay
First to the dram-house and then to the card-house,
Got shot in the breast and I am dying to-day.

Laredo town in Texas   *the Nation* The United States
                                (Texas not having become one of
                                the United States till 1845).

Get six jolly cowboys to carry my coffin,
Get six pretty maidens to bear up my pall.
Put bunches of roses all over my coffin,
Put roses to deaden the sods as they fall.

Then swing your rope slowly and rattle your spurs lowly,
And give a wild whoop as you carry me along,
And in the grave throw me and roll the sod o'er me,
For I'm a young cowboy and I know I've done wrong.

Oh bury beside me my knife and six-shooter,
My spurs on my heel, as you sing me a song,
And over my coffin put a bottle of brandy
That the cowboys may drink as they carry me along.

Go bring me a cup, a cup of cold water
To cool my parched lips, the cowboy then said;
Before I returned his soul had departed,
And gone to the round-up, the cowboy was dead.

We beat the drum slowly and played the fife lowly,
And bitterly wept as we bore him along;
For we all loved our comrade, so brave, young, and
    handsome,
We all loved our comrade although he'd done wrong.

112

SWEET BETSY FROM PIKE

Did you ever hear tell of sweet Betsy from Pike,
Who crossed the wide prairies with her lover Ike,
With two yoke of cattle and one spotted hog,
A tall shanghai rooster and an old yaller dog?
    Sing-too-rall-i-oo-ral-i-oo-ral-i-ay,
    Sing-too-rall-i-oo-ral-oo-ral-i-ay.

One evening quite early they camped on the Platte,
'Twas near by the road on a green shady flat;
Where Betsy, quite tired, lay down to repose,
While with wonder Ike gazed on his Pike County rose.

They swam the wide rivers and crossed the tall peaks,
And camped on the prairie for weeks upon weeks.
Starvation and cholera and hard work and slaughter,
They reached California spite of hell and high water.

Out on the prairie one bright starry night
They broke the whisky and Betsy got tight,
She sang and she shouted and danced o'er the plain,
And showed her bare arse to the whole wagon train.

The Injuns came down in a wild yelling horde,
And Betsy was skeered they would scalp her adored;
Behind the front wagon wheel Betsy did crawl,
And there she fought the Injuns with musket and ball.

The alkali desert was burning and bare,
And Isaac's soul shrank from the death that lurked there:
'Dear old Pike County, I'll go back to you.'
Says Betsy, 'You'll go by yourself if you do.'

They soon reached the desert, where Betsy gave out,
And down in the sand she lay rolling about;
While Ike in great terror looked on in surprise,
Saying, 'Betsy, get up, you'll get sand in your eyes.'

Sweet Betsy got up in a great deal of pain
And declared she'd go back to Pike County again;
Then Ike heaved a sigh and they fondly embraced,
And she traveled along with his arm round her waist.

They went to Salt Lake to inquire the way,
And Brigham declared that sweet Betsy should stay;
But Betsy got frightened and ran like a deer,
While Brigham stood pawing the earth like a steer.

The wagon tipped over with a terrible crash,
And out on the prairie rolled all sorts of trash;
A few little baby clothes done up with care
Looked rather suspicious, but it was all on the square.

One morning they climbed a very high hill,
And with wonder looked down on old Placerville;
Ike shouted and said, as he cast his eyes down,
'Sweet Betsy, my darling, we've got to Hangtown.'

Long Ike and sweet Betsy attended a dance,
Where Ike wore a pair of his Pike County pants;
Sweet Betsy was covered with ribbons and rings,
Said Ike, 'You're an angel, but where are your wings?'

A miner said, 'Betsy, will you dance with me?'
'I will that, old hoss, if you don't make too free;
But don't dance me hard. Do you want to know why?
Doggone ye, I'm chock-full of strong alkali.'

Long Ike and sweet Betsy got married of course,
But Ike, getting jealous, obtained a divorce;
And Betsy, well satisfied, said with a shout,
'Good-by, you big lummox, I'm glad you backed out.'

lummex clumsy creature

113

FRANKIE AND ALBERT

Frankie wuz a good woman,
Everybody knows,
She spent one hundred dollars
For to buy her man some clothes,
Oh, he wuz her man,
But he done her wrong.

Frankie went down to de corner,
Went there wid a can,
Ast de lovin' bartender:
'Has you seen my lovin' man?
He's my man,
But he's a-doin' me wrong.'

Frankie went down to de corner,
Didn't go dere for fun,
Underneath her raglin,
She had Albert's 41 –
He was her man,
But she shot him down.

Frankie went down to de whore-house,
Rang de whore-house bell,
Says, 'Tell me, is my lovin' Albert here?
Caze Frankie's gwine to raise some hell –
Oh, he's my man,
But he's a-doin' me wrong.'

When Albert saw Frankie,
For the back door he did scoot,
But Frankie pulled dat forty-fo',
Went root-ta-toot-toot-ta-toot-toot –

raglin Raglan, overcoat

En she shot him down,
Yes, she shot him down.

Well, when Frankie shot Albert,
He fell down on his knees,
Looked up at her and said,
'Oh, Frankie, please
Don't shoot me no mo', babe,
Don't shoot me no mo''.

'Oh, tu'n me over, doctor,
Tu'n me over slow,
Tu'n me over on my right-hand side
Caze de bullet is a-hurtin' me so.'
He was her man,
But he's dead an' gone.

Frankie follered Albert to de graveyard,
Fell down on her knees.
'Speak one word, Albert,
An' git my heart some ease —
You wuz my man,
But you done me wrong.'

Albert raise up in his grave,
To old Frankie he said,
'You bein' my lovin' woman,
Kindly put some cracked ice on my head —
I wuz yo' man,
But I done you wrong.'

Now Frankie's layin' on old Albert's grave,
Tears rollin' down her face,
Says, 'I've loved many a nigger son of a bitch,
But there's none can take Albert's place —
He wuz my man,
But he done me wrong.'

En now it's rubber-tired carriages,
An' a rubber-tired hack,
Took old Albert to de graveyard
An' brought his mother back –
His soul's in hell,
His soul's in hell.

COCAINE LIL AND MORPHINE SUE

Did you ever hear about Cocaine Lil?
She lived in Cocaine town on Cocaine hill,
She had a cocaine dog and a cocaine cat,
They fought all night with a cocaine rat.

She had cocaine hair on her cocaine head.
She had a cocaine dress that was poppy red:
She wore a snowbird hat and sleigh-riding clothes,
On her coat she wore a crimson, cocaine rose.

Big gold chariots on the Milky Way,
Snakes and elephants silver and gray.
Oh the cocaine blues they make me sad,
Oh the cocaine blues make me feel bad.

Lil went to a snow party one cold night,
And the way she sniffed was sure a fright.
There was Hophead Mag with Dopey Slim,
Kankakee Liz and Yen Shee Jim.

There was Morphine Sue and the Poppy Face Kid,
Climbed up snow ladders and down they skid;
There was the Stepladder Kit, a good six feet,
And the Sleigh-riding Sister who were hard to beat.

Along in the morning about half past three
They were all lit up like a Christmas tree;
Lil got home and started for bed,
Took another sniff and it knocked her dead.

They laid her out in her cocaine clothes:
She wore a snowbird hat with a crimson rose;
On her headstone you'll find this refrain:
'She died as she lived, sniffing cocaine.'

snow cocaine

WILLY THE WEEPER

Hark to the story of Willie the Weeper,
Willie the Weeper was a chimney sweeper,
He had the hop habit and he had it bad,
O listen while I tell you 'bout a dream he had.

He went to the hop joint the other night,
When he knew the lights would all be burning bright,
I guess he smoked a dozen pills or more,
When he woke up, he was on a foreign shore.

Queen o' Bulgaria was the first he met,
She called him her darlin' and her lovin' pet,
She promised him a pretty Ford automobile
With a diamond headlight an' a silver steerin' wheel.

She had a million cattle, she had a million sheep,
She had a million vessels on the ocean deep,
She had a million dollars, all in nickels and dimes,
She knew 'cause she counted them a million times.

Willie landed in New York one evenin' late,
He asked his sugar for an after-date,
Willie he got funny, she began to shout,
BIM BAM BOO! – an' the dope gave out.

hop habit opium habit

THE GRESFORD DISASTER

You've heard of the Gresford disaster,
The terrible price that was paid,
Two hundred and forty-two colliers were lost
And three men of a rescue brigade.

It occurred in the month of September,
At three in the morning, that pit
Was racked by a violent explosion
In the Dennis where gas lay so thick.

The gas in the Dennis deep section
Was packed there like snow in a drift,
And many a man had to leave the coal-face
Before he had worked out his shift.

A fortnight before the explosion,
To the shot-firer Tomlinson cried
'If you fire that shot we'll be all blown to hell!'
And no one can say that he lied.

The fireman's reports they are missing,
The records of forty-two days;
The colliery manager had them destroyed
To cover his criminal ways.

Down there in the dark they are lying,
They died for nine shillings a day.
They have worked out their shift and now they must lie
In the darkness until Judgement Day.

The Lord Mayor of London's collecting
To help both our children and wives,
The owners have sent some white lilies
To pay for the poor colliers' lives.

Farewell, our dear wives and our children,
Farewell, our old comrades as well.
Don't send your sons down the dark dreary pit,
They'll be damned like the sinners in hell.

117

SAM HALL

Oh, my name it is Sam Hall, it is Sam Hall,
Yes, my name it is Sam Hall, it is Sam Hall;
Yes, my name it is Sam Hall, and I hate you one and all,
Yes, I hate you one and all, God damn your eyes.

Oh, I killed a man, they say, so they say;
Yes, I killed a man, they say, so they say;
I beat him on the head, and I left him there for dead,
Yes, I left him there for dead, God damn his eyes.

Oh, the parson he did come, he did come,
Yes, the parson he did come, he did come;
And he looked so bloody glum, as he talked of Kingdom
    Come —
He can kiss my ruddy bum, God damn his eyes.

And the sheriff he came too, he came too;
Yes, the sheriff he came too, he came too;
Yes, the sheriff he came too, with his men all dressed in blue —
Lord, they were a bloody crew, God damn their eyes.

Now up the rope I go, up I go;
Yes, up the rope I go, up I go;
And those bastards down below, they'll say, 'Sam, we told
    you so,'
They'll say, 'Sam, we told you so,' God damn their eyes.

I saw my Nellie dressed in blue, dressed in blue;
I saw my Nellie in the crowd, all dressed in blue:
Says my Nellie, dressed in blue: 'Your triflin' days are
    through —
Now I know that you'll be true, God damn your eyes.'

And now in heaven I dwell, in heaven I dwell,
Yes, now in heaven I dwell, in heaven I dwell;
Yes, now in heaven I dwell – Holy Christ! It is a sell –
All the whores are down in hell, God damn their eyes.

118

THE LAY OF OLIVER GOGARTY

Come all ye bould Free Staters now and listen to my lay
And pay a close attention please to what I've got to say,
For 'tis the tale of a winter's night in last December drear
When Oliver St John Gogarty swam down the Salmon Weir.

As Oliver St John Gogarty one night sat in his home
A-writin' of prescriptions or composin' of a poem
Up rolled a gorgeous Rolls-Royce car and out a lady jumped
And at Oliver St John Gogarty's hall-door she loudly
    thumped.

'O! Oliver St John Gogarty,' said she, 'Now please come
    quick
For in a house some miles away a man lies mighty sick.'
Yet Oliver St John Gogarty to her made no reply,
But with a dextrous facial twist he gently closed one eye.

'O! Oliver St John Gogarty, come let yourself be led.'
Cried a couple of maskèd ruffians puttin' guns up to his head.
'I'm with you boys,' cried he, 'but first, give me my big fur
    coat
And also let me have a scarf – my special care's the throat.'

They shoved him in the Rolls-Royce car and swiftly sped away,
What route they followed Oliver St John Gogarty can't say,
But they reached a house at Island Bridge and locked him in a
    room,
And said, 'Oliver St John Gogarty, prepare to meet your
    doom.'

Said he, 'Give me some minutes first to settle my affairs,
And let me have some moments' grace to say my last night's
    prayers.'

To this appeal his brutal guard was unable to say nay,
He was so amazed that Oliver St John Gogarty could pray.

Said Oliver St John Gogarty, 'My coat I beg you hold.'
The half-bewildered scoundrel then did as he was told.
Before he twigged what game was up, the coat was round his
    head
And Oliver St John Gogarty into the night had fled.

The rain came down like bullets, and the bullets fell like rain,
As Oliver St John Gogarty the river bank did gain,
He plunged into the ragin' tide and swum with courage bold,
Like brave Horatius long ago in the fabled days of old.

Then landin' he proceeded through the famous Phaynix Park,
The night was bitter cold and what was worse, extremely dark,
But Oliver St John Gogarty to this paid no regard,
Till he found himself a target for our gallant Civic Guard.

Cried Oliver St John Gogarty, 'A Senator am I,
The rebels I've tricked, the Liffey I've swum, and sorra the
    word's a lie.'
As they clad and fed that hero bold, said the sergeant with a
    wink,
'Faith, then, Oliver St John Gogarty, ye've too much bounce
    to sink.'

WILLIAM DAWSON

sorra not at all, never

119

WALTZING MATILDA

Once a jolly swagman camped by a billabong,
　Under the shade of a coolabah tree;
And he sang as he watched and waited till his billy boiled,
　'You'll come a-waltzing Matilda with me!'

'Waltzing Matilda, Waltzing Matilda,
　You'll come a-waltzing Matilda with me,'
And he sang as he watched and waited till his billy boiled,
　You'll come a-waltzing Matilda with me.'

Down came a jumbuck to drink at the billabong,
　Up jumped the swagman and grabbed him with glee;
And he sang as he shoved that jumbuck in his tucker-bag,
　'You'll come a-waltzing Matilda with me.'

'Waltzing Matilda, Waltzing Matilda,
　You'll come a-waltzing Matilda with me,'
And he sang as he shoved that jumbuck in his tucker-bag,
　'You'll come a-waltzing Matilda with me.'

Up rode the squatter mounted on his thoroughbred;
　Down came the troopers – one, two and three.
'Whose the jolly jumbuck you've got in your tucker-bag?
　You'll come a-waltzing Matilda with me.'

'Waltzing Matilda, Waltzing Matilda,
　You'll come a-waltzing Matilda with me,
Whose the jolly jumbuck you've got in your tucker-bag?
　You'll come a-waltzing Matilda with me.'

swagman tramp carrying his swag
　or bundle
billabong blind channel of a river
coolabah tree species of gum tree
billy can

waltzing Matilda carrying a swag
　around
jumbuck sheep
tucker-bag food bag
squatter owner of a sheep station

Up jumped the swagman, sprang into the billabong,
  'You'll never catch me alive,' said he.
And his ghost may be heard as you pass by that billabong
  'Who'll come a-waltzing Matilda with me?'

'Waltzing Matilda, Waltzing Matilda,
  You'll come a-waltzing Matilda with me,'
And his ghost may be heard as you pass by that billabong,
  'Who'll come a-waltzing Matilda with me?'

THE KEEPER OF THE EDDYSTONE LIGHT

My father was the keeper of the Eddystone Light
And he slept with a mermaid one fine night,
And of that union there came three,
A porpoise and a paugie and the other was me.
    Yo ho ho the wind blows free,
    O for a life on the rolling sea.

One night as I was trimming the glim
And singing a verse of the evening hymn,
A voice from the starboard cried Ahoy,
And there was my mother sitting on a buoy.

Then my mother she asked of me
'What has become of my children three?'
'One was exhibited as a talking fish
And one was served up in a chafing dish.'

With a phosphorous flash in her seaweed hair
I looked again and my mother wasn't there,
And a voice came echoing out of the night
'To hell with the keeper of the Eddystone Light.'

paugie sea-bream (US)   *glim* candle

THE STREETS OF LAREDO

O early one morning I walked out like Agag,
Early one morning to walk through the fire
Dodging the pythons that leaked on the pavements
With tinkle of glasses and tangle of wire;

When grimed to the eyebrows I met an old fireman
Who looked at me wryly and thus did he say:
'The streets of Laredo are closed to all traffic,
We won't never master this joker to-day.

'O hold the branch tightly and wield the axe brightly,
The bank is in powder, the banker's in hell,
But loot is still free on the streets of Laredo
And when we drive home we drive home on the bell.'

Then out from a doorway there sidled a cockney,
A rocking-chair rocking on top of his head:
'O fifty-five years I been feathering my love-nest
And look at it now – why, you'd sooner be dead.'

At which there arose from a wound in the asphalt,
His big wig a-smoulder, Sir Christopher Wren
Saying: 'Let them make hay of the streets of Laredo;
When your ground-rent expire I will build them again.'

Then twangling their bibles with wrath in their nostrils
From Bonehill Fields came Bunyan and Blake:
'Laredo the golden is fallen, is fallen;
Your flame shall not quench nor your thirst shall not slake.'

'I come to Laredo to find me asylum',
Says Tom Dick and Harry the Wandering Jew;
'They tell me report at the first police station
But the station is pancaked – so what can I do?'

Thus eavesdropping sadly I strolled through Laredo
Perplexed by the dicta misfortunes inspire
Till one low last whisper inveigled my earhole –
The voice of the Angel, the voice of the fire:

O late, very late, have I come to Laredo
A whimsical bride in my new scarlet dress
But at last I took pity on those who were waiting
To see my regalia and feel my caress.

Now ring the bells gaily and play the hose daily,
Put splints on your legs, put a gag on your breath;
O you streets of Laredo, you streets of Laredo,
Lay down the red carpet – My dowry is death.

LOUIS MACNEICE

122

VICTOR WAS A LITTLE BABY

Victor was a little baby,
    Into this world he came;
His father took him on his knee and said:
    'Don't dishonour the family name.'

Victor looked up at his father
    Looked up with big round eyes:
His father said; 'Victor, my only son,
    Don't you ever ever tell lies.'

Victor and his father went riding
    Out in a little dog-cart;
His father took a Bible from his pocket and read;
    'Blessed are the pure in heart.'

It was a frosty December,
    It wasn't the season for fruits;
His father fell dead of heart disease
    While lacing up his boots.

It was a frosty December
    When into his grave he sank;
His uncle found Victor a post as cashier
    In the Midland Counties Bank.

It was a frosty December
    Victor was only eighteen,
But his figures were neat and his margins straight
    And his cuffs were always clean.

He took a room at the Peveril,
    A respectable boarding-house;
And Time watched Victor day by day
    As a cat will watch a mouse.

The clerks slapped Victor on the shoulder;
    'Have you ever had a woman?' they said,
'Come down town with us on Saturday night.'
    Victor smiled and shook his head.

The manager sat in his office,
    Smoked a Corona cigar:
Said; 'Victor's a decent fellow but
    He's too mousey to go far.'

Victor went up to his bedroom,
    Set the alarum bell;
Climbed into bed, took his Bible and read
    Of what happened to Jezebel.

It was the First of April,
    Anna to the Peveril came;
Her eyes, her lips, her breasts, her hips
    And her smile set men aflame.

She looked as pure as a schoolgirl
    On her First Communion day,
But her kisses were like the best champagne
    When she gave herself away.

It was the Second of April,
    She was wearing a coat of fur;
Victor met her upon the stairs
    And he fell in love with her.

The first time he made his proposal,
    She laughed, said; 'I'll never wed';
The second time there was a pause;
    Then she smiled and shook her head.

Anna looked into her mirror,
    Pouted and gave a frown:
Said; 'Victor's as dull as a wet afternoon
    But I've got to settle down.'

The third time he made his proposal,
        As they walked by the Reservoir:
She gave him a kiss like a blow on the head,
        Said; 'You are my heart's desire.'

They were married early in August,
        She said; 'Kiss me, you funny boy';
Victor took her in his arms and said;
        'O my Helen of Troy.'

It was the middle of September,
        Victor came to the office one day;
He was wearing a flower in his buttonhole,
        He was late but he was gay.

The clerks were talking of Anna,
        The door was just ajar:
One said; 'Poor old Victor, but where ignorance
        Is bliss, etcetera.'

Victor stood still as a statue,
        The door was just ajar:
One said; 'God, what fun I had with her
        In that Baby Austin car.'

Victor walked out into the High Street,
        He walked to the edge of the town;
He came to the allotments and the rubbish heaps
        And his tears came tumbling down.

Victor looked up at the sunset
        As he stood there all alone;
Cried; 'Are you in Heaven, Father?'
        But the sky said 'Address not known.'

Victor looked up at the mountains,
        The mountains all covered with snow:
Cried: 'Are you pleased with me, Father?'
        And the answer came back, No.

Victor came to the forest,
    Cried: 'Father, will she ever be true?'
And the oaks and the beeches shook their heads
    And they answered: 'Not to you.'

Victor came to the meadow
    Where the wind went sweeping by:
Cried; 'O Father, I love her so,'
    But the wind said, 'She must die.'

Victor came to the river
    Running so deep and so still:
Crying; 'O Father, what shall I do?'
    And the river answered, 'Kill.'

Anna was sitting at table,
    Drawing cards from a pack;
Anna was sitting at table
    Waiting for her husband to come back.

It wasn't the Jack of Diamonds
    Nor the Joker she drew at first;
It wasn't the King or the Queen of Hearts
    But the Ace of Spades reversed.

Victor stood in the doorway,
    He didn't utter a word:
She said; 'What's the matter, darling?'
    He behaved as if he hadn't heard.

There was a voice in his left ear,
    There was a voice in his right,
There was a voice at the base of his skull
    Saying, 'She must die tonight.'

Victor picked up a carving-knife,
    His features were set and drawn,
Said; 'Anna, it would have been better for you
    If you had not been born.'

Anna jumped up from the table,
　　　Anna started to scream,
But Victor came slowly after her
　　　Like a horror in a dream.

She dodged behind the sofa,
　　　She tore down a curtain rod,
But Victor came slowly after her;
　　　Said: 'Prepare to meet thy God.'

She managed to wrench the door open,
　　　She ran and she didn't stop.
But Victor followed her up the stairs
　　　And he caught her at the top.

He stood there above the body,
　　　He stood there holding the knife;
And the blood ran down the stairs and sang,
　　　'I'm the Resurrection and the Life.'

They tapped Victor on the shoulder,
　　　They took him away in a van;
He sat as quiet as a lump of moss
　　　Saying: 'I am the Son of Man.'

Victor sat in a corner
　　　Making a woman of clay;
Saying: 'I am Alpha and Omega, I shall come
　　　To judge the earth one day.'

W. H. AUDEN

SONG ABOUT MARY

Mary sat on a long brown bench
Reading *Woman's Own* and *She*,
Then a slimy-haired nit with stripes on his collar
Said: 'What's the baby's name to be?'

She looked across to Marks and Spencers
Through the dirty window pane,
'I think I'll call him Jesus Christ,
It's time he came again.'

The clerk he banged his ledger
And he called the Cruelty Man
Saying: 'This bird thinks she's the mother of Christ,
Do what you bleeding well can.'

They took Mary down to the country
And fed her on country air,
And they put the baby in a Christian home
And he's much happier there.

For if Jesus came to Britain
He would turn its dizzy head,
You'd see him arrested at the next sit-down
And he'd raise the poor from the dead.

So if you have a little baby
Make sure it's a legitimate child,
Bind down his limbs with insurance
And he'll grow up meek and mild.
   Meek and mild ... meek and mild ... meek and mild.

ADRIAN MITCHELL

FIFTEEN MILLION PLASTIC BAGS

I was walking in a government warehouse
Where the daylight never goes.
I saw fifteen million plastic bags
Hanging in a thousand rows.

Five million bags were six feet long
Five million bags were five foot five
Five million were stamped with Mickey Mouse
And they came in a smaller size.

Were they for guns or uniforms
Or a dirty kind of party game?
Then I saw each bag had a number
And every bag bore a name.

And five million bags were six feet long
Five million were five foot five
Five million were stamped with Mickey Mouse
And they came in a smaller size

So I've taken my bag from the hanger
And I've pulled it over my head
And I'll wait for the priest to zip it
So the radiation won't spread

Now five million bags are six feet long
Five million are five foot five
Five million are stamped with Mickey Mouse
And they come in a smaller size.

ADRIAN MITCHELL

SOURCES AND NOTES

'Child', below, refers to *The English and Scottish Popular Ballads*, edited by Francis James Child, five volumes, 1882–98; reprinted 1965 by Dover Publications, New York.

1. Child 22. Fifteenth century.
2. Child 54A; Sandys, *Christmas Carols* (1833).
3. Child 21A.
4. *Oxford Book of Carols*, 43.
5. *Notes and Queries* (1905).
6. Gillington, *Songs of the Open Road* (1911). Taken down from a gypsy singer.
7. *Journal of the Folk Song Society*, Vol. V.
8. Child 57.
9. Sandys, *Christmas Carols*.
10. Child 1C. He prints an English version of the fifteenth century entitled 'Inter Diabolus et Virgo' ('Between the Devil and the Virgin').
11. Ernest Rhys, *Fairy Gold* (1907). Several versions are given by Child (38).
12. Child 4A.
13. Robert Chambers, *Popular Rhymes of Scotland* (1858); cf. Child 3.
14. Child 3A.
15. Child 2A.
16. Child 43A (Sir Walter Scott's *Minstrelsy of the Scottish Border*).
17. Child 35.
18. Child 200 BA, as taken down (see Child, Vol. V, p. 252).
19. Robert Bell, *Ancient Poems, Ballads and Songs of the Peasantry of England* (1861), cf. Child 18C.
20. Child 36. The last line in stanza 11 added from the Skene MSS (Child, Vol. V, pp. 214–15).
21. Child 41B. In other versions the point is that Margaret and Hind Etin's children manage in spite of everything to 'get christendame', to be baptized.
22. Child 37A.
23. Child 39A. Perhaps touched up by Robert Burns, by whom it was contributed to James Johnson's *The Scots Musical Museum* (1787–1803).

24. Child 79A (Sir Walter Scott's *Minstrelsy of the Scottish Border*).
25. Child 44.
26. Child 34A.
27. Child 20B, with conclusion from Child 20C.
28. Child 26A (Ravenscroft's *Melismata*, 1611).
29. Sir Walter Scott, *Minstrelsy of the Scottish Border*; cf. Child 106.
30. Child 69A, reunited with the final fifteen stanzas printed as Child 77B, Child having divided the ballad as given in David Herd's MSS, in the British Museum.
31. Child 78A. The conclusion of a lost ballad.
32. Child 11A.
33. Child 7H.
34. Child 70A.
35. John Bell, *Rhymes of Northern Bards* (1812). A version of 'The Baffled Knight', from Child 112D. Child's earliest version is from Ravenscroft's *Deuteromelia* (1609).
36. Child 81A, from *Wit Restored* (1658).
37. Child 269A.
38. Child 51A.
39. Child 73A.
40. Child 65B ('Lady Maisry').
41. Child 67A.
42. Child 5A.
43. Child 96A.
44. Child 68A. In the last line 'hoky-gren' has been changed to 'holly gren'.
45. Child 100A.
46. Child 178D.
47. Child 63B.
48. *Roxburghe Ballads* (1884), Vol. V, from a broadside of 1738.
49. Child 7B (Sir Walter Scott's *Minstrelsy of the Scottish Border*), less three concluding stanzas added by Scott from another source.
50. Child 62A (Sir Walter Scott's *Minstrelsy of the Scottish Border*).
51. Child 223.
52. Child 15A.
53. Child 72A.
54. Child 114A.
55. Child 90A (Sir Walter Scott's *Minstrelsy of the Scottish Border*).
56. Child 186 (Sir Walter Scott's *Minstrelsy of the Scottish Border*).
57. R. A. Smith, *The Scottish Minstrel* (1820–24); cf. Child 210.
58. Child 97A.
59. Child 84A.

60. Child 88B. Stanza 24 inserted for the sense from Child 88E.
61. Child 173A.
62. Child 215A.
63. Child 13B (Percy's *Reliques of Ancient English Poetry*).
64. Child 93A.
65. Child 243F (Sir Walter Scott's *Minstrelsy of the Scottish Border*).
66. Child 58A (Percy's *Reliques of Ancient English Poetry*).
67. Child 190 (Sir Walter Scott's *Minstrelsy of the Scottish Border*).
68. Child 138.
69. Child 141 (Appendix).
70. Child 144A.
71. Child 162B.
72. Child 156A.
73. Child 273.
74. Child 113.
75. David Thomson, *The People of the Sea* (Barrie & Rockliff, 1965), from the MSS of John Campbell of Islay.
76. Haliwell, *Early Naval Ballads* (1841). Admiral Benbow died from his wounds after an action with the French in 1702. He had been deserted by Captain Wade and Captain Kirkby who were subsequently court-martialled and hanged.
77. Stone, *Sea Songs and Ballads* (1906).
78. John Masefield, *A Sailor's Garland* (1906). The pirate Edward Teach was shot in 1718 by Lieutenant Robert Maynard after Maynard's frigate had closed with his ship at Bathtown, North Carolina.
79. John Masefield, *A Sailor's Garland* (1906).
80. J. A. and Alan Lomax, *American Ballads and Folk Songs* (1934). It should be William, not Robert, Kidd. William Kidd, pirate, of Boston, Mass., was brought from Boston to London in 1700, tried on charges of piracy and murdering his gunner Moore, and hanged at Execution Dock on 23 May 1701.
81. Edward Thomas, *Pocket Book of Poems and Songs* (1907); one of many versions of an early eighteenth-century ballad.
82. David Herd, *Ancient and Modern Scottish Songs* (1776). Ascribed to the Scotch ballad poet Francis Sempill (?1616–82).
83. Pinto and Rodway, *The Common Muse* (Penguin, 1965), from a printed sheet. A ballad much tidied and sharpened in favourite modern versions.
84. A. L. Lloyd, *The Singing Englishman* (Workers' Music Association, London, n.d. [1944]).
85. Robert Graves, *English and Scottish Ballads* (Heinemann,

1957). Cf. the version in Samuel Butler, *Alps and Sanctuaries* (1882).

86. Frank Purslow, *Marrowbones* (English Folk Dance and Song Society, 1965). Taken down from a singer in Hampshire in 1908.

87. By George Colman the Younger (1762–1836), from his *Broad Grins* (1872).

88. By George Colman the Younger; included in his play *Love Laughs at Locksmiths*, it became rapidly popular as a printer's ballad, to music by Mozart's onetime friend Michael Kelly. Text from *Broad Grins*.

89. By Thomas Love Peacock (1785–1866). From his *Maid Marian* (1822).

90. ibid. Cf. No. 70.

91. Colm O Lochlainn, *More Irish Street Ballads* (Dublin, 1965).

92. Colm O Lochlainn, *Irish Street Ballads* (Dublin, 1952).

93. P. W. Joyce, *Old Irish Folk Music and Songs* (1909).

94. H. H. Sparling, *Irish Minstrelsy* (1887).

95. ibid.

96. MacAlister, *Old Pioneering Days in the Sunny South* (Goulburn, 1907). For Jack Donohoo, see No. 99.

97. D. Stewart and N. Keesing, *Old Bush Songs* (Sydney, 1957).

98. ibid.

99. Maureen Jolliffe, *The Third Book of Irish Ballads* (Cork, 1970). Cf. W. R. Mackenzie, *Ballads and Sea Songs of Nova Scotia* (1928). Jack Donohue was transported in 1823, and shot by the police in 1830.

100. Stan Hugill, *Shanties of the Seven Seas* (Routledge, 1966).

101. John Ashton, *Modern Street Ballads* (1888).

102. ibid.

103. By Sir W. S. Gilbert (1836–1911). From his *Bab Ballads* (1874).

104. Stokoe, *Songs and Ballads of Northern England* (1892). In the dialect of Co. Durham.

105. By Sir W. S. Gilbert. From *Bab Ballads*. Published in the magazine *Fun* in 1866; and before long in separate circulation as a ballad with music.

106. From *Barrack-Room Ballads* (Methuen, 1961), by Rudyard Kipling (1865–1936).

107. ibid.

108. As given by W. H. Auden, *Oxford Book of Light Verse* (1938).

109. J. A. and Alan Lomax, *American Ballads and Folk Songs* (1934).

110. ibid.

111. B. A. Botkin, *Treasury of American Folklore* (Crown, New York,

1944). An American adaptation of the English eighteenth century ballad, 'The Unfortunate Rake', of which there are many descendants, the rake – soldier or sailor – having caught his death from flash girls with syphilis. See Louis MacNeice's re-adaptation, No. 121, prompted by London burning after incendiary raids in the Second World War.

112. J. A. and Alan Lomax, *American Ballads and Folk Songs* (1934).

113. ibid. A ballad now more familiar in the various versions of 'Frankie and Johnny'.

114. As given by W. H. Auden in the *Oxford Book of Light Verse* (1938).

115. J. A. and Alan Lomax, *American Ballads and Folk Songs* (1934).

116. A. L. Lloyd, *Come All Ye Bold Miners* (Lawrence & Wishart, 1952). On the explosion down the Gresford pit, in Denbighshire, 1934, in which 268 miners were killed.

117. J. A. and Alan Lomax, *American Ballads and Folk Songs*, (1934). American version of an English ballad.

118. By a Dublin journalist, William Dawson. From Colm O Lochlainn's *More Irish Street Ballads*. Oliver St John Gogarty (1878–1957), was an Irish surgeon, poet and senator, friend of Yeats and of James Joyce, and the original of Buck Mulligan in Joyce's *Ulysses*.

119. *Australian Encyclopedia* (Angus & Robertson, 1958, Vol. 9). This, perhaps best of Australian ballads and poems, has usually been ascribed to the poetaster A. B. Paterson (1864–1941), and was first printed in 1903, in an advertisement for Billy Tea. Paterson wrote nothing – or nothing else – of such rhythmical and coherent virtuosity, and it seems likely there were earlier versions. But there is no proof of its descent, which has been claimed, from an English ballad called 'The Bold Fusilier', dating from Marlborough's wars. Nothing is known of this ballad except the opening stanza, which is perhaps a modern invention, based actually on 'Waltzing Matilda'. See the article on 'Waltzing Matilda' by Russel Ward, in *Australian Signposts*, ed. T. A. G. Hungerford (Angus & Robertson, 1956).

120. Current pop ballad, ? of American origin.

121. From *Holes in the Sky* (Faber, 1948), by Louis MacNeice (1907–1963). On the fires in London in the Second World War. Based on No. 111, 'The Cowboy's Lament'. William Alwyn wrote an arrangement of the tune for the 'Lament' to fit MacNeice's ballad.

122. From *Another Time* (Faber, 1940), by W. H. Auden.

123. From *Poems* (Cape, 1964), by Adrian Mitchell (b. 1932).

124. ibid.

INDEX OF TITLES